Because of Her

BECAUSE OF LOVE SERIES 1

DEVON MAY

Edited by: Natalie Liddell at NLBooks
Ashleigh Van Arkkels at AVA Book Editing

Cover Design: Books and Moods

Formatted by: Stacey at Champagne Book Design

Books by
DEVON MAY

BECAUSE OF LOVE SERIES
Because of Us (Novella)
Because of Her
Because of Them (November)

Author's Note

The Because of Love series is a steamy contemporary romance set in Melbourne, Australia. To stay true to the characters and the author, it is written in Australian English. There may be times you spot a *u* where you weren't expecting one, or an *s* instead of a *z*. It is my hope that you are so invested in Callum and Cassidy's story that you don't notice them.

Trigger Warning: *Because of Her* is a story of finding love and accepting all the baggage that comes with second chances. It involves sexual content between two consenting adults who are learning to accept their flaws. If any of the below is potentially triggering for you, please read on with care.

- Infertility, including mentions of failed IVF and miscarriages (not on page).
- Anxiety, including panic attacks (on page).

For the teachers who said stop making up stories.
For the friends who said reading was for nerds.
For the high school boyfriends who said writing fan-fiction was lame.

But mostly for the girls who had to hear it all.

Because of Her

Chapter One

CALLUM

"Will you be home for dinner?"

I've been up for hours, loading my belongings onto the truck, but Maisie is still in her pyjamas as we hug goodbye. Rubbing away the sleep dried in her lashes, she steps back from our embrace to look at me. With me crouched in a squat position, we're almost eye to eye, but the quiver of her lower lip has me looking away.

"Ahh, no." I run my palms along my thighs, taking a moment to find the right words before looking back up at her. "I'm going to live in another house now, Maisie."

"Why?" Her eyes scrunch together, and a crack forms through the centre of my chest. I knew this morning was going to be difficult for the both of us, but I had no idea how much it would hurt.

"Well, remember how we said mummy and daddy weren't going to be married anymore?"

When she nods, I continue. "It means we're going to have our own houses. You'll live with mummy most of the time, but soon you'll be able to come stay with me."

Behind Maisie, my ex-wife, Audrey, scoffs. These were details we still had to work out. The divorce papers list that we share custody. In my ideal world, the 50/50 agreement would start immediately, but Audrey has been adamant we all have a little time to settle.

She believes Maisie needs stability for the short term; that we should focus on one change at a time. To her, it means Maisie staying in her home and not being 'shipped from house to house every fortnight'. And while I agree in principle, I'm also not willing to give up all custody of the most important person in my life. Once I have convinced her mother I am settled in my new place, and spending time with me is what's best for Maisie, she will be spending half her weeks with me.

When a tear forms in the corner of Maisie's eye, I drop my knees to the ground and pull her in for another bear hug. "I love you, chicka," I whisper into her ear. "No matter what, know that I love you, and I'm going to miss you. So much."

Tears of my own start forming, but I need to be the strong one, for Maisie. I blink them away as I draw in a long breath. The scent of the sweet coconut from her hair calms me; the dark waves being the only thing she got from me.

When I try to pull away, she clings tight to my shoulders and cries. "Don't go Daddy."

I wish I didn't need my ex-wife's support, but when Maisie refuses to let go, I know I do. I shift my gaze up to Audrey, forcing a slow blink when she stares back down at me. As much as it pains me, I know the best thing for Maisie is for me to make a quick exit. Audrey scoops her up, carrying her inside and offering to put *Bluey* on.

I wait until Maisie's laughter travels through the open window and onto the porch where I stand. When the melodic sound hits my ears, I soak it in. Turning toward the rental truck, my heart splits in two, and I know, without a doubt, it will never be whole again.

My love for my ex-wife evaporated long ago, and in the aftermath, I decided she can have all the material possessions she wanted. She wanted the house, she could have it. She wants all the furniture, fine. The one thing she cannot take, and the one thing I will never forgive her for trying to take; what matters most to me; my daughter.

The truck beeps as I reverse into the lobby drop off zone. Each piercing sound is a needle straight to the temple, but even after I pull to a stop, the pain continues. I don't want to be here.

It's a temporary stop while I find a new house, but the apartment building is nothing like my old home. Instead, it is full of couples, old ladies, and single friends. The last tenant report stated there are no kids in the building, and I worry about how my daughter will handle the move once her mother finally lets her stay.

Standing on the sidewalk, I stretch my limbs and gesture for my family to get out of their car. I'll be forever grateful for their support.

"Woah, Maisie is so lucky," my nephew calls out as he stares up at the building in adoration. "There must be loads of stairs in this house."

My brother-in-law claps a hand on my back. "Speaking of stairs, just how many flights are we talking about?"

"Three, but I paid extra for the furniture delivery so they'll get the heavy stuff. We just have the boxes."

He moves to wrangle the kids off the retaining wall. Passing them each a sweet before giving them each a small bag of ... something. It's my stuff, but I lost track of what was put where hours ago.

He calls to my mum, "Do you want to take them up and we'll help Callum with the boxes?"

"If they get one flight of stairs in, I'll be happy," my sister, Isobel, muses from beside me.

She wraps an arm around my middle, leaning some of her weight onto me. Isobel and I have always been close, thanks to the strong family values our parents instilled in us. Despite the usual teenage hatred we shared, I now consider her to be one of my best friends. Without her support throughout the past year, and the past month of house hunting, I would have crumbled.

I pass my mother the key to the building so she can let herself in. Watching them, I picture Maisie walking in their place. Once she gets through the changes, my daughter will love it here. The stairs, the people—even if they aren't kids her own age. I feel a pang in my chest at the thought of not putting her to bed tonight, the hurt reaching deep in my soul.

Maisie is a firecracker. Even though she's only recently turned five, I can tell she's going to rule the world one day. From the moment she was born, she became my first priority, and that's exactly how she'll remain.

Her mother and I realised our marriage was dying over a year ago, but through the separation process, I'd stayed with them in our old family home. It worked, for us, to have both Maisie's parents under one roof. With the divorce finalised, we realised it was time for one of us to move out.

We'd tried to talk to Maisie about how we weren't going to be married any more. She knew we were no longer sleeping in the same room, but I don't think she understood what any of it meant until this morning.

My heart aches, remembering how confused and hurt Maisie was.

A large part of me is still grieving my marriage, the ideals I had in my head and the future I always envisioned. Family has always been the most important thing in my life, my parents made sure my sister and I knew to always stick together. When she got married, we all welcomed her husband into our tight knit group, even though his dark red hair makes him stand out like the only deciduous tree in the botanic gardens during autumn.

When my relationship with Audrey was still young, I wanted nothing more than for her to join our family group as well. In hindsight, the fact she never put in much effort probably should have been red flag number one. No one goes into a marriage thinking divorce is a possibility, but I never imagined my marriage might be the one destined to break down. I thought I had found the love of my life and would spend the rest of my years with her by my side. Instead, I'll spend them alone.

I shake off the reflective thoughts and the sorrow adjoining them.

Refocusing on my family and the move, we form something that resembles a plan, but mostly involves one person waiting with the truck while the others carry a load in.

I move to the back of the truck, and as I lower the tailgate, goosebumps form on the back of my neck. An odd feeling washes over me and tingles spread down my spine. I look back to my family, but they stand in place, ready to help once we can get into the truck.

"You've got admirers," Isobel calls from the sidewalk as I walk onto the truck bed.

I glance around. From a balcony above us, two women stand in the sun. I'm not surprised my new, third floor neighbours are watching. I don't blame them, I would, too, and they aren't the only ones.

My eyes are only drawn to them, though, and I watch them through my peripheral so they won't shy away. One woman wears a bright, oversized dressing gown and has her hair tied in a long braid over her shoulder. But it isn't her who catches my eye, it's the other one. Wearing a simple sundress, her chocolate hair falls in soft waves to her collarbone. Sunlight surrounds her, and I can't look away, or explain the way my spine continues to tingle at the sight of her. My insides flop at her beauty, even from this far away. More interesting than that, though, I can't shake the feeling I know her.

Chapter Two

CASSIDY

The hypnotic smell of coffee hits me at the same time as the ridiculous level of chatter. My ears buzz with the noise, and I pause to remind myself why I'm here.

Scanning the room, I'm drawn to the giant floral backdrop along the far wall, and the gaggle of women crowding the space. Men stand back, scattered through the tables, cradling handbags and occasionally stepping forward to take a social media worthy photo.

I spot Mike seated as far from the back wall as possible. I should feel relief, seeing the man I'm here to meet, but I don't. Dread flows through my veins instead, as I realise he is far larger than his photos implied. He isn't just fit, or well built. He is immense. Veins protrude from every bulging muscle on his crossed arms, and his neck is so wide it seems as though his shoulders are in a permanent shrug. The blond, beachy hair is long, tied back in a ridiculous ponytail. The kind of luscious waves that years past, would have made me jealous.

If I didn't so desperately need a double shot latte, I would turn on my heel and remove myself from this ridiculous scenario.

I wonder, for the tiniest of moments, if I could order a sneaky coffee to go before bailing. *Would he recognise me? Would he care if I never showed?* To my dismay, Mike spots me, stretching up a hand to wave me over. His face twists into a goofy smile, and I catch a glimpse of the humorous man I've been chatting to. Maybe this date won't be so bad after all.

On paper, or phone screen, I suppose, Mike ticked all

the right boxes. The banter between us flowed well. His messages made me chuckle and I'm sure my lame puns had him cringing.

"Hey." I greet him with my own tight-lipped smile after zigzagging through the crowded room.

He doesn't stand up when I approach the table.

When I pull out my chair to sit down, I notice how reserved his smile really is. His eyebrows pinched in a frown despite the upturn of his lips.

"You're late," he scoffs, as I pick up the menu and sit down.

When Mike recommended this café, I looked up the menu online. The website gave a cutesy, romantic vibe, and I hadn't minded it would involve a twenty-minute tram ride to get here. I figured it would give me time to read my romance novel in peace. Now though, I feel like all it did was make me late and give me additional time to develop my already unrealistic expectations in men.

Like Mike.

Because although I'm not counting, I'm pretty sure I'm up to red flag number five, and I haven't even ordered my coffee. I try to keep my expression sympathetic.

"Sorry, the tram was overcrowded so I waited for a second one."

Mike responds with a blank stare.

"Which was late," I add, trying to keep my tone light. "So, I'm late. Sorry."

Without a word, Mike waves a waitress over and orders himself an oat milk cappuccino before gesturing for me to order.

"I'll have a double shot latte please." After she writes my drink order on her little notepad, I add, "and the bacon avocado smash with a poached egg."

Her grin is wide as she writes down the order. When she turns to Mike, her slick high ponytail flips over her shoulder.

"Would you—"

"No food for me, thanks." He cuts her off, his voice blunt and growly.

While we wait, I attempt to make small talk, but his flat monosyllabic answers wear me down. I hadn't exactly expected it to, but the incessant chatter and giggles never quietens down. Eventually, it pulls my attention away from my failing date.

From this side of the café, the flowers and greenery look real, and I can't help but wonder how the café keeps them looking fresh. Influencers and wannabes are taking turns snapping photos and filming ridiculous short videos. Girlfriends peer pressure their partners into lovey photos. The constant high-pitched laughter and ceaseless chit chat are like tiny needles in my brain.

By the time my food arrives with our coffees, I've given up trying to make any conversation with Mike. I wonder what I did wrong before our date even began, and the more I wonder, the more my head fills with self-doubt. I thought the sundress and boots were cute together, but maybe I should have worn something 'prettier'? Or was it my comment about children when we were chatting last night?

I try my best to shut out the wave of insecurities, instead, looking around, I take mental notes of things I could incorporate in my boutique, perhaps something similar to the café's floral wall. At this late stage in the season, I'm willing to try anything to bring in some extra customers and spread awareness of my company. Whilst contemplating the small posies on each table, I add cafés to my mental list of companies to approach for weekly deliveries.

"Hey, um, how much longer do you think you'll be?"

Ah, so he can speak in full sentences. Such a shame it was for a rude question, I'm not even halfway through my food; my egg still waiting to be split open so I can test the yolk.

He leans back in his chair, thick arms rested up with his hands linked behind his head. He looks firm in a way that seems uncomfortable to touch, and his grey tee strains across his obscene muscles.

"Not long I think," I reply, furrowing my brow. "Have somewhere you need to be?" I add a laugh, attempting to keep the conversation light-hearted.

"Ah, yeah actually." He strokes a hand through the ends of his long, blond hair before bringing it down to check his watch. "I'm meeting someone in twenty minutes for lunch."

We haven't even been here for more than an hour, and he's already close to being late to another commitment. Even if I hadn't been five minutes late, we would have been pushing for time. *No thanks.*

"Not like a date," he adds, somehow raising his shoulders even closer to his ears. "Just a girl I've been chatting to."

"Chatting to, like me?" My stomach twists and I no longer feel hungry.

"Well, yeah I guess."

"Oh."

I can't believe I fell for the thought of a brunch date. I thought it meant our day was open to extend the date if we felt we clicked, but Mike obviously had other ideas.

"You don't have a dinner date as well, do you?" I spit out.

His lack of care the whole time we'd been here, the noise that still won't stop, and my sudden anger, swirl like a storm inside me. I press my lips together, holding it all in until I can calm myself enough to avoid making a scene.

An icy lump is forming in my throat. The longer he sits there sipping at his coffee without answering me, the more my skin crawls. I stare him down, waiting for a response, not wanting to be the pathetic single girl I already feel like.

"Oh my God, you do!" I blurt out when the pressure of silence becomes too much. I push out my chair, standing up as I run my hands down my face. "Have fun Mike, this was … interesting." I pull twenty dollars from my purse and slam it on the table. As I storm away, a heavy sigh escapes and I wonder if I'm overreacting.

The anger settles as I make my way to the nearest tram stop. It's not Mike I'm upset at. Well, I am, but it's more than that. We hadn't spoken about the idea of spending the afternoon together, and not once did either of us hint at the idea of us being any kind of exclusive. Maybe I was … am, overreacting to a guy whose only crime is playing his cards.

But I'm over my dates crumbling. Each time it happens, I spiral, and can't help but think of all the times people I care about, or love, leave me. It's irrational, it was just a date, I barely knew him, but I think it regardless. It hurts, and all I want to do is find my person. For real this time.

Arriving home, I slam the door behind me as hard as I can and dump my bag so it lands on the floor with a thud. Following suit, I sink to the ground and bang my head against the wall behind me.

"Argh," I moan, as loud as possible, banging my head again for dramatic effect.

When my flatmate Amira doesn't call out with sympathy, I kick off my shoes, allowing them to clunk into the wall on the other side of the hallway. I wince, thinking about the damage I might have caused. To the shoes, not the wall. They're nothing fancy, but they are my favourite pair of boots and with the winter season coming, I can't afford to replace them.

"Aaargh." I try again, with more force this time. I'm

mopey, and I know it. But if there is one person I can act like a spoiled brat around, it's Amira. I really, *really,* wanted my date with Mike to go well. There had been so much promise, and it feels like a kick straight to the kidney for it to have gone so bad.

"I'm not coming down there for you to bitch about your date, you can come here," Amira calls out from our open plan, kitchen-slash-dining-slash-living area.

I crawl my way along the hallway and reach up to pull myself onto the couch.

"That bad?" Amira asks as she sits down next to me and pulls my feet into her lap.

She's still in her pyjamas, her legs wrapped underneath the oversized sleep tee. Her long brown hair is tied into a braid that rests over her shoulder, and although her eyes are always dark, there's a shadow about them today. She'd been out to dinner with her parents last night, coming home late. She was still asleep when I left this morning, but I know how draining conversations with her father are for her.

"Did I tell you I turned down a job for this date?"

As a florist who specialises in weddings, Saturdays are a valuable trade. Especially now, as the wedding season nears its end. It was insane, and a little concerning, that I had today off in the first place to be able to make plans. And when a last-minute opportunity came up to help another florist, saying no had been a difficult decision. I had thought things with Mike would go well, and after my string of bad dating luck since returning to Melbourne, I couldn't say no to the one guy I thought had potential.

I even closed the boutique for the day, and although I *should* go open up and hope for a few walk in customers, my mood is now far too sour.

"Why were you so keen on him, anyway?"

I pause, because in truth, I don't really know the answer.

Sure, we got along well enough while we were chatting on-line, but we didn't share a heap of interests or have the same life goals. There was nothing special about Mike besides his stance on children.

I wanted it to go well like I want anything to go well. I want someone to call me after a stressful day, I want someone to snuggle up to on cold winter nights. But most of all, I want someone to buy me flowers for a change. It feels ridiculous to be this hung up on wanting to find love, and I'm pretty sure the reason I can't find it, is because of how hard I'm looking.

Every terrible date makes me wonder a little more about what I did to deserve ending up here. What I did to deserve the heartache, and the gut wrenching break up that followed.

Things had been going well with Blake for years. After meeting and dating at university, we moved interstate so he could follow his dream of being a national journalist. As our relationship progressed, and the hard questions became more important, we realised our lives no longer aligned as well as we had hoped. It's not that I never wanted children. I always had a picture in my head of how my life would go, and eventually the idea of being a parent forced its way out of the image. No matter how much I once wanted one, a baby wasn't in my future. And I grew to accept that. Blake told me he wished he could say the same, but he couldn't.

Despite his career ambitions and all the goals he was smashing in the journalism world, he couldn't picture his future without 'fathering an heir'. He had said it with a mountain of seriousness, but I couldn't help cringing at his self-righteousness.

It broke both our hearts when we realised our paths were ultimately separating. But it tore mine in two learning after all we had been through, he valued me no more than my ability to be a mother.

Two years later, I still often wonder how he is doing. If

he found someone who could give him what I couldn't. And with every failed fling and shitty date, I wonder how different my life could be if I hadn't been dealt these cards.

"I don't know," I admit. "I just feel like I should have moved on. Found someone. It's been years since I moved back to Melbourne. Otherwise, what was the point?"

"Well, for starters, you wouldn't have met me." She laughs, leaning down to squeeze me in a hug.

"I don't understand why I attract all the crazies," I whine.

Amira quiets her laugh.

Before Mike, there was Brad. He had seemed nice until I discovered not only did he want children one day, he wanted a whole tribe of them. The joke, about having a soccer team, was said without a hint of sarcasm.

There was also Justin, who had a wife on the side. And Trevor, who openly told me he was gay but was trying to hide it from his very old-fashioned grandmother. It's ok though, he had said, she will die soon, and he'll be free to live how he wants. The list of terrible flings and dates went on and on.

"Maybe you're trying to fill a hole that doesn't need filling."

I give a short, dry laugh and nudge her rib cage. "What if I really want my hole filled, though?"

Amira shakes her head with an eyeroll. "I was talking about the hole in your heart you filthy whore."

Pulling a pillow from behind me, I throw it at her face. I don't have a hole in my heart, I just want someone to snuggle with after a long day. I want someone to choose me over everything, and everyone. Forever, not just for now.

Amira and I met not long after I moved back to the city. I had returned to my parents' place, but soon realised I needed a place of my own. Only, living alone is not exactly affordable on a florist's income, so I started looking for a housemate.

Amira was a cousin of a friend of a friend, whose old

housemate had moved out. So, I moved in. Our apartment is a small two-bedroom unit, close enough to the city to be trendy, without being so close that we live in a high rise with rent as high as the rooftop courtyard.

A little over a year ago, we got permission to paint the hospital white walls a homier shade of eggshell grey, and together we have started adding colour to the decor. My grandma's pink, hand-knit, blanket drapes the back of the couch, and the bird paintings we did at a 'Paint 'n' Sip' class take pride of place on the wall behind it. The small round dining table is surrounded by four different chairs, each its own vibrant colour. My favourite is the royal blue upholstered dining chair. Amira prefers the traditional style wooden one she painted red.

"Maybe it's time I stopped actively trying to find a man," I admit, more to myself than to Amira.

"You could swear off dating like I have?"

I snuggle into her shoulder, whispering "deal", even though I'm not so sure. Amira flitters between swearing off relationships and cosying up to her latest fling weekly. I know better than to take her seriously.

We hug for a while, and I soak up Amira's golden energy. I swear it flows through the woman like the honey of her skin. When I'm feeling a little better about my miserable start to the day, I stand up and walk to the balcony. We can't have many more pleasant days left before winter hits, and I plan to soak in every ounce of sun I can.

I step out into the sun, expecting to hear the sounds of a busy inner suburban street. Instead, the steady beeps of a truck reversing ring in my ear, flooding the apartment.

"I think our new neighbour is moving in," I announce, moving towards the handrail and hoping to catch sight of the person, or people, we are bound to cross paths with countless times from here on out.

Amira joins me on the balcony, but I shove her back inside.

"Don't make it obvious," I hiss. "Go make coffee or something so it looks like we're just two women enjoying the midday sun."

She laughs at me but walks over to the kitchen and flicks the machine on. While she grabs our favourite mugs from the drying rack next to the sink, I lean over the rusted railing a fraction to see if I can spot the new resident of apartment thirty-two.

The unit across from ours has been empty for more than a few months. We suspect the owners were trying to charge too much rent, because despite hundreds of people walking through during the openings, no one came to stay. Until now. The big "FOR RENT" sign in front of the block was taken down last weekend.

Amira comes out with two mugs of her perfectly brewed coffee. I grab one from her as she leans on the railing with me.

"See anyone yet?"

Before I can answer her, the driver's side to the rental truck opens and a man with dark scruffy hair steps out. It's not until he is standing on the footpath, I realise how ridiculously tall he is, and I wonder if he would have to stoop to avoid the low ceilings in the communal hallways of our building. He calls out to someone in the car in front, and soon a whole family is on the sidewalk. Two young kids start to play on the retaining wall, while five adults gather and, I assume, form a plan.

"Mum, Dad, grown-up kids, grandkids?" I look to Amira.

"Or is one of them an in-law? They all have really dark hair except that guy."

She raises a finger off her bright green mug to point. We're too far away to see them clearly, but I can tell she is referring to the man wrangling the children off the wall. His dark auburn hair stands out in the sea of deep browns.

I laugh. "I wonder who's moving in."

Together, we watch as the tall one opens the tailgate of the vehicle and starts lowering the ramp. His shirt is tight against his broad shoulders and muscular back. A sleeve of tattoos spirals around his right arm. His hair has a slight wave to it, sitting messily on the nape of his neck. A glimpse of the side of his face reveals a short beard, long enough to be on purpose, but trimmed and tidy in a way the rest of his hair isn't. I can't explain why, but there is something familiar about him.

"I feel like a creep," I whisper, turning to walk back inside.

Amira follows. "We can find out who has moved in later, but if it's the guy with the tatt, I call dibs."

"What happened to you swearing off men?"

She cocks her eyebrow at me. "Like you weren't checking him out, too."

She's right, but it's more than his muscular frame that has me intrigued. Maybe it's something about the dragon tail wrapping around his forearm. Or how the thought of him having to stoop in the hallway feels oddly nostalgic, bringing back memories of hiding in the storage room during my teenage job as a supermarket cashier. Whatever it is, I'm determined to work out why I can't shake the nervous tingles spreading from my fingers.

Chapter Three

CASSIDY

The cockatoos are swarming, and as afternoon turns into evening, I'm well and truly out of ideas to fill the time, and my stomach is rumbling.

Amira and I had been hanging around the apartment for most of the afternoon, torn between wanting to sneak a better glance at the new neighbours, and not wanting to appear nosey. In my indecisiveness, I'd rearranged our bookshelves, emptied out the cupboard under the bathroom sink, and tidied my room. A box of books and two garbage bags of old clothes sit in the hallway, ready to be donated.

Amira spent the afternoon in the kitchen. The smell of freshly baked treats fills the apartment, and the contents of the pantry are mostly back in place after her decision to deep clean the cupboards.

"Unless you're cooking, let's go get dinner," I say to Amira.

She peels herself off the couch. "You can eat macarons for dinner. Pretty sure I made enough to last months."

I grab one off the bench. "As tempting as that is," I say, taking a bite. I savour the sweet strawberry flavour before adding through chews, "I don't think it will fill me up."

My stomach growls again. This time, the sound escapes the confines of my body, travelling across the room like the rumble of a train. I probably shouldn't have skipped lunch during my hyper fixation on decluttering the house.

"Geez lady, I heard that from here." Amira feigns concern

as she pulls on her sneakers. "Let's go, I want to try out the new Italian place on the corner."

I pull my boots back on and grab a jacket from the hooks at the entrance. Despite the sun this afternoon, Melbourne's weather is forever unpredictable and I suspect I'll need it by the time dinner's done.

"Truck's gone," Amira states from the window. "We might not even see them."

"Shame, that was my plan all along."

I sigh in jest. It would be nice to see who it is we'll be sharing a hallway with, but after a day of lugging belongings up three flights of stairs, I imagine whoever it is will have retreated to their couch by now. Maybe even their bed.

Stepping into the hallway, I find my assumptions were wrong.

My heart stops. Standing across the hall from me with a large box propped against his hip, is Callum Wilson.

I feel dizzy. Reaching a hand back to Amira to steady myself, I glance between the two of them, knowing social conventions dictate I do something here, but my brain doesn't work. It isn't sending signals to my arms or face or mouth. With no rational thought telling my limbs what to do, they fall in on themselves. Pins and needles race up from my toes, my lip quivers, and my hand clings to the front of Amira's loose top.

I haven't seen Callum in more than ten years, but he is still as drop-dead gorgeous as I remember. Reaching above his head, he rests an arm on the door frame. While my body runs a sprint against itself, Callum's is casual and relaxed. Only a hint of surprise can be seen in the way his wide eyes reflect the fluorescent light tube above us.

As he allows a fraction of his weight to hang, the muscles in his forearm bulge. My gaze darts over him, pausing on the dragon curling down from his elbow. His tight t-shirt

20

shows off the muscular shoulders Amira and I had admired like creeps from the balcony. Up close, I can't take my eyes off the way his muscles flow down into edible pecs, then to perfectly defined abs and finally to the 'v' that draws my attention further down.

I can't help but compare his physique to Mike's. Where Mike was over the top gym buff and looked stiff all over, Callum looks fit but somehow cosy, like I could sink into him and be subjected to the kind of hug I've only ever read about.

"Cassidy?"

His voice is gruff, not as loud and boisterous as I remember, but it still holds the deep rumble that haunts my dreams. His face twists into something between a grin and a smirk. Smaller than the grins I remember from our youth, but it still reaches his eyes, making the steel blue sparkle.

"Callum, hi." I wave, feeling a little like the shy, awkward teenager he must remember. Shit, I suppose I still am a shy, awkward teenager to him. Here I am, stumbling over my words, waving to a man no more than a metre away from me and solidifying that impression. "Um, this is Amira."

I shove my best friend in front of Callum, hoping her outgoing personality will hide my mixed emotions. She nods politely and turns back to me. "Definitely calling dibs."

Her faux whisper screeches across the hall, but it's the harsh "no" that escapes my lips that shocks me. I don't blame her for attempting to claim the man, but God, what I wouldn't give to be that box propped on his hip. To feel his arms wrapped around me, supporting my weight while I rest around his waist.

I suck in the thought, spluttering on the sharp inhale and choking on a bead of saliva. *Didn't I just swear off men? Didn't the man in front of me break my heart ten years ago? I* shouldn't be thinking about wrapping my legs around him, or how safe I would feel in his arms.

Callum sees through my soul as he rakes his eyes over me. The tingle of a blush spreads up my neck.

Despite not seeing him since I was a teenager, despite the way his absence hurt me so deeply and the long-term relationship I'd been in since then, Callum still takes my breath away. I wonder how I ever managed to maintain a friendship with the man standing in front of me.

I'd met Callum and all his broad-shouldered, strong-armed goodness when I was fifteen and working at the local supermarket. Somehow, he had seen past my raging teenage hormones, and we'd become friends. Good friends. In the three years we worked together, he became my safe place. I dreaded work when he wasn't rostered on and lived for the days our shifts collided. I told him all my deepest secrets, except the one where I found him unbearably attractive.

Callum lets out a loud exhale, the kind of half laugh half snort that says he clearly heard Amira. He shrugs and brings his arm down to run a hand through his dark scruffy hair. The adjustment makes his tight black t-shirt hug his bicep, and it rises above the waist of his pants just enough to make my mouth water. He smirks again, raising his eyebrows as if knowing exactly what the movement was doing to my insides.

I cough, spluttering, before composing myself. "So, you're our new neighbour?"

"Yeah, I guess so," he grunts. I melt. I'm in trouble.

"Well." Amira takes over, picking up on my stuttering. "We were just going to grab dinner, if you want to come?"

I cough again, choking on more of the saliva in my mouth. Heat rushes up to my ears and I'm sure my whole face goes pink. It's hard to compose myself around Callum, and I wonder how I survived my teenage years around him.

I would have stuck his poster on the wall next to Justin Bieber if I'd been able to.

Every time he would come to hang at my house, I would create imaginary scenarios where he would have to stay the night and share my bed. I mentally wrote my own fanfiction romance story where we were the main characters and 'only one bed' was the defining trope. But, somehow, I managed to keep my senseless attraction at bay while we hung out, and we had a close friendship for many years.

"Or we could bring you back some?" Amira adds.

"Ahh yeah sure, I was going to get UberEats, but if you're offering?"

"Italian okay?" Amira lists off some classic dishes, not knowing the menu of the new restaurant.

"Lasagne," he answers. "I don't have cash though?"

"It's okay." She laughs, patting his arm. "I know where you live."

And with a wink, she turns to walk down the hallway, leaving me to lock up. I'm still in shock; my mouth is dry and it feels as though I'm wearing lead shoes. Although Amira's quick thinking with the dinner delivery got me out of Callum's immediate attention, her swift exit has left me alone with him.

"Ahh, good to see you again," I manage, as I glance down the hall towards Amira.

"You too, Rogue." Callum's deep voice as he utters my old nickname melts away the tiny fraction of composure I had left. "I suspect I'll be seeing a lot more of you now?"

Avoiding his piercing gaze, I scrape out something resembling a 'yes' before tripping over my own feet as I chase Amira down the hall. Like the best friend I've always known her to be, she stretches her arms out to catch me, disguising my tumble as a friendly embrace.

In the street, Amira and I settle into a steady pace. There is little warmth left in the sun as it sets, and the southerly breeze is cool off the water. I can tell Amira's cold by the way her arms are wrapped around her middle. That, and the fact she is power walking down the street.

"I always say you should bring a jacket just in case."

"But it was such a nice day." She drags out the word 'day' in complaint.

I rub my hands against her arms and stifle a laugh. We've had this conversation hundreds of times. Even with her years of living in Melbourne, Amira hasn't quite caught on to the 'four seasons in one day' concept. She still seems to think her thin, cotton, long sleeve shirts will be enough once the sun goes down. If I haven't convinced her otherwise by now, I doubt I ever will.

As we step in front of the trendy Italian restaurant, we're hit by a steady warm glow from the outdoor gas heaters. Amira snuggles up to one, cocking an eyebrow as she rubs her hands up and down her arms.

"Can you order?" she requests, stepping closer to the red glow.

Amira nudges my side with her elbow when I return after ordering our food. "So?"

"So what?" I ask, even though I know full well what she is referring to. After living with her for nearly two years, I've never acted as lustful and embarrassing as I had earlier.

"You and Callum?" Another nudge.

I bring my hands up to my face to hide the blush I can feel forming.

"Was it that obvious?" I groan while Amira hums her agreement.

"We worked together as teenagers," I start. "Well, I was a teenager. He was pretty much an adult when we first met."

I think back to those days, the stories we used to share in between stocking shelves or serving customers. Although at first we hadn't spent much time together outside of work, our friendship blossomed over time. Shortened text messages became longer phone calls. Online chats became hours long. Eventually, we were best friends. The few years between us meant nothing, and we spent more time together than we did apart. I think about how much of a slap in the face it was when we lost touch after I quit. I had hoped me starting my own career would allow him to see me as more of an adult and less of the acne-covered teenager under his supervision.

I shudder at how wrong I had been.

"I had a massive, like *massive*, crush on him when we worked together," I tell Amira. "But he was promoted to shift supervisor, and I had to back off."

She stares at me, her brows furrowing, and I know she sees through the little white lie.

"Okay, so he was promoted to shift supervisor and I used to imagine that was the only reason he hadn't asked me out." I shake my head.

Despite the huge crush I had on Callum as a teenager, I can acknowledge how unrealistic I'd been at the time. Three years doesn't seem like a big gap when you're over thirty, but at fifteen I can only imagine how young I seemed to him.

"It was ridiculous, I don't think he ever gave any clues he was into me, but we did get along really well. I thought we were friends, at least."

"Until?" Amira prompts.

"Until I quit. The next time we hung out, I kissed him." I wait for a response, but instead, Amira looks at me with a cocked eyebrow, urging me to continue.

"Nothing happened. We kissed, and it was terrible. Not

the kiss, but everything that happened after. I was so embarrassed. And we just, I don't know, plateaued. He moved to the other side of the city for another promotion, and eventually, we lost contact. I guess I'd hoped once he was no longer my 'boss' things would be different." I use air quotes around the word boss, because in reality, he was hardly that.

"They were, but not in the way I had hoped."

"He never tried for anything more than friends?"

A large puff of air escapes. "No, he never did. And it's been more than ten years since I've seen him."

Rubbing my hands together under the heater, I fiddle with the spinning ring I always wear.

"So why did you act like a lovesick teenager again?"

"Argh, I did, didn't I?" The blush spreads back up my neck and onto my cheeks.

A lot has changed in the past ten years, and I wonder what my younger self would think if she knew we would end up neighbours with Callum Wilson. I'm sure she would be giddy with excitement, dreaming up all the ways to rekindle our friendship. Hoping yet again it would lead to something more. But strangely, I don't feel any of that. Instead, the thought of living across the hall from my teenage crush creates a well in my stomach, and I'm afraid if I think too much about it, I won't be able to eat my dinner.

Callum may have been my best friend once, years ago, when he was the person I trusted the most. But he became another in the ever growing list of people who leave me behind. The thought of him being back in my life is overwhelming.

"But he is pretty fucking hot," I admit. Because history aside, I can acknowledge some eye candy when I see it.

"Now that, I can agree with."

By the time my ticket number is called, the sun has finished setting behind the buildings. It's cold as we walk home. Amira hugs the hot food, and fusses when I detour into the bottle shop to grab some cold beers and seltzers. I have vague memories of Callum preferring pale ales, so that's what I grab.

"It's going to be an interesting few weeks isn't it?" Amira scoffs as I step back outside.

I meet her side eye by rolling my own.

Chapter Four

CALLUM

After Cassidy went running down the hall in a coughing fit, I collapsed on the couch. I'm exhausted, physically and mentally, but mostly, emotionally. Today's move was always going to take it out of me, and I'm glad my family came along to support me, but seeing Cassidy at the end of it all felt like a solid kick to the balls. It's been years. Many, many years. Years that on my side, include a failed marriage, and a complete lifestyle change when I became a father. Seeing Cassidy again reminded me of how carefree I used to be. How I used to dive into anything I wanted. Except Cassidy. And now she is back in my life. I'm wondering why that was.

She's still as gorgeous as I remember, if not more so. The years have treated her well. She grew into her teenage lankiness and now owns her petite frame. Her brunette hair is longer, and a shade lighter in the sections framing her face. When she looked up at me through her thick lashes and I saw the deep green of her eyes, my memory flashed to all the times I spent blindly staring into them.

We had been two anxious teenagers, finding solace in each other's company. The comfort grew as we did, until the difference in our age was no longer significant. Friendship grew into love, but the anxiety remained, and I was so worried I would screw everything up if I told her how I felt.

Looking back, I can't believe how utterly idiotic I had been not to. Even when she literally sat on my lap and gave me the chance I'd been waiting for. Memories of how my pulse raced in all the wrong ways and I forgot how to breathe threaten to tip me back over the edge of my anxiety.

I've never believed in fate, but my sister would say the universe shoved Cassidy back into my life for a reason. Something about reigniting my inner child, rediscovering myself after divorce. If she was here, I'd tell her it's a load of crock. But I have to admit there is something about Cassidy coming back into my life at this moment that feels ... right.

If I'm thinking this deeply into fate and destiny and gifts from the universe, I'm clearly exhausted. And hungry. Which is why I jumped at the chance when Cassidy's friend offered to bring dinner home. I have, quite literally, zero food in the apartment. This time on a Saturday, UberEats would have taken hours, even so close to Main Street. I was not looking forward to the wait. My stomach grumbles in agreement.

As I drift about, waiting for the women to return, I'm regretting my decision. The last thing I need is to force small talk for the sake of being social, and pretending my life isn't one big happy never after. Especially with Cassidy, considering how seeing her has turned my brain into hippy goo.

Part of me wonders if my body is waiting until the sun goes down before the emotions come flooding out. Just like they have most nights for the past six months.

I check the time, calculating how long it's been since the women left to get food against how long I assume it will take. They didn't mention how far this Italian place was, or even how they were getting there. But, waiting for food would have been at least twenty minutes.

I decide to make the phone call. If I don't, it'll be Maisie's bedtime before I've had a chance to finish my food. Calling to tell her goodnight, knowing I won't be there when she wakes up in the morning, is almost too painful.

My hand trembles as I pick up my phone, scrolling down the messenger app until I find Audrey's name and hit the call button. After she picks up, the video is loading but I can hear her calling out.

"Maisie, Daddy is on the phone!"

A second later, the video comes on, and a smile brighter than the sun fills the screen.

"Hey, chicka," I say, choking on the lump forming in my throat.

"Daddy I had a bath with *sprinkles!*"

"Bath salts!" Audrey calls out from somewhere off screen. I appreciate the way Audrey has made something as mundane as a bath such a fun experience for Maisie.

Despite how incompatible we were as partners, I hold so much respect for Audrey, and how devoted she is to motherhood.

Maisie pulls the phone back a little until I can see *most* of her face.

"Wow, sprinkles! That sounds fun." I put on a cheerful expression, even though I don't feel it. "I called to say goodnight."

"Oh." The light drains from her face. "I forgot you weren't coming home."

"I know, Maisie, I'm sorry."

Suddenly, the screen is full of bubbles, and fish swim around Maisie's face.

"Heehee." She giggles. "Look Daddy, we are swimming."

I laugh, too, because Maisie's giggle is the sweetest sound I'll ever hear. The screen changes and we become fruits, animals and clowns, until eventually Maisie turns us into princesses.

"Can I come visit you?" she asks. She puts one hand on her cheek, pouting her lips and raising her eyebrows.

It's her 'please' face, and it kills me every time.

"Soon, Maisie. I promise."

"You can never break a promise," she states, pointing one finger at the screen.

"I know."

Audrey's face pops onto the screen behind Maisie's. "We gotta get you to bed, Maisie."

"No, I'm talking to Daddy." Maisie is defiant, and for once I'm not mad about it.

Audrey is right though, it's getting close to Maisie's bedtime, and ending this conversation is likely to be as hard on her as it will be on me. Probably harder.

"It's alright, Maisie, I'll talk to you tomorrow, okay?"

Her tiny brown eyes go red, and tears fill them as her bottom lip pops out. Sensing she is about to cry, I call out a final "goodbye, I love you," before hanging up the phone.

I'm sure Audrey will have a hard time settling Maisie, but I needed to speak with her. It's the first time I've not been around to put her to bed, and it's breaking me in two. I drop the phone and lean back on the couch, rubbing the heels of my palms against my face.

My pulse quickens and the tremors in my hands become more intense. Anxiety I haven't felt since before my marriage pumps through my veins, forcing me to move.

As I stand to stretch my limbs, a knock echoes from the hallway and Amira calls out, "We've got food!"

"And beer," Cassidy adds. "Or vodka, depending on what you'd prefer!"

Her voice floats into the room, and a fraction of the anxiety starts to melt away. Hearing her voice, even after all these years, brings an air of calm. Moments ago, I was ready for bed and a week's worth of sorrowful sleep. Now, I only want her company.

"Beer," I reply as the women let themselves in.

"Thought you could do with one of these after moving

day," she says, walking to the kitchen. She slides a pale ale across the bench to me and puts the rest in the fridge.

Grabbing my favourite beer, I spin the can in my hand. I mumble a thanks before taking a long sip. Pale ales have always been my beer of choice. I wonder if Cassidy remembered my favourite brewery, or if it was a fluke.

She flicks her hair in triumph and struts back around the island bench, glancing back at me for a second. My heart does a weird flop at her smug grin, and I'm torn between wondering what it means that she remembered after all these years, and why it feels as important as it does.

"We won't stay," she says, walking back towards her own apartment. She tries to drag Amira out of the chair she made herself comfortable in.

"Why? We brought the food, he doesn't need to do anything but eat," Amira protests. But Cassidy is insistent.

"He spent the whole day lugging boxes up three flights of stairs. Remember when I moved in, it was exhausting."

I gulp down a mouthful of beer and clear my throat to get their attention. "Do I get a say in this?"

I don't want them to go. Cassidy's instinct to leave reminds me of how thoughtful she always was. *Is,* I suppose. Even as a teenager I remember her putting other people first.

The women freeze.

"I am exhausted," I start. "And I might not be *great* company right now, but please, sit." I gesture to the table. After they brought me food, the least I can do is sit and eat it with them.

Amira plonks back down in her seat and opens her own lasagne. Cassidy hesitates, but once I'm sitting at the table, she follows suit, pulling out a creamy pasta dish and a pizza.

"This is to share," she states, opening the pizza and placing it in the middle of the table. The smell of garlic fills the room and I reach my hand out to take a slice.

"Thanks." I look up, smiling a fraction at the girl who visited my dreams and fuelled my fantasies for years before my marriage. Sharing a meal with her has me wondering if we can get back what we lost. "Remember the kid who ate garlic bread every day for lunch for like a year?"

It's a meagre attempt to break the ice, but Cassidy lights up at the memory.

She groans but reaches across the table to take a piece of the pizza. "The smell got into *everything*, I swear it was imbedded into my uniform. I thought I wouldn't be able to eat garlic ever again."

"That clearly didn't last," Amira jests, but I barely register her words.

My eyes meet Cassidy's over the table, and she smiles back at me before looking down at her food. The shared memory is a gentle reminder of how close we used to be. She makes quick work of pulling her hair into a messy bun low on her neck, before shrugging off her puffer jacket. A small piece of lightened hair falls over her face. I fight a strange urge to reach out and gently tuck it behind her ear. It would be inappropriate on a huge number of levels, but I can't escape the intimate feeling between us.

I'm starved after a long day of heavy labour, and as soon as the food starts to settle, I feel my eyelids droop. The effort of lugging my belongings up three flights of stairs has hit me hard. Amira yawns beside me.

"What are you tired for?" I can't help but question. "Not like you uprooted your entire life today."

It comes out snappy and sour, but I can't help it. My social filter is wavering thanks to the exhaustion creeping into my limbs, and I yawn, too.

"Well, thanks, guys, I wasn't tired until you all started yawning." Cassidy's yawn is exaggerated as she stretches her arms above her head.

"I think they are contagious," Amira says through a second yawn. "And I'll have you know, I was up very early this morning for yoga." She waves her glass of water in my face.

I snort, a little of the beer I just sipped bubbling up into my sinuses. "Yoga," I say with a cough, "how laboursome."

"Screw you, neighbour." Amira climbs out of her chair and carries her dishes to the sink.

"Dishwasher isn't hooked up," I say over my shoulder. "Leave it in the sink, I'll do it tomorrow."

I add the task of connecting the dishwasher to my ever growing long list of things to do tomorrow. I'm regretting my decision not to take any time off work, but I was determined to carry on with normal life as much as possible.

Now though, life feels anything but normal, and a few extra days to settle in would have been welcome.

"I'm off," Amira states, halfway out of the apartment. In another situation, I would have walked her out, but the space is tiny, and the exact layout as the one she lives in across the hall. Instead, I call out, "night" with a wave.

"I should go, too." Cassidy is standing, gathering our dishes into neat piles.

"You could stay for another drink?" I shock myself when I say it.

Two minutes ago, I was yawning, feeling tired and grumpy. But now, with just Cassidy in the room, I'd give anything to keep her here. We had been such good friends, and I could use one of those right now. "It's been so long, we should catch up."

With the table cleared, Cassidy pauses in front of the fridge. "Another beer then?"

I always regretted the way Cassidy and I left things. After we lost contact I always wondered if we could have been more. What we might have become if I hadn't been such an awkward, anxious young adult. We had been friends for so long,

I was scared to ruin what we had. Turns out the wedge that formed between us was my fear.

Cassidy had finally quit Supers to pursue her creative career, and for whatever reason, it was the push that encouraged me to kiss her at the party. Her phone ringing and interrupting us was a cold washer to my face. All the anxiety that had rushed through me before we made out flooded back. I couldn't breathe the same air as her any longer, and instead of explaining myself, I ran. Almost literally.

I hate how my actions made her question herself, and I was so sick with embarrassment that the next few times we saw each other were increasingly awkward. It didn't take long before our friendship started to fizzle out.

"You know, I never quit working at Supers," I admit.

I'm trying to take my mind off how I rejected her ... by talking about the time around when I rejected her. I can't make sense of the logic.

She looks at me, confusion spreading across her face as she places an open beer on the table in front of me. "Hmm?" It's a prompt, nothing more, as though she needs to see where this is going before making judgement.

"I was what, shift supervisor when you left?" When she nods, I continue. "I moved stores to become a Pantry Manager, then third in charge. Eventually I was running the whole store. I moved around the state, hopping from store to store, trying to get ahead and make a name for myself within the Supers group. It sucked."

"So did they fire you?" Cassidy smirks as she takes a sip of her drink. The clear liquid wets her lips and I try to ignore the desire to lick it off.

It's apparent that after so long, the slightest amount of interest from another woman will send inappropriate thoughts into my brain, and extra blood to my groin. I cringe inwardly, reminding myself Cassidy is, and always has been, off limits.

The crush I once had on her should be a distant memory, and I can't afford to get caught up in anything more than a friendship.

"Nah, I moved into head office after finally deciding management wasn't for me."

Wondering how we got on the topic of my career, I curse myself for talking about something so drab. "Admin first. After a year I started buying shares. I run the board now."

"Wow." She sounds genuinely impressed. "I've got to say, when you said you never quit, I was worried for a minute."

We laugh together, and the sound brings back some warmth to my cold heart. After all these years, I wonder if I'll ever get back to the carefree guy I used to be. If I'll remember how to push the anxious thoughts to the side and enjoy myself. It feels like too much has changed; so much that changed me.

As the laughter fades, she sighs.

"Sometimes I regret quitting." She says it so quietly I barely hear her, and wonder if that was her intent.

"Why?" I ask, reaching across the table to place my hand on hers. My heart has not beat in this haphazard way since the day I met Audrey. It feels exciting and off-putting all at once. I must be more tired than I thought, because emotions are swirling around in my brain like thunderclouds and I need to work out how to get them under control.

"I lost a lot of friends." She looks down and pulls back her hand. "A really good friend."

It feels like a knife through my chest, and where it was beating fast, it now feels like it stopped. It's fallen to my stomach and left an ache where it once was. My younger self had no idea how much my lack of contact had hurt her. My current self feels atrocious for ever thinking we could have been something more. Clearly, in her eyes, we were friends. I pull my hand back in response and take a long sip of my beer.

"I know it doesn't mean much now, but I'm sorry. I was a dick."

"That we can agree on."

All day, my shoulders have been lifted with tension, but the muscles ease a little at Cassidy's light-hearted tone.

Cassidy flicks at the metal pull ring of her can. "Anyway, what's a hot shot, board executive doing renting a tiny, two bedder in the inner suburbs?"

I take a long pull of my beer, savouring the taste and remembering all the beers we shared as teenagers, before either of us should have been indulging.

"I'm not," I finally choke out.

She raises her perfectly arched eyebrows and gestures around the room.

"Did someone else move in today then?"

I shake my head. The wealth I built myself still feels extravagant, and I'm not sure how to tell Cassidy I'm her landlord.

"I, uh, own the building. This apartment was empty and I needed a temporary place while I look for a new house."

Cassidy stares at me with wide eyes and forced smile. I hate that I've made her feel uncomfortable, but appreciate the lack of follow-up questions. There is so much of my history I'm not ready to share with her.

After we've finished our drinks, and Cassidy has retreated across the hall, I wash the dishes. As exhausted as I am, it'll be even worse if I wake in the morning to a sink of dishes. While I'm rinsing glasses I attempt to straighten the storm cloud of emotions before I settle in for the night and attempt to sleep. Yes, I used to have a massive crush on Cassidy, but it was a long time ago. We barely know each other as adults, and she made it clear how upset she was when we lost contact. I can't do anything to jeopardise the chance of our friendship rekindling, regardless of how absolutely stunning the woman is.

Not to mention, how fresh the pain over my marriage breaking up still is. I'm in no place to pursue any kind of relationship. All it will lead to is pain and heartache for everyone, and I've had enough of that to last me a very long time.

Chapter Five

CALLUM

By the time a whole week has rolled around, I'm missing my daughter more than I ever thought possible. The phone calls every night have done little to ease the aching that has spread through me. The way she giggles at the smallest of things, and how she is the only person in the world to appreciate my dad jokes. The way she always demands an Elsa braid even when she knows my attempt will fall out within minutes. The songs she loves to create, blending lyrics of all her favourites into a Kidz Bop worthy mashup.

And the way she finds her calm in my arms, and how when she snuggles in close, I feel every single worry of mine melting away.

I've always found comfort in knowing I'm Maisie's safe place. Spending so much time apart, I'm realising just how much she is mine, too. I never realised how much I depended on her to cheer me up after a long shitty day punching numbers. But as much as I miss her, I hate thinking about how hard the past week must have been on her.

As I rush to tidy my small apartment, I have a skip in my step knowing I will get to see my daughter soon. Audrey is going to drop her off after breakfast. Maisie and I will be spending the whole day together. I had tried to convince Audrey to let her stay, especially considering how tired she will be after my nephew's birthday party. But my ex-wife had held her ground, still convinced Maisie deserved the stability her old room provided. I'm hopeful when she sees the place I've set up for Maisie here, I'll be a little closer to nudging her over the line. I hate the thought of getting lawyers involved in such a personal situation, but if she doesn't agree to start following the terms of the custody agreement, I might have to.

Without a child in the house, there's not a lot to tidy up, but I find myself straightening the picture frames I placed on the TV stand and refolding the tea towel hanging under the sink. I mock myself as I fluff the bright cushions I ordered to make the clinical grey couch look more appealing. I doubt Maisie will notice, or care, before she jumps all over it.

My goal is to show Audrey I've set up a perfect little space for Maisie, and I'm not giving her anything to pick at.

The second bedroom has been set up as Maisie's space. A repeating ballet shoe pattern covers the bedspread, and a doll's house sits in the corner. I've asked Audrey to bring over a couple of soft toys and Barbies to live here, but bought a small selection just in case. Everything Maisie could need to express her creativity is set up on the table under the window. Scrapbooks, felt tip pens, pencils, glue, scissors, and the like, are all neatly placed in desk organisers. She's always bringing her creations home from kindergarten, asking to stick them on the fridge or the wall. I have a good feeling she will love being able to create things here, too. I've also loaded the shelves of a small bookshelf with some picture books and puzzles. My favourites, Julia Donaldson and Dr Seuss, as well as Maisie's favourites like *Frozen* and other Disney tales.

The place looks perfect, but it's not *right*. Sitting on the edge of the ballerina bed, I glance around the room and run a hand through my hair. Any five year old would love this room, but it feels like something out of a catalogue. It's too neat, not lived in, and lacks Maisie's creative flare. I hope that in time, she feels comfortable here. That it starts to feel like home.

The intercom buzzes, interrupting my contemplation. I jump up to answer it. The grainy video shows Audrey standing outside the lobby with Maisie clinging to her leg. Her favourite toy ballerina tucked under her arm.

I hit the button to unlock the entrance, and push the speaker button. "Come in, I'll start heading down to meet you."

As I slide on my shoes and head for the stairwell, I find myself staring at Cassidy's apartment door. Guilt spreads through me, leaving a tingling feeling in my fingers. I should have told her about Maisie when we had dinner last weekend. But I didn't. *How do I tell a girl from my past that my present is so different to what she knows?* I've never had to casually bring up the fact I have a child, and I have no idea how to do it.

I find Maisie and Audrey near the first floor, and it shouldn't be as awkward as it is. Maisie shuffles her feet, still clinging to her mother as I resist the urge to collect her into a bear hug. I look to Audrey for guidance, and she shrugs.

"She's missed you," she says, her tone sweet, not at all like the bitter one liners I'd gotten used to over the past few months. "Honestly, it's been a hard time for her. This is a lot."

"I know," I answer, as I squat down to put myself at Maisie's level. "Hey, chicka," I whisper.

"Hey, Daddy." Her voice is the quietest I've ever heard it, and holds an uncertainty I've never heard from her.

"I know it's been hard, okay, but I've missed you *so* much." I gently reach my hand towards hers, respecting her boundaries and waiting until she reaches towards me with her own hand before I grab hold of it.

"Wanna come see the new house?"

Maisie looks side to side, before settling her eyes on the stairs and letting go of Audrey's leg. The three of us walk up the next two flights of stairs and head down the corridor. Maisie's mouth hangs open as she swivels her head, taking in everything.

"Is this all your house?" she asks.

Audrey chuckles behind us.

"No, no, Maisie." I laugh. "Just this one." I pull my keys from my pocket. Turning the key in the lock I add, "Can you help me open it?"

Maisie lets go of my hand, placing both her palms flat on the door in front of her.

"One, two, three!" I roar with a fake grunt. We've played this game for as long as I can remember. Her giggles flood my ears and as we walk into the apartment together, it finally feels like home.

I give Maisie and Audrey a tour of the place, highlighting all the things I think Maisie will love, like the balcony and how I've hooked the console up to my new TV. When we get to the bedroom I've set up for Maisie, she runs inside and spins with her arms out wide.

"Is this my room?!" she calls out, her eyes flicking from the ballerina bed, to the craft table, to the doll's house.

From my peripheral, I can see Audrey giving me a death glare. I force a slow breath before answering Maisie in what I hope is a fair and age appropriate way.

"Yes, but the bed is only for naps or resting today. I'll drop you back at Mummy's after dinner, and you'll go to bed there."

Audrey releases the puff of air she must have been holding, and I wonder if she thought I was going to manipulate Maisie, encourage her to beg her mother to stay here.

"You can sleep here soon."

I whip my head around to face my ex, astounded at her sudden change of mind.

"Not just yet," she clarifies, taking the few steps towards Maisie and picking her up. "But yeah, one day. I think Daddy needs to settle in a little bit more, and we all need to get used to living apart first."

I try not to let her words about me needing to settle

hit me. I do feel settled, and although her justifications don't make sense to me, I'll give her a little more time to come around.

Maisie grabs Audrey's face in her hands and plants a sloppy kiss on her nose, before wriggling back down to the ground.

"I love it," she exclaims, as she runs towards me and leaps into my arms.

"And I love you." I kiss her forehead.

After Audrey leaves, Maisie and I get ready for her cousin's fifth birthday party. The two have always been close, less than a year apart in age, and I love how they managed to bring my sister, Isobel, and I closer together. Although we were friendly enough as young kids, our relationship took a hit during our teenage years. It wasn't until we bonded as adults that we reconnected. Once we both settled down and had kids of our own, our relationship continued to grow. Now, I'd say she is one of my closest friends and she is the first person I turn to for advice.

"We have to buy a present on the way, okay, Maisie," I say, as she puts her blue sparkly shoes back on.

"I think he would like blue shoes, too," she responds, "or Lego."

"Lego sounds like a good choice." And easier, since I have no idea what size shoe Jackson would wear.

It's late in the afternoon before I finally get to relax a little at Jackon's birthday. Almost as soon as we arrived, my brother-in-law roped me in to manning the BBQ, after which I somehow ended up as the only adult supervising the jumping castle. I had thought the call of cake would bring the kids running in an instant. I was wrong, and ended up having to climb in, chasing after kids whose names I didn't even know. I've always prided myself on being the 'fun dad', but it sure is tiring on days like these.

With the party mostly calmed down, the few stragglers left are all family or close friends. The jumping castle company has been and gone to collect the blow-up castle and slide, so the kids run laps of the yard. Fits of laughter and squeals fill the air. I have to get Maisie back to her mum by dinner, but figure after all the sweets, cake and juice, another half an hour burning off energy won't hurt.

"Here." My sister passes a cold beer over my shoulder and sits on the lounger next to me. It's already open, and I take a long sip, appreciating the cool frothy bubbles.

"How are you?" Isobel asks. Before I can answer, she adds, "Like, don't just say 'yeah good', I mean *really* how are you?"

I take another sip of beer to fill the gap as I consider her loaded question.

"I'm okay, really," I answer. "It's been hard, but today was good. I needed today, with Maisie."

"I can't imagine not being with the kids every day." Isobel leans back in her chair, pressing her thumbs against her temples. As if her ears were burning, my niece comes running over and climbs onto her mother's lap. At only two years old, she looks worn out after the party, yawning as she snuggles into Isobel's shoulder.

"Bedtime soon, I think," Isobel whispers down.

Nothing makes me prouder as a little brother, than seeing my sister with her kids, and her husband. She has the kind of family I dreamed of. The kind I once thought I would have with Audrey.

More than that, though, my sister excels at being a mum. Isobel's hand caresses her daughter's long hair, getting caught in the knots I can only assume have come from all the running and jumping.

"I know you said you didn't want to go to court, but you know he'd fight for you, right?"

She jerks her head, and I follow her line of sight to where her husband is packing up the last of the party decorations. My brother-in-law is a family court lawyer, something I never imagined would come in handy until Audrey and I were finalising the divorce. Although I've been adamant I didn't want to go to court, it's soothing knowing I've still got his support if I need it.

For now, I'm giving Audrey a few weeks to adjust. The whole situation is complicated, and she is only doing what she thinks is right for Maisie. And although I miss my daughter terribly, Audrey's decision comes from a place of love and care. I don't want to make my move messier than it needs to be. Not yet.

"I know," I respond after a pause. "But I hope he won't need to. I'm giving her a little bit of time."

A few weeks. That's all. Then I'll fight. If I have to.

I watch as my brother-in-law hauls a garbage bag around the backyard, rounding up the kids. Isobel closes her eyes, enjoying the moment of peace as her daughter falls asleep in her arms.

Isobel turns to me after her husband has taken their daughter inside. "Aside from, you know," she waves her arm around, "everything. What's been going on?"

The change of topic is welcome. It seems all anyone ever talks to me about is the separation, the pending divorce, or how hard it must be on Maisie. Although it makes sense they are offering me a chance to talk things out, it gets draining, hashing out the same conversation countless times.

"Good, I guess. Work is work. They have been pretty

flexible with me when I need it and I've finally set a work from home space up again which is easier."

"And what about the new place? Have you met the neighbours?"

I choke on my drink. Because yes, I've met the neighbours, and I haven't stopped thinking about one of them since.

Isobel gives me a side eye. "Do tell."

"Do you remember Cassidy?"

She jolts up from her laid-back position, feet kicking the half full bottle I'd placed on the ground. The bottle tinkles as it rolls away, but Isobel doesn't take her eyes off me. "From the supermarket? The Cassidy you were in love with for years?"

I nod.

"Well, what about her?"

"She lives across the hall."

Gaining composure, Isobel takes a sip of her drink. "Okay, and?"

"And I don't know," I answer, because I don't. I don't know if I'm rebounding onto an old crush because it's convenient. I don't know if she even feels the same. I don't know what any of the swirling, conflicting emotions mean, but I do know I shouldn't be ready for anything like that right now.

At the very least, I want to get back to the level of friendship Cassidy and I used to have. If I could hold back my lust as a teenager, then surely I can hold it back as an adult. At least until I have a better grip on my life.

I explain it all to Isobel, hoping she has some magic words of wisdom to share. Leaning forward again, she places a hand on my knee.

"You're allowed to move on," is all she says, before finishing the last swig of her bottle and leaning back. With her face in the setting sun, she closes her eyes. Her hands fold across her waist, holding the cardigan she wears close. We got lucky this time of year, to have such a lovely day for a backyard party, but as the sun lowers, the cool breeze has picked up. As a flurry rushes over us, I feel goosebumps prickle on my arms and wish I'd brought a sweater.

"Just because I'm allowed to, doesn't mean I want to," I spit back after contemplating Isobel's statement. The look on her face has me regretting my mini outburst. I run a hand over my face, hating the snappy person I've become lately.

"Sorry," I say. "I'm still getting over what I had with Audrey. You know more than anyone I never wanted things to work out this way."

What Audrey and I had was great, until it wasn't. When I first noticed our growing issues, I had tried to convince her we needed to work a little harder to find our relationship again. I found a couple's therapist, organised date nights, and tried my hardest to romance Audrey; to be the man she fell in love with again. But nothing I did convinced her we were worth fighting for, and eventually, I resigned to the fact we had grown too far apart. We had become housemates who shared a child and a bank account, and the longer it went on, the harder it was to bring our love back.

Despite no longer loving Audrey, I'm not ready to move on. It's not just my heart on the line anymore. I have to think about Maisie and what is right for her. Introducing a new woman into my life, into Maisie's life, is simply not on the cards. No matter how much my heart flutters over the woman across the hall.

I lean forward, resting my elbows on my knees and staring into the now empty backyard. I realise I'll have to get Maisie back to Audrey soon.

For a while, the only sound between us is the gentle fizz from the small puddle of beer and the rush of leaves from the trees.

"Issy?"

"What?"

"I thought you were asleep."

"Nah just thinking about all the cleaning I'll have to do tomorrow." She sighs, sitting up.

"Yeah, good luck with that." I laugh. "I've got to take Maisie back."

She stands up with me and we share one of those awkward adult siblings' hugs. As we pull apart, she reaches around to whack the back of my head with her palm.

"Ow, what was that for?"

"It doesn't matter, it's in the past."

Her attempt at a Swahili accent is terrible, but I pick up on the Lion King reference and one side of my mouth creeps up. What started as a couple of kids finding a sneaky excuse to hit each other, eventually morphed into our coded way to remind each other to look forward, instead of back.

"Thanks," I say. I appreciate the reminder, even if it has left a subtle sting under my hair.

Despite my sister's nudge, I'm not sure the way forward is with Cassidy. Our history aside, I can't bounce from one shitty marriage to another half-hearted relationship.

So I'll look forward, but not across the hall. I'll focus on gaining Audrey's trust and showing her how Maisie can thrive with two homes. I'll focus on making sure my days with my daughter are full of love and joy. I'll focus on moving on from the life I thought I would have, and my future as a single dad.

Chapter Six

CASSIDY

Sweat trickles down my forehead as I load the last pile of empty buckets into my van. It's my last wedding of the season, but instead of relief at a quiet few months ahead, I'm nervous as all hell. The landlord increased rent on my tiny storefront, and unless I magically sell twice as many bouquets as I did last winter, it's going to be a tough run.

Other florists would be settling in, enjoying a little peace before the craziness that always comes with Mother's Day. But I refuse. Although it might be detrimental to my business, it's the one day I refuse to open. It feels wrong in far too many ways. The fear my business will fail sweeps through me as a cool breeze raises the tiny hairs on my arms. Mother's Day might be my only way out this year, and I hate the thought.

As glad as I am that I was able to secure a Friday wedding, self-doubt has me wondering why I hadn't been able to secure an event for tomorrow as well.

My self-doubt creeps in a lot.

Especially since last weekend. Funny how one conversation with Amira about my sucky love life had me so confident to step away from dating and men, and one guy from my past made me question my decision. As much as Amira was right when she said I needed to take a break from dating, there's something about the timing of Callum's reappearance that feels like fate.

Either my head wasn't screwed on tight enough, or part of me was still a messy teenage girl with a giant crush. I need to pull myself together. We're not teenagers anymore, and a quick conversation with Callum showed he was still well and truly out of my league. Maybe even more than he used to be. What did he say his job was, running the board? It seems important. White collar, upper management style professional. Very unlike little old me getting her hands all green and wet cutting flowers every day.

And that's without thinking about the conversations we used to share in the tearoom. Callum was all 'when I'm a dad' and 'imagine a little me running around', and at the time, I was the same. But things change, life happens and what we thought we wanted doesn't always pan out.

Fate aside, I need to remember those conversations.

Closing the van, I pull my phone out of my pocket and head back towards the ceremony location. I've never done a wedding at this winery, but it's stunning. I remind myself to thank my cousin for recommending me to the bride. He is the new event coordinator, and I'm hopeful he'll continue to recommend me as a vendor. Either way, photos of all the different arrangements and locations will be great for all my socials.

My Betty Blooms pages have thousands of followers, and I regularly get shared across other vendor pages. But if I can grow it even further, it could mean that next wedding season, my services are highly sought after, and fully booked out. I chuckle at the thought. *A florist can dream, right?*

Realistically, I doubt my fading view of love is going to get me far in this industry.

Taking snaps of the floral arbour, I start wondering how I can shift some focus to special occasion flowers and standard bouquets. I already offer free local delivery, but I'll have to find a same day courier service if I want to expand my customer base. I flip to the messages app and write a note to myself to look into Uber Couriers when muffled footsteps make their way along the grass aisle behind me.

A gruff voice coughs. "Ahh, we need to clear out, the groom is due to arrive any minute."

I must have taken longer with the photos than intended, it's not surprising when getting lost in my thoughts is one of my best, or worse, qualities.

"Sorry," I reply as I wave my arm at the floral arrangements. "I was getting some snaps, but I'm done."

Looking up, I see one of the few people that always manages to brighten my day. He looks almost unrecognisable in such dark and professional attire. Pushing his mop of sandy blond hair off his face, my cousin squints his bright blue eyes. His hand rests on his forehead, shielding his face from the sun with his hand.

"You look ... different." I laugh.

Noah looks like he belongs on the sand, like he would be more comfortable on Bondi Beach than down here in Melbourne. He was comfortable there, I suppose, until he wasn't. The singlet and board shorts I'm used to seeing him in are gone, replaced with slimline black pants and a dark button down shirt. His sleeves are rolled up, revealing the sun-tanned skin of his forearms; the kind of glow women pay for, but it won't last forever. We are blessed, or maybe cursed, with the same pale skin from our mothers.

My aunty moved up to Sydney back in her university days, fell in love, and never left. While I was living up there with my ex, Noah and I connected and started the foundations of a solid friendship. He hasn't told me what prompted his move down to Melbourne earlier this year, but we've become closer than ever before. Along with Amira and my sister, I'd trust him with anything.

"It's all the black I think, had to buy a whole new wardrobe." His hands glide up and down his sides while he pops his hips and shoulders like a model.

"I'd say it suits you ..." I start.

He laughs. "But it doesn't," he says, finishing my sentence for me. "Anyway, we finished setting the tables if you want photos of the centrepieces too?"

I'll never say no to more photos, so we walk across to the restaurant together. Inside has been transformed. When I was setting up, the four long tables were bare. The long centrepieces of twined dollar gum are spotted with florals. The greenery pops against the woodgrain tables. White native daisies are scattered amongst the leaves, with the occasional white Waratah. Native Australian flora is my speciality, and I'm particularly proud of what I've created today. The terms 'white' and 'Aussie natives' don't typically work well together when it comes to floristry, but that's what today's bride had briefed. Admiring my work in the fully set reception area, I'm confident I pulled it off. I stand a little taller as I walk between the tables, taking photos of all the little details.

The winery staff have added golden charger plates, white linen napkins, and gorgeous wooden name cards to the table. The final look is something out of a bridal magazine, and not at all the rustic vibe the space usually exudes. With only my phone to take photos with, I wish I had a better camera on me. I'm hopeful the photographer not only takes some great shots but is also willing to share them with me. I add a note to track down who it is.

My text message to-do list is getting longer by the hour, and I need a better way of managing my tasks. I add researching mobile planner apps before hitting send and quickly closing out of the message. I need to see the red notification every time I open my phone if I want to remember the list is there at all.

"Here." Noah walks back towards me with a glass of ice water. "I'd offer you wine, but we aren't allowed to pop the bottles until the guests arrive."

I can't help but laugh at his suggestion of wine this early

in the day, although the thought of having a drink with Noah sounds inviting. It's been too long since we had a night out.

"We'll have to have wine another time."

"We should," he replies, leaning back against the bar that lines one side of the event space. "I feel more settled in here, and the season is starting to calm down. We should both have some more time."

"You're telling me," I scoff. Regardless of how busy or quiet the season is, Noah is a contracted employee with a secure wage. Not all of us are so lucky.

As I enter my apartment, I can smell Amira's cooking. She makes the most delicious middle eastern meals, recipes passed down through generations with ingredients I wouldn't even know where to buy.

"Whatever you have made smells delicious," I call out. Hints of nutmeg and turmeric blend with something fruity, filling my nostrils. I might as well be salivating, and I don't even know what she's made.

Ducking into my room, I strip off my green stained work wear and slip on an old t-shirt dress. It's so worn it's almost see-through, and I often wear it to bed, but it's comfy and the exact amount of coziness I need after a long day. Friday mornings always start at the crack of dawn for the flower market, and typically end long after dark. With the added wedding in today's normal schedule, I'm exhausted. Once I was finished at the winery, I returned to open the physical shop front for the rest of the day. Customers were few and far between, but I spent a lot of time working my way down my list of tasks. Uber Couriers is still a maybe, but I found a better app for to-do lists and reminders and found a social media agency I might be able to squeeze into the budget. Once I was in the creative mood, I started a Pinterest board of florist 'extras' that I want to start looking into stocking at the shop.

When I walk out of my room, I hesitate in the hall. Sitting on the couch, a comfortable distance from Amira, is Callum. I want to rush back into my room, fix my hair, and put on something far more attractive but instead, I pull at the hem of my oversized tee.

My shoulders turn down, but I force my head high, hiding my embarrassment and trying to embrace the comfort that oozes from his presence. It's only been a week, but it already feels as though Callum is inserting himself into our circle. The picture before me feels so seamless he could have been living in the building forever. It gives me hope the years between us, all the missed moments after we parted ways, will eventually melt into nothingness. After all this time, it's impossible to take off exactly where we left, but it's nice for someone to have returned to my life, rather than leaving it forever. I hope we can be friends again. Close friends.

I decide to lean into the newfound familiarity and announce my presence, "Oh, hi."

Callum looks up, and a wide smile spreads across his face.

"Hi, Rogue."

At my old nickname, butterflies find their wings in my stomach. It's impossible to ignore the sensation. I instinctually rub against the feeling, willing it to calm down. Although our friendship is taking a slow rebirth, the attraction and giddiness is back in full force, and I'd do anything to make sure Callum never finds out about it.

"Hmm," I groan, feigning a sniff. "What have you cooked us, Amira?"

She jolts up and darts across to the kitchen stove, where

two big pots sit. Cooking is Amira's love language, and on days like these, I'm glad she loves me.

"Pomegranate chicken." She lifts the lid of one pot, sticks her nose in, and gives it a stir. Using the wooden spoon she pats the second pot. "And wild rice." Even with my limited knowledge about cooking, I know she can't remove the lid until the rice is fully cooked. Something about water absorption and not wanting the rice to end up gluggy.

"Drink?" She walks to the fridge and pulls out one of my favourite watermelon seltzers. "Another beer, Cal?"

Cal? Since when were Amira and Callum close enough for abbreviations? But also, I'm sure he used to hate being called that. He used to say it was reserved for special people only. I was the only one at work allowed to shorten his name. I pivot to face Amira in the kitchen, my eyes wide with shock and question. She smirks, and I'm hit with a pang of unease. It feels like jealousy, but I force the emotion away, knowing it has no place in our friendship.

"Please," he calls out from the couch.

Amira hands me both drinks with a wink before sitting down on her favourite red dining chair. I stand, stunned for a few seconds before Amira adds an extra nod towards the couch. Turning, I pass Callum his drink. A thin pink band stretches around his wrist, out of place next to his plain black tee. My eyes linger on it, trying to figure out the odd fashion statement. If I took a guess, I'd say it's a hair tie, but his hair is too short to need one.

I sit at the opposite end of the couch. Pulling my grandma's knit blanket onto my lap, I curl my legs underneath me.

"You're just in time," Amira states, "dinner will be ready in about five more minutes."

"I could smell it from across the hall." Callum's voice is low, almost a growl, and he looks like he might start drooling.

"Get used to it." Laughing, I stretch my leg out to gently

kick his thigh. He catches my foot, and when I try to pull it back he holds tight. I regret my playfulness, until he presses his fingers into my aching muscles, massaging my calf. Although he used to rub my feet all the time, the intimacy feels intense after so long of not knowing one another. But my legs are sore after a long day on my feet, and the massage is welcome. I stretch the other leg up as well, encouraging him to continue.

"Why Rogue?" Amira questions as we eat.

"From an old game we used to play. I called her Rogue, she called me Master."

Amira chokes on her rice. "I don't want to know what kind of kinky games you guys were playing as teenagers."

I kick her shin under the table. The game was about as innocent as they come, never mind the double entendre.

"It was nothing," I mutter, stuffing my face with food.

The rest of the evening feels comfortable, familiar in a way it shouldn't after one week. It's as though Callum never left my life.

I snort at the thought, and when the two of them look up in sync, I try to brush it off as a bit of food down the wrong pipe. Sitting, eating, and chatting with Callum has brought back all levels of nostalgia, along with all kinds of inappropriate thoughts.

Like what other kind of spots he could massage with those strong fingers of his, or how close my feet were to his crotch and whether he had a foot fetish. I push my hands into my eyes and try to get the thoughts out of my head.

After dinner, we return to the couch. Without intention, my legs end up back in Callum's lap. Fighting the return of the inappropriate thoughts from earlier, I attempt to shift my focus.

"So, Cass," Amira says, before I have a chance to think of an appropriate conversation topic.

I glance at her with raised eyebrows. I know that voice.

Taking a deep breath she adds, "Remember how you swore off men and I said I wasn't going to date anyone?" She laughs, and I feel Callum's hands slow down and hesitate. "Well I have to take it back."

I gasp in feigned shock, knowing all along her vow of celibacy was never going to last.

"I have a date to go on." She leans back on her chair with a smirk. Of course she does.

My eyebrows drop as I roll my eyes at her.

"Is this normal for her?" Callum turns to ask me. His hands have stopped massaging and I wonder if I should take my feet from his lap.

"Pretty much. She goes on a date, has a terrible time, probably sleeps with them anyway, then swears off dating when they don't call her. Rinse, repeat."

"I do not sleep with them *all*." Amira folds her arm across her face.

"You sleep with enough of them that I sleep with earplugs so I won't get jealous."

Callum clears his throat, his eyes flashing between us as we bicker.

Deciding I'm not finished with the massage, I wiggle my feet, inviting him to continue. But instead, he tickles my soles, causing me to shriek. Lurching backwards I pull my feet out of his grasp.

Amira slaps her hand on the table as she stands. "Oh, girl." She laughs. "I was right when I said it would be an interesting few weeks."

"Meaning?"

"Meaning a lot of things."

Pushing herself to a stand, she mocks a bow and starts walking out. "I'm off," she yells over her shoulder.

"Now?"

"Yes now."

"Don't forget your—"

"Coat, yes, I won't forget my coat," she finishes for me as she pulls a black jacket off the hook. "Have fun, don't wait up!"

Callum and I sit, the ticking of the clock and the occasional car horn from outside the only sound between us. He stretches his arms behind his head and leans back with a sigh.

"I'm pretty sure that was my coat," I blurt out to fill the silence, at the same time he says, "So you swore off men?"

Shifting my legs, I hug them to my chest. "Yeah," I whisper, feeling childish about the oath. Talking about it with the man I considered breaking it for feels unnecessary, and highly embarrassing.

Callum's mouth falls thin and soft lines form between his brows. When he shifts, part of me expects him to leave, but instead he leans forward, resting his elbows on his knees.

He drops his head, running both hands through his hair.

"Okay," he says, although he doesn't sound convinced. It comes out as almost a squeak, and he hasn't looked up. "I mean." He clears his throat, "Cool. That's cool."

Laughing, I try to relax my legs.

"Yeah," I respond, although the air still feels static, "until the right guy comes along of course."

"Fair." He chokes on his breath as he tilts his head to the side before pushing himself to stand. "I should go."

In only a few strides he has one foot in the hall. "Tell Amira thanks for the meal?"

"Sure." My heart cracks, wondering why he feels the need to rush off. There's no reason me swearing off men should ruin the friendship that is fast re-forming between me and Callum.

He gave me advice when the coolest boy in my high school grade took me to formal, and I stood by him when he nervously told me he wanted to ask out his neighbour. Why should our friendship now be any different?

"Goodnight," I call out.

"Night."

Chapter Seven

CALLUM

Maisie sobs against my leg on the doorstep of what was once my family home, and it's taking all I have not to fall to my knees and cry with her. I don't want to say goodbye either. The past couple of weeks have been beyond difficult. Knowing I won't see her for another seven days weighs my limbs down like concrete. Sure, there are men, and women, out there who don't see their kids for varying chunks of time. And sure, they make it work and somehow get through their days without crumbling. But my foundations are sinking, and I don't know how much longer I can sustain this.

Maisie and I spent so much time together. I worked from home when she was younger; when Audrey returned to work part time and had to be onsite. Somehow, I managed to juggle my career and caring for a toddler. It was tough, but we made it work. I grew so used to Maisie being around. It was hard enough when she started kindergarten earlier in the year, but nothing compares to not seeing her throughout the week.

I don't want to leave her here and return to my apartment. It feels too clinical through the week. Bitterly quiet despite the traffic sounds that waft in through the windows. It stays too tidy and my workdays are too uninterrupted. There is a giant Maisie sized hole in my life.

"I want to take Maisie to see my parents next Saturday," Audrey announces after we manage to peel Maisie off me and settle her in front of the TV.

Leaning her weight on to one leg and placing a hand on

her popped hip, Audrey's tone has an odd flare. It's like she threw a concrete slab at my chest, and she knows how off guard I was when it hit me. I take a step back, rubbing my fist against my breastbone in a futile attempt to ease the tension.

"What?"

I want Maisie to have a strong relationship with her maternal grandparents just as much as I want her to have a strong relationship with my family, but I'm not okay with missing out on my time with her for it to happen. This feels like the final straw, and my lenience around our custody arrangement is about to crack.

"She hasn't seen them in months," Audrey says, her hand flying around in front of her face as though she can wave off my shock.

"But we agreed I would see her Saturdays." I fumble the response, my teeth grinding as I draw in a long, slow breath.

"And it's not fair you get all the fun Saturdays and I get all the hard work during the week."

"So we'll start following the custody agreement you *agreed* to. We alternate weeks, swap out picking her up from Kindergarten Friday afternoons. You know I'm settled now, I've got a space set up for her."

I tap my knuckle against my sternum before bringing my hand up to pinch the bridge of my nose. I can't keep having this same conversation and getting nowhere. We discuss our so-called 'custody agreement' almost weekly, but Audrey still hasn't budged from her belief that Maisie needs more time to settle. If anything, it's Audrey who's not ready to let go. Which isn't fair on Maisie. Or me.

"I can't keep doing this," I add once I have my breathing under control.

Disney songs blare through the house and I silently curse knowing one will be sure to end up stuck in my head all day. Audrey stands, frozen, staring at me.

"So don't," she jabs. "If you don't want to be part of Maisie's life, don't be."

Her arms fold across her heaving chest. "I should have known this was coming," she adds, shaking her head.

"That's not what I meant." I take a step closer, towering over her just enough so she has to tilt her head to look me in the eye.

"I mean," I drawl, "I need to see her more. The custody agreement was signed by both of us, you need to follow it."

"She needs consistency, stability. Your leaving has been enough of a change. I won't have her living out of a backpack."

"Me leaving?" My muscles tighten in response, hands flexing to ease a fraction of the tension. I remind myself not to raise my voice above the Disney tunes coming from the living room. "It was not my choice to leave." My jaw clenches as I stare down at Audrey. "*You* decided it makes more sense for me to move since I was travelling furthest for work. *You* are deciding how little Maisie sees me. *You* wanted this. Not me."

I take a few steps back, walk out of the front door and down the step onto the porch. My blood boils, but my rational brain knows an outburst of anger will not win me any favours. Audrey huffs as she follows me, stopping at the entrance to the house.

"Take her to see your parents on Saturday, but I'll come pick her up Sunday morning. You need to let me see her more, or you'll be hearing from my lawyer." I state over my shoulder as I walk down the driveway. I don't like threatening Audrey with lawyers and family court, but I'm done playing nice when it comes to my daughter. I will do whatever it takes to see her more.

And I'm starting to think I'll have to use my family connections again after all.

Returning to the apartment, the adrenaline is still flooding through me. I want to punch something. To scream. Balling my hands into fists, I squeeze as I stomp up the stairs to my apartment. Emotion flickering and wavering with every step, it hits me when I reach the third floor landing. So close to my new place, yet so far from anywhere that feels homely. I place my hands on the wall under the tiny window and lean forward. My forehead rests against the cool glass as I rake in breaths and try to blink away the moisture in my eyes.

And then I smell her.

Hints of lavender first, followed by something fruity and sweet. It smells like home, and a wave of reassurance that doesn't belong creeps along my spine.

I push myself to stand upright, but not before Cassidy rounds the corner and sees me heaving like the contents of my stomach are making their way back up. My heart feels like it forgot how to beat, and with every short breath, my lungs feel tighter. I focus on the rapid rise and fall of my chest as I work to prevent my lunch from making a reappearance.

"Callum?"

There is concern in her far away voice as she rushes over and guides me to the floor. My vision fades.

Cassidy's hands are on my legs, pulling them up. I try to focus on the feeling, willing my body to calm down.

"Breathe," she whispers, as she moves her hands to my cheeks. Slowly, she guides my head down until it's between my knees.

She's behind me, her legs on either side of me with her chest pressed against my back. I can feel her rise and fall with each breath she takes.

"Breathe with me," she says as she starts counting. "One ... two ... three ... four."

She inhales deeply, counts again as she stills, and once more as she exhales. Reaching around, Cassidy taps her knuckles on my sternum. In time with her counts, the steady beat gives me something to focus on. Just the way I used to do it. She repeats the process until my breaths fall in line with hers.

"I think you had a panic attack," she whispers.

"You remembered the tappy thing."

She draws her arm back from around my body to rest on my side. "Do you think you can stand?"

"I can try."

Cassidy wraps her arm around my back to help me up. Balancing more of my weight on her petite frame than I should, we stand. She guides me to my apartment, fumbling around my pockets for the key.

"Up," I groan, reaching my hand above my head to grab the spare key I keep 'hidden' on the door frame.

Grabbing it from my hand, Cassidy laughs.

"Very safe," she says with an eye roll as the door swings open.

Inside, she guides me to the couch. I fight the urge to crawl into a ball.

"Drink," she demands, placing a glass of water on the coffee table in front of me, adding "slowly," when I lean forward and take a gulp.

When she sits next to me, a wave of her lavender scent wafts my way. I choke on the water.

"That's why I said slowly." She nudges my side softly, not realising it's her that made me splutter.

The sun has started to set, the sky outside the big window a dull grey. As we sit, the only sounds are Cassidy's slow, counted breaths, and my shaky, too quick ones.

My pulse returns to its normal rhythm and my lungs start to work again, but my mind still swirls with the unwelcome storm of leftover emotions. The panic attack hit me hard and fast, and left me more worried than I was before. It's been years since my anxiety made an appearance, but since the divorce, I've felt it creeping back. Frankly, anxiety is a distraction I don't need; a weapon I'm sure Audrey will use against me if she finds out about it.

"Is everything okay?"

I don't know how to tell her that nothing is okay. That my life started crumbling a little over a year ago, and I don't even think I've reached the bottom. I don't know how to tell her that her reappearance in my life has only added to the boulders I carry. And I certainly don't know how to tell her I miss my daughter. Every. Single. Day.

Because I realise, not for the first time, I haven't even told Cassidy about Maisie. I glance over Cassidy's shoulder to Maisie's room. It's open, and I can see her childish bedspread and the giant doll house, but Cassidy hasn't noticed it. Or she noticed it, but hasn't said anything. I've never been more glad of my reputation as the tidy one. I always make Maisie help me pack things away before she goes, so at least there are no Barbies spread across the floor or art supplies on the table.

I should tell Cassidy about Maisie, but now is a terrible time to open the can of worms I'm sure will follow. Cassidy is like a reminder of my old life, of the old me. And I'm not ready to bring her into my present reality. Not just yet.

So instead, I close my eyes and shrug. As I lean back on the couch, I feel Cassidy move closer. Her touch is slow, almost trembling, as she rests her head on my shoulder and lays her hand above my heart. It's warm, and comforting, and it feels safe. So, I wrap my arm around her, somehow finding comfort in the closeness.

"You don't owe me an explanation," she whispers. "I'm here for you either way."

"Like old times?"

"Yeah," she whispers.

While we rest, my mind wanders through the many what-ifs of my life.

I'll never take back the choices I made. Without meeting Audrey, I wouldn't have had Maisie, and she is far too special to wish away. But I can't help wondering where my life would be if things had taken a different path.

None of my old friends have kids. Most of them joke about never feeling like enough of an adult to contemplate having a child, but most of them are also single. I can't remember the last time I went on a big night out with them. After meeting Audrey, and especially after Maisie came into our lives, I never felt like joining guy's night.

As the course of my life changed, so did my friendships. And when I'm honest with myself, I don't know if I'd even call most of those guys my close friends anymore. It really, truly, painfully, sucks. My life veered off the main path and away from them. Or they veered off the main path away from me.

Either way, it still hits like a brick when I think about how all my friends are just the dads of Maisie's friends. And all of Maisie's friends are the children of Audrey's friends. Which means, as Audrey and I started to drift apart, and when we finally, officially, called the divorce what it was, those so-called friends had drifted, too.

I turn my head towards Cassidy's to rest my cheek on her head. Her hair tangles in the coarse stubble of my beard—the perfectly maintained short style I keep tidy enough not to push the limits of my corporate job. As I rasp in unsteady breaths, I realise Cassidy's hair is giving off the sweet aspect of her scent. I can't quite put my finger on it. Something tropical and fruity that on paper shouldn't blend well with the lavender of her perfume, but somehow it does.

My eyes are still closed when my stomach grumbles and I realise the last thing I ate was lunch; Maisie's crusts, and the apple half she decided she didn't want.

"Hey, Cass," I mumble into her hair.

"Hey, Cal," she whispers against my shoulder. Her head bobs with a giggle. "I thought you hated that name, but that's what Amira called you."

"I don't hate it so much coming from you."

The moment feels more intimate than either of us intended. I lean back, the movement prompting her to push up so she can look at my face.

"You hungry?"

She nods, laughing when her own stomach rumbles at the thought of food.

"Let's go get something," she says as she stands.

I spot her coat and bag on the floor. She must have been on her way out when she found me in the hall. The sky outside is pitch black, too close to the city for any stars to shine through. I wonder how long we've been sitting on the couch, knowing how easy it is for me to get lost in my thoughts.

"Cass, were you going somewhere? I'm sorry."

"It doesn't matter. You needed me."

She picks up her bag and hangs her coat over her shoulders before adding, "I am starving though, so you better take me to get food before I get hangry."

My mind flicks back to a much younger Cassidy, overworked, tired, and hangry when our boss at the time forgot to open a second register so she could have her break.

Not wanting to see her hangry ever again, I rush to move off the couch.

Chapter Eight

CALLUM

Restaurants are buzzing with activity, lines queuing outside the entrances. We walk the length of main street without talking, because all I can think about is the panic attack I had in the hall.

It's been years since I had one. Many, many, years. Although if I'm honest with myself, I'm surprised I haven't had more recently. As it turns out, your whole life being flipped upside down, and the one person you care most about in the world being ripped away from you, will really play on your mental health.

While I'm glad to be out getting food, I also desperately crave my bed. I'm exhausted from the adrenaline that surged and the crash that has hit me.

"Argh, everywhere is booked," Cassidy groans as we are turned away from yet another restaurant.

"We'll find somewhere," I mutter, despite knowing at this time on a Saturday night, we probably won't.

Continuing down the length of the street, the eateries get further and further apart, until we are standing on the corner at the end of the main strip. Everywhere was either booked for the night, closed for a function, or had a forty-five minute wait time.

"Those Golden Arches sure look appealing." She is staring wistfully at the McDonalds across from us, and I don't blame her.

"Chicken and Cheese?" I ask, reaching out to hit the button to activate the pedestrian lights.

Cassidy moans, leaning towards the building. "How did you know?"

Inside, it smells like deep fried potatoes and greasy burgers. Families scatter throughout the dining space with kids squealing in excitement. Across from me, chicken burger in one hand and fries in the other, Cassidy looks like she has barely changed from when we were teenagers.

Her hair, although longer than it was back then, still sits in loose waves over her shoulder. Her skin still glows, and the golden flecks in her green eyes are sparkling against the fluorescent tubes overhead.

I hate the way our friendship ended. I hate that I was so bitter, angry, jealous and, honestly, scared that I let her walk away. All over a stupid teenage job. I should have known she would quit eventually, we all wanted to quit back then.

"I'm glad we circled our way back to one another," I say. I mean it, too. Despite all the what-ifs, despite my confusing feelings, having Cassidy back in my life feels like it means something. It's only been a few weeks, but we've fallen back into an easy friendship I'm incredibly grateful for.

"Me, too." She looks up, a glint in her eyes as she smiles before shoving a handful of fries in her mouth.

"Couldn't think of anyone else I'd rather stuff my face with McDonalds with than you." Her mouth is still full of food when she says it, tiny bits of chewed up potato flying out of her mouth and onto the table.

I can't stop the way my whole body vibrates with laughter. I throw my head back and enjoy the way my cheeks hurt. It feels good. I haven't laughed this hard, and genuinely felt it, in a long time. I clutch my sides, enjoying the feeling. Teenagers sitting a table away from us stare over before sniggering amongst themselves. I ignore them, no longer concerned over what strangers think of my actions.

We eat the rest of our grease filled meal in between gross

displays of talking with food in our mouths and numerous fits of laughter. It feels playful, childish, but also intimate in a way I struggle to make sense of. Even in the peak of our relationship, I wouldn't have acted like this around Audrey. And I doubt Cassidy would act like this around many other people. Together, we know it's a judgement free zone. We can be our goofy selves, reminiscent of our teenage personalities, and it works. Together, we work.

I'm still thinking about it as we head back to the apartment. I'm still thinking about it when Cassidy ducks into the bottle shop on our block corner. And I'm still thinking about it when she walks out with a six pack of Pirate Lifes and a pack of her vodka fruity whatevers.

"You're obviously coming in for a drink," she says. Juggling the drinks against her hip, she rummages through her bag for her key.

I grab them before they fall, hand lingering on her waist a fraction too long. Her knit dress is soft under my fingers. Cassidy turns to me, holding my gaze. The air has been sucked out of the hallway, and I should move my hand away, but I can't. It's like a magic xylophone has dinged. Only this time I'm not pretending to be frozen, I am. Because I can't decipher the look in Cassidy's eyes. The golden flecks have darkened as she looks up at me through thick lashes. Heat spreads across the back of my neck, and I fight the urge to sweep my hand around her waist and pull her close.

Before I can act on the impulse, Cassidy pulls her attention away from me as she pushes her way into her apartment. I wrench my hand away from her waist, flexing my fingers and shaking out my wrist. The electricity of the touch still lingers on my hand, and I take a second to count my breaths before following her inside.

By the time I reach the couch, Cassidy has cracked us each a drink, removed her shoes, and snuggled up under a knitted blanket. The scrappy pink stripes clash perfectly with the deep earthy green of her dress, but she looks cosy. I love how comfortable she is with me, and I'm reminded of movie nights at her place when we were younger. How we would innocently snuggle under the blanket together, sharing popcorn and laughing over the cliched jokes.

Is that what she wants now?

I shake my head at the thought. Even if she did want to, it's not appropriate. Not anymore. Not now we are adults. Not now when blood surges to my groin at the thought of rubbing up against her under the blanket. Not now I have so much to work out in my personal life and I'm not sure I can contemplate bringing her into the mix.

Cassidy deserves someone who is sure of themselves, sure of how they feel about her. She deserves someone who she can start a family with, not someone whose family she would be stepping into. And she definitely deserves someone who isn't blindly lying by omission every day. Because fuck, I need to figure out how to tell her I have a daughter.

My fingers toy with the hair tie on my wrist. Even when I don't have Maisie with me, I can't break the habit of always having one. It's a small piece of her I take everywhere, and fiddling with it eases a fraction of the anxiety I constantly feel these days.

I need to tell Cassidy about Maisie. And Audrey. But any time I come close to thinking about it, fear clouds my vision. I think of all the mates I drifted away from after starting a family, and I can't bear the thought of Cassidy drifting away, too. It happened once before, and I will do anything to make sure it never happens again. Even if it means always holding her at arm's length, waiting for a little longer before I let my two worlds collide.

"Movie?" Cassidy looks up from the TV. She's holding the remote, and when I sit down, action movie after action movie fly across the screen. She's speeding through the titles and I can barely make out the posters as they flash past. I reach over to snatch the remote out of her hands.

"Hey." She laughs as she kicks my waist.

I grab her foot, reaching under the blanket to tickle it. In these moments, it feels like no time has passed at all. She kicks back at me, and I shrink away to avoid a foot to the nose.

She yanks her foot out of my grip and I shift my attention to the TV, pulling up an old favourite and hoping she still loves it as much as she used to.

"Oh, we're having a sing off are we?" Her voice is airy and boastful as she sits up straighter. I grin to myself, knowing I've made the right choice.

Nature Boy plays as the Moulin Rouge opening credits appear on the screen. We both settle in, and Cassidy's feet find their way back onto my lap. I rub at her calves as we sing along to all the songs. We get more and more dramatic as the movie goes on.

My throat is sore from singing as the credits start to roll. Cassidy sits up as she stretches her arms out with a yawn. She turns to place her feet on the floor. I expected her to stand, but instead she leans her head on my shoulder. I reach my arm around her, pulling her in tight. The instrumental tune fades out. All I can focus on is Cassidy, curled up in my arms and looking up at me with her beautiful green eyes. The golden specks are dark again, and her pupils are wide. Her breaths turn heavy as she adjusts herself, sitting up more so we are closer to eye level.

"Cal."

She whispers the shortened version of my name. The one I only really like when it comes from her lips. The intimacy sends shivers down my back. I reach my other hand up and brush my knuckles over her cheek. She closes her eyes, leaning into the touch. Her tongue darts out to wet her lips, and now I'm the one whose breaths are heavy. My rational brain melts into a puddle on the floor as my body takes over. Despite everything I know about our relationship, everything I'm not telling her and everything I'm not ready for, I want her. My body wants hers, and I think she might be willing to give it to me.

"Rogue?"

She looks up at me through her lashes and I watch as her gaze drops to my lips. My hand reaches the back of her neck and she nods, the tiniest of movements I wouldn't have noticed if I hadn't been so hyper focused on her.

We are so close, I feel the wet warmth of her exhale on my lips. I try to count to four and calm my nerves, but I get stuck after one. My lips crash into Cassidy's, and I hold back the desire to devour her. I kiss her bottom lip, then her top lip, and she kisses me back.

She opens her mouth, and I dive in. Our kiss becomes frenzied, years of teenage longing drives me as I savour her taste, sucking at her tongue and biting her lips. Cassidy is just as uncontrolled, her hands gliding up my arms towards my hair. I pull her closer, but the feeling of her pressed against me isn't enough.

I need … more. I grab the back of her head, tilting her and deepening the kiss. Desire clouds my judgement as I explore her mouth. Cassidy flips her leg over mine to straddle me. I grab at her ass, pulling her body toward mine.

A quick knock breaks our connection, and reality hits me with enough force I push her back with a gasp. My racing pulse scatters, and my fingertips tingle, but not in a good way. I'm out of breath, and by the way her whole body rises with each inhale I'd say Cassidy is, too.

"Cassidy?!" An old, rusty, unfamiliar voice calls through the apartment.

"Not now, Mrs Kelly!"

The voice in the hall huffs in response, but her unsteady footsteps retreat.

Cassidy leans back into the kiss, but the moment is gone. All I can think about is the myriad of untold truths between us.

"I'm sorry I—" I fumble to make a sentence as I try to find the words to explain.

I'm not ready for this with anyone, let alone with Cassidy. Last time we hooked up it completely ruined our friendship, and I can't go through that again. Not when my life is so messed up. I need to tell Cassidy everything if I want to make something more of the friendship we have. My body fights my brain, still hot with desire, and I'm sure she can feel it through my jeans.

"No, it's fine," Cassidy cuts me off as she climbs off my lap. Standing in front of me, she composes herself, pulling the hem of her dress back down and running a hand through her hair.

"I shouldn't have, I'm sorry." The corners of her lips tilt upward as she apologises, but her cheeks are flushed and her eyes downturned.

Gesturing to the empty cans on the table she adds, "vodka," with a forced giggle. We've only had one drink each, but I allow her the little white lie. We both got swept up in a feeling. I'm not mad about it, but I can tell she is embarrassed.

Cassidy grabs the empty cans from the table, and I can't help but stare at her when she bends over to pick up a bottle-cap that had fallen to the floor.

I sit, caught between disappointment, anger, and arousal. Closing my eyes, I'm greeted by memories of the last time we kissed. Of the last time I let fear get the better of me. Of the last time I pushed her off my lap.

I had no reason to be afraid back then, but I was. When her phone rang and formed a tiny crack between us, I couldn't stop thinking about what that meant. I became terrified of how far we might have fallen, of what would happen if we carried on with that little crack in our foundations. Afterward, I hated myself for breaking the kiss and running away.

But now? I can't dive into something like this. I want to, more than anything. The interruption doesn't feel as devastating as it did the first time, but the old lady knocking was a swift reminder to slow down. Just like they did that day when we were young, my words jumble inside my head. I wish I had the words to tell Cassidy how I feel, but I can't form the sentences I need.

"I, uh, I'm pretty tired," Cassidy says.

She stretches her arms wide as she drops her mouth open in what is clearly a fake yawn.

"Sorry," I mumble as I stand.

Letting myself out of her apartment and into my own, I collapse onto my couch.

I can still taste her on my tongue, the sweet remnants of her fruity drinks. I can still feel how perfectly she fit in my lap, and parts of my body are still protesting. I shudder, grasping my cock through my jeans to ease the pressure. It's no use.

Unbuttoning my jeans and tugging down the waistband of my jocks, I let the hard length spring free. My eyes roll back in my head as I stroke it, imagining Cass bouncing naked on my lap until I spill onto my shirt. It feels dirty and wrong, and none of the tension I felt has been relieved.

Jerking off has never felt so unsatisfying.

Chapter Nine

CASSIDY

Not once have I understood movie scenes where the main character literally *paces* around a room. It seems fruitless, an unnecessary use of energy designed to show emotion in what felt like an unauthentic way. And yet, that's exactly what I find myself doing. As I mutter expletives and furious questions to myself, I storm laps around my tiny apartment. I've gone mad. Callum Wilson has wiped any manner of reasonable thought from my brain. I'm fit for a mental institution.

After Callum left, I retreated to the bedroom to get changed. When I returned to the living room, I curled back up on the couch in my cosy tee dress. I tried wrapping myself in grandma's blanket to read a book, but the words blurred. I turned the TV back on and scrolled for something to watch, but nothing felt appealing. I couldn't distract myself. Wanting to get rid of the lump in my throat, I stood to get a glass of water from the kitchen. But when I made it to the counter, I just kept walking, the movement helping burn off the built-up energy in my limbs.

I made an absolute fool of myself. I want to cry with embarrassment, and simultaneously pull my hair out at the stupidity of my actions. Right when Callum and I were rebuilding our friendship, I had to ruin it by climbing on top of him.

The heat from my core is still racing through me, but I also feel teleported back in time to the last time I kissed Callum Wilson.

"I can't believe you quit." Callum stands with a drink in one hand. The other rests on the wall above my head. "Good for you." He tips his drink toward me before taking a swig.

Words have escaped me for the first time around Callum. In the three years I've known him, we've become incredibly close. We tell each other everything. Well, almost everything. The only thing I've ever been afraid to tell him, is how I really feel.

He was eighteen when I met him. At three years younger, I'm sure he looked at me like a little sister, but the way I looked at him was far from brotherly. Now though, I'm older, and I'm ready for him to stop looking at me like a sister, or a friend. I want him to look at me the way he used to look at his neighbour. When she dumped him, it took everything I had not to crawl onto his lap and kiss away his tears.

Tonight though, that's exactly what I plan to do. Minus the tears.

"I'll miss working with you though." I look up at him through my lashes. I'm trying to flirt, but I've never really tried to get a guy's attention before. I don't know if it's working, or if I look downright ridiculous.

"It's pretty loud here," he says into my ear. His breath is hot, sending a shiver down my neck.

Grabbing my hand, he leads the way out of the garage towards the back corner of the yard. We're at a friend of a work friend's party, and I doubt anyone will miss us. There's a cute little bench seat surrounded by bottle brush, and I follow as Callum turns to sit down. Beside the chair is a pottery bird bath, and my mind wanders to the lorikeets that must love this little set up during the spring.

"It's cute here," I say as I sit down. I stay close, my leg up against Callum's and our shoulders touching. His hands are under his legs, and his knee bounces up and down. I know him, and I know how he acts when he is nervous. I just don't understand what it is about this moment that is making him feel that way now.

"Cass," he whispers.

I turn towards him and place a hand on his jittering knee. My touch calms him.

"Yeah," I whisper back, looking up at him.

This is my chance. We've both had enough drinks to feel relaxed, but not so many we can't make smart choices. And since we don't work together, there's nothing holding us back from being together in the way I want. In the way I hope he wants. I flick my gaze down to his lips and see him do the same.

"Is this ... are we ... do you ..." Reaching for my cheek, he fumbles over his words. The way he struggles to form a sentence feels like the moment I've been waiting for. It's now, or it will probably be never. I cut him off by crashing my lips against his.

I should go slower, savour the moment, try to show him how much I care. But I can't. Years of wishing and dreaming and waiting have left me starved. Our lips tangle together in a frenzy, and when he runs his tongue along my lip, I open my mouth to let him in. I stretch my body up against his, bracing my hands on his shoulders as I climb onto his lap.

Before I can seat myself against him, my pocket vibrates. I want to ignore it. I want to ignore the world and get lost in Callum's embrace. I grab the back of his head to show him I don't care about my ringing phone, but he breaks us apart.

"You should get that," he says through bated breaths.

As I climb off him, I scratch at my fingers. Callum's knee starts bouncing again.

I stand, watching him until my phone finally stops ringing.

"Callum," I say.

"Rogue, I ... I'm sorry," he says as he shakes his head. Standing, a visible shiver runs up the length of his spine. His breaths become raspy as he tries to slow them down.

Knocking his fist against his chest in the way he always does when panic overrules him, Callum reaches to the ground to grab his beer.

"I'll, um." He stumbles over his words as he walks past me.

"I'll see you around," he finally says over his shoulder as he walks away. I fight the urge to race after him and check he is okay.

I don't think I can be his rock. Not anymore.

Eventually, I tire my legs out and collapse on the couch. As I brush my hands through my knotted hair, I change my mind and get up to open a bottle of wine. I forego a glass, and slump back into the couch to take a long swig before looking at the bottle. Rosé … not as great at room temperature as it would be chilled, but right now, I couldn't care less.

All those years ago, that kiss with Callum marked the end of our friendship. I'd known before I threw myself at him that he was moving to the other side of the city, but I didn't care. I thought we were worth the travel. But to him, we weren't. He left me.

I sob into the silence. My heart aching at being rejected, again.

Keys rattle as Amira calls out to announce her arrival. She walks down the hall with one hand covering her face. "La la la," she sings, "I'm just running to my room."

The idiocy of her actions after how my night ended turns my sobs into laughter. "No one's here," I squeak through sobs.

"Oh." She ends her crazy dance-slash-run and moves to collapse onto the couch next to me. Catching herself before gravity takes over, she gestures to the wine bottle on the table.

"No glass?"

She side steps to the kitchen cabinet, pulling two cheap stemless wine glasses out. "I thought … Cal?"

I shake my head.

"Well at least I'm not the only one sleeping alone tonight," Amira whines as she places the glasses on the table. In one swift movement, she falls back onto the couch beside me. Her legs stretch up as she places her feet on the coffee table.

"You have no idea." I elbow her in the ribs. "But you go first."

Grabbing my hand she massages my palm the way she does when I complain my fingers hurt from twisting bouquets.

"Eh, there's not much to tell. It was … awkward."

"What? How?" I question, pulling my hand away. She's been out with this guy a couple of times in the space of just a week. I figured any potential awkwardness would be gone.

"It was just … I don't know … weird. Neither of us knew she was coming, but his mum was there the whole time."

"His mother?" *Wow.*

"Yeah." She grabs my hand back and continues her massage. "Anyways, it was super awkward, obviously, so in the end we called it a night and went our separate ways."

"Argh, that's shit. I'm sorry."

"Don't be, I should have known what I was getting myself into when I let my parents set me up. It'll work out." She reaches out for my other hand, grabby fingers pulling at my sweater until I adjust how I'm sitting. She presses her thumb between my fingers, massaging at the pressure points to relieve some of the tension still caught in my body.

"Or it won't, and I'll swear off men again. I'm okay." Leaning her head back with a sigh, she drops my hand in her lap.

We sit, each musing about our own miserable dating lives, until the lump in my throat threatens to resurface. I sit up to pour us both a glass of my room temperature Rosé. I push back into the couch, prompting her to sit up and take the wine.

"Ugh," she sputters after taking a swig. "What happened to you that was bad enough for *room temperature* wine?"

"In my defence, I didn't check the bottle before opening and assumed it was a red." I laugh.

"Just as bad, honestly."

"To you maybe." In the few years we have lived together, I'd yet to convince her to build up her taste for a good red wine.

She pinches the soft skin between my thumb and forefinger firmly until I yelp and pull away.

"What was that for?"

"For trying to change the subject. Tell me what happened with Callum."

I place my glass back on the table and lean my head back onto the couch. Letting out a long breath, I go limp and slide down to a slouch.

I tell her all about how I found Callum in the hall mid panic attack, and how that's why I'd had to cancel our afternoon coffee plans. I tell her about how Callum and I spent a comfortable evening as friends once he had calmed down. When I get to the kiss, Amira jolts upright, hands over her mouth as she gasps in shock.

She squeals in excitement before catching my eye. Realising there is more to the story, she places her hands politely on her knees.

"Sorry, go on."

"It was dumb, I was dumb," I whine. "I'm so embarrassed."

When I tell her how Callum practically threw me off his lap when I straddled him, Amira's hands jump back up to cover her mouth.

"He did *not*," she says in shock.

"He did," I reply. "And now all I can think about is the last time I did something as stupid as make a move on him."

"You were basically kids then." Amira speaks softly as she moves closer to me. Pulling me into one of her trademark comfort hugs, she rubs the back of my head.

"What happened then isn't necessarily going to repeat itself," she adds.

I nod with a sob, hating that I've let myself get this worked up over the man. Again.

"Maybe I should go back to the whole 'swearing off men' thing," I say before downing the rest of my wine. I reach forward to fill up the glass.

"Yeah, me, too."

Amira grabs her own glass. When she takes a sip, her face scrunches up and she jerks her shoulders in disgust. She forces a gulp as she swallows the drink.

"Nup, still gross."

"Still don't care." I laugh as I take the glass off her. I finish her leftovers and slouch back into the pillows.

Amira has long gone to bed by the time I do.

The Rosé bottle sits empty on the coffee table, the wine churning in my gut in a way I know is a bad sign for tomorrow morning. I'm still angry, still embarrassed, still worried about my friendship with Callum and if we ruined it tonight. There was no coming back from the first time we kissed, and although we are adults now, I don't see any way it's going to be different this time around.

I can't explain why I feel so deeply about Callum's rejection. There could be a million reasons why he broke the kiss and stopped us from taking anything further. And I have no idea what any of them are. I didn't think I felt so strongly about him, but I do know the knife of embarrassment has been forced even deeper this time around.

I can't keep him on an imaginary pedestal any longer.

We used to be friends, and I had a silly crush. Our lives grew apart, and that's just a part of growing up.

Now, he is nothing more than the guy who lives across the hall. Who I used to work with many years ago and who occasionally comes over for beers. The guy who, sure, I'm still insanely attracted to, but whom I don't actually know all that much about.

Chapter Ten

CALLUM

I drop to my knees on the porch, collecting Maisie as she runs out of the house and barrels into me. I scoop her into my arms, lifting her off the floor and somehow keeping my balance as I stand. Audrey holds her arm out to steady me. The gesture feels kind, friendly in a way she hasn't shown in the past few weeks. Months, really.

"How was Nanna and Poppy's?" I ask Maisie.

Her high-pitched squeal hurts my ears. Good, I think that means.

"She missed you though." Audrey gestures for me to come in, so I step across the threshold before placing Maisie down.

"Go get Pavlova," I tell her. She skips off through the house to find her favourite doll.

The click of the kettle sounds from where Audrey has made her way to the kitchen.

"Tea?" she calls out through the house.

The photos along the hall have been removed, replaced with artsy landscape pictures of wide sweeping fields. The array of navy pillows on the couch in the living room are gone, shades of pink in their place. Everywhere I look, I notice the small changes Audrey has made. All the little ways she has turned our old house into a place that's uniquely hers. I don't blame her, but it feels … odd.

I walk toward the kitchen, the hairs on the back of my neck standing tall. Since I moved out, Audrey has never so much as asked if I wanted to come inside, let alone offer me tea. Every instinct tells me she is up to something. She already swapped the one day I got to see Maisie this week. I refuse to let her get away with something like that again.

We sit at the table we used to share, drinking tea out of mugs that were once ours. Now, they're just Audrey's, even the dragon mug she got me for a birthday many years ago. She never asked if I wanted it back, but now I'm using it to warm my hands again, I realise I don't. It feels tainted, like most of the memories in this house.

I'm ready to fight my case, to tell her we'll go to court, when she catches me by surprise.

"You were right."

Looking up at Audrey, I give her pause to continue. She could be talking about almost anything, and it's unlike her to start by admitting she is wrong.

Taking a long sip from her floral mug, Audrey slurps at the hot liquid before smacking her lips together. "Maisie deserves to see you more. Even though it will kill me to be away from her."

"It kills me to be away from her."

"I know. But honestly, I don't care about you. I care about Maisie."

Her words don't hurt the way I think she intended. I don't need her to care for me. I drink my tea, hoping the warmth will slow the rapid beating of my pulse. I think of all the places I want to take Maisie now we will have more time. About how much more homely my little apartment will feel, and how I should probably start looking for a house again. One with a backyard for Maisie to play. Maybe I'll even get her a dog.

I can see it playing out in my head, and I drink my tea as I contemplate my new life. I hadn't realised my eyes were closed, but when Cassidy shows up in my daydream I throw them open.

"We'll start with a weekend? Give her time to settle. Next week." Audrey's voice adds another layer of fuel to the firepit in my stomach.

I gulp at my tea, hoping to smother the flames. I need to focus on right now, not an imaginary scenario. But I can't erase Cassidy from my thoughts. I can't escape the feel of her weight on my lap, or the taste of her tongue. I can still feel the tingle in my lips from where her teeth bit down in excitement. Kissing Cassidy so soon was a mistake, but I can't take it back. I can only make it right. And to do that, I need to sort my own life out.

Audrey has given me a thread, and I intend to pull it.

"I want to take her to that ballet exhibit." My shoulders tense and the warm liquid in my gut boils as I think about the next part to what I'm about to say.

"Okay." Audrey taps her fingers on her mug.

"I want to take someone."

The tapping stops. I can hear every forced breath Audrey takes.

"An old friend, my neighbour. I don't want to take her like a date, but I think she would like it, too."

"Not a date," Audrey repeats.

I nod.

"But she will be there. With Maisie."

I nod again.

"I'm not ... I don't ... she needs ..." Audrey tries. Her nose twitches.

"I'm not asking, I'm telling you. Out of courtesy. I wouldn't do anything that could make things awkward, or harder for Maisie. But I'm allowed to have friends, I'm allowed to see people. That doesn't stop when Maisie is with me. Just like it shouldn't stop for you when she is here. I'm telling you, not to get your blessing or to ask for permission, but so you aren't caught off guard."

Pushing her chair back, Audrey folds her arms on the table, resting her head in the crevasse they make.

"Thank you for telling me," she mumbles.

"I think I really like her," I admit, although I'm not sure why.

"Okay, but will she like Maisie?"

"I hope so."

"I can't believe I agreed to cancel our park date for this."

I push Isobel's pram through the mall, loaded with all the clothes and toys Maisie chose. Isobel is holding Pavlova while Maisie lags behind, shuffling her feet. She's had enough shopping, even though today was all about her and I said yes to everything she asked for. Well, almost everything. We did not get the $400 glitter dress or the teddy bear that was bigger than me.

"There's a family coffee shop up here. We can let the girls play." Isobel nudges me as she marches forward toward her caffeine.

We sit at a table next to the enclosed play area. Maisie helps her younger cousin up and down the tiny slide.

Isobel drinks most of her large latte in one long gulp. "At least I didn't have both kids with me today."

In another gulp, she finishes her drink. Scanning the code on the table, she orders another.

I don't know how they do it. Isobel and her husband. Two kids sounds like a nightmare. Sure, it mustn't be *that* bad, considering how many families have more than one child. But after Maisie was born, I knew she was it for me. One round of sleepless nights. One round of baby led weaning and sleep regression and potty training. I don't need to go through that again. Besides, Maisie is more than enough to fill my heart.

"I need your help."

"Say that again so I can record it." Isobel holds her phone toward my mouth.

I bat it away. "Ha. Ha. But I'm serious. I don't know how to tell Cassidy about Maisie without scaring her off."

Isobel turns in her chair to watch the girls as they play. The slide has been left behind as they build towers with the big foam blocks. I've never seen Maisie so patient with her younger cousin, but I'm not about to complain.

"How much does she know? How close are you?"

"I kissed her."

Isobel slaps me across the head. "Fuck, Callum. How could you kiss her without telling her?"

"I didn't mean it." My elbows rest on the table and I drop my head into my hands, rubbing the sore spot.

I did though. I did mean it. That kiss with Cassidy was incredible, and I want more of them. But I got a little ahead of myself, and now I don't know how to crawl back to the starting line.

"How do you think she will react?"

"Good, I hope. She always loved kids. But it's different to just loving kids, right? To end up with a guy who already has a daughter, that has to be rough."

But shit, I hope Cassidy is okay with it. I hope she is still willing to give this a proper try once she finds out about Maisie. I hope this is our chance to get things right.

"I think you need to be honest with her. Tell her how you feel, tell her about Audrey, first. Then Maisie. Then introduce them. But tell Audrey about that bit first."

Already done, but my gut still pains when I think about how defeated Audrey looked. After everything, I still don't want to hurt her.

"What if it all goes to shit?" I ask, pressing my thumbs into my temples to alleviate some of the pressure. "What if Maisie doesn't like Cass? Or Cass doesn't like Maisie? What if Audrey cracks the shits and stops me from seeing Maisie because of it? What if I lose everyone all over again?"

My knees start shaking and I feel my pulse quicken. Spots appear in my peripheral vision, and the sound of the girls laughing and other customers chatting fades into the background.

"Knuckles."

Her voice is from a distant, far-off land, but I recognise the signal. Tapping my knuckle against my sternum, I focus on the steady rhythm and count my breaths. Four in, four hold, four out. When the panic settles, I look up at my sister. My eyes feel glassy and my fingers are still tingling, but my pulse has settled. At some stage, Isobel must have switched my coffee for a glass of water. I take a small sip, focusing on the cool sensation as I swallow the liquid.

"You really need to talk to Cassidy."

Chapter Eleven

CALLUM

My feet pound against the footpath as I suck in as much air as my lungs will allow. It's been months, possibly years, since I've had time to go for a run, and my body is reminding me. I might have spent plenty of time in the old home gym I used to have, but getting out for a run was near impossible with Maisie around. Lifting a few weights might have allowed me to maintain a physique I'm proud enough of, but it certainly did nothing for my cardio fitness.

The sun is low in the sky, rising late thanks to the transition towards winter. Long shadows stretch out from the trees lining the road. The air carries an unexpected warmth, and despite the smell of rain in the air, the sky is clear. Above me, a regatta of hot air balloons drifts peacefully across the sky. They add a pop of colour to the powder blue sky.

Rounding the corner to return to the apartment, my legs slow their assault. A sharp pain stretches under my ribcage, my body's final protest against my new morning routine.

After my recent panic attacks, and the realisation my anxiety was forcing its way back to the surface, I decided I need to get on top of things. Staying active was one of the first things my old therapist told me would help, so it's the first thing I'm trying.

I've been tied down by the inky blackness of anxiety before, and I let it ruin plenty of good things in my life. I refuse to let that happen again. Although I know it might not be quite so easy, I'm crossing everything that this time, I've seen the signs and can take the right steps before the darkness takes hold.

I have Maisie now, and she is worth fighting for. Knowing this afternoon will be the start of us spending more time together, a weight has lifted from my shoulders. I won't let it settle back down.

I double over, gasping air into my lungs as the apartment building comes into view. My pulse pounds through my limbs, although I can't be sure if it's due to the run, or the woman standing outside the lobby. She's worth fighting for, too. Anxiety ruined any chance I had of being with her once, and our friendship ceremoniously died along with my pride. She might be a distraction I can't afford, but I know how much it hurt her when I pushed her away all those years ago. I won't let that happen again. Until I figure out how to be honest with her about Maisie, I can't be the romantic partner she deserves, but I can be a friend. And I'll do anything to make sure she knows that. No matter how much I might want more.

Cassidy's hands are on her head as she leans against the brick wall. It's not until I've closed the gap between the street corner and the building that I see the twisted look on her face.

A fine crease sits between her brows and her lips form a thin straight line across her face. Her hands aren't just on her head but are pulling at her hair. Even so, I'm in awe of her beauty. The morning sun reflects off the chocolate brown of her hair and leaves her skin glowing. Her black jeans hug her hips, reminding me of how they felt under my hands.

When I notice what she is staring at in disbelief, I force the memory of our kiss out of my head. Outside the building sits a full, wrapped pallet of boxes.

"Did you order 100 instead of 10?" I jest, leaning against the wall beside her.

She releases her hair and drags her hands down her face. Pushing herself off the wall, she steps towards the pallet. Her hands press on the top boxes, testing their stability before she pushes up to sit atop the pile.

"It's for my store," she says. Her legs dangle below her, and I fight the urge to slip myself between her thighs. Hadn't I just decided to be her friend? I can't keep up with my rotating emotions. Every time I see her, I want her more and more, despite the baggage I'm carrying.

"But it's here?" My hand scratches at my beard. The delivery label on the pallet clearly lists the apartment building as the address. "Did you give them the wrong address?"

Cassidy kicks me. "No. I triple checked the order before the driver left a whole damn *pallet* on the footpath. They sent it to the billing address, but the driver couldn't take it back because according to all his paperwork he was at the right place."

Jumping down from her misplaced throne, she paces back and forth. Her arms wave about as she huffs and puffs.

"Did you try call—"

Storming towards me, she cuts me off.

"Yes, I tried calling the company, but they are in Perth and they aren't open yet." She yells the words in my face. I can handle a little raised voice if it means she can blow off some of the steam. "So now I have to figure out how to get a pallet worth of boxes to the shop. The van is getting a service, and it'll take three trips in my car."

"The Gnome?" I ask, using her car's old nickname.

Memories of her tiny two-door hatchback resurface. She was so proud of how much money she saved and how she could afford a brand new car when she turned eighteen. It didn't matter that it was the smallest car on the market, she loved it all the same. I wouldn't be surprised if she still had it.

Her giggle breaks through her tension, the melodic sound doing something unnatural to my insides.

"No, he went into retirement years ago. But my new car

isn't much bigger." Her shoulders droop as she turns to look back at her stock. "What am I going to do?"

My watch vibrates with an alarm, reminding me I'm supposed to be getting ready to head into the office today. Although I can work remotely, the nature of my role means I'm often booked with meetings. Today is no exception.

After turning the alarm off, I look back up to see Cassidy picking at the plastic wrapped around the boxes.

"Will you wait here while I get my car?"

When my brows pinch and a gruff sound escapes my throat, she adds, "Not for all the trips, just to help me figure out the best way to get as much in the car in one go."

"Wait here."

Racing up the stairs, I grab my keys and phone from my apartment before heading down to the parking garage. I send a quick text to my assistant, asking him to reschedule all my morning meetings, before jumping into my oversized SUV.

As I pull up out the front of the building, Cassidy's face twists. Frustration melts away as her cheeks puff up and the corners of her lips start to turn.

"You have a big car," she squeals. She leaps towards me and I throw my arms up to catch her. She stops herself though, stepping back before our bodies collide.

"Sorry," she mumbles, her cheeks red as she stares at her feet.

I wrap my arms around her and pull her body against mine. I soak in the feeling as she relaxes into me. Her closeness warms a part of my heart I thought had been frozen forever. When the thawing spreads lower in my core, I force myself to think of anything but how Cassidy feels in my arms, but I can't seem to let her go. The sweet smell of her hair wakes me up more than my run did, more than a coffee ever could. It speaks to my soul.

"Morning, love birds!" The old lady from apartment

thirty-one whistles as she exits the building. There's a spring in her step as she walks off down the street, crochet shopping bag swinging on her wrist.

"Morning, Mrs Kelly!"

Cassidy pulls away from our embrace, and I allow her to drop. She slides down, creating friction in all the best places. All the places that don't need that sort of friction while wearing running shorts.

She turns away, and I reach down to tuck my growing length away before striding over to help her.

We unwrap the pallet and move all the boxes to my car. The boxes are light, but even with the seats folded flat, the boot space fills quickly. I break into a slight sweat under the autumn sun, but Cassidy grins the whole time. Knowing I'm the reason her morning mood shifted, adds another layer of heat to my body, this one spreading from my heart.

Once the car is full, I look down at the empty pallet.

"Do you need that?"

She shakes her head, so I drag it around the back corner. I lean it against the large blue dumpster, hoping someone picks it up for firewood. If not, I'll have to pull it apart to fit it in the bin before collection day.

"As much as I want to ride in a Mercedes, I need my car at the shop," Cassidy says as I head back to my SUV. "I texted you the address and I'll meet you there."

I wave her off as she heads toward the car park. I climb into the car that yesterday felt a bit old but now feels too flashy.

Betty Blooms Boutique isn't far from the apartment building, but by the time I pull up, I'm beyond late for my workday. A hint of concern over my tardiness furrows at my brow, until I see Cassidy inside her shop. The way her hair shines in the morning sun, the way her face lights up when she sees my car parked out the front, it makes everything else melt away.

I leap out of the car when she opens the boutique, gesturing for me to come in. The space is perfect. White, pink, and neutral flower decals scatter the front windows. The double wooden doors reach the ceiling, opening inward to create a passage past the windows. I can picture the fresh blooms spreading into the space, and pride swells in my chest. I can't believe she created all this from nothing.

Cassidy was always creative, and as a teenager I admired her ability to turn the mundane into something beautiful. Napkins folded into swans, receipt roll snowflakes decorating the tearoom at Christmas, collages of magazine cutouts that looked suspiciously like annoying customers. The break room used to be filled with her creations. It seems fitting she built a career in such a creative industry.

"This place is amazing," I tell her as I haul the first two boxes out of the car.

She shrinks a little, picking up a box of her own and following me in.

Inside is somehow even more perfect. The walls are lined with exposed brick, and a large modern chandelier hangs from the centre of the ceiling. A wooden slab bench forms the counter to one side, and large low tables are dotted through the rest of the space. Metal buckets filled with various flowers and greenery are scattered through the space.

"I still need to set up after the weekend," she mumbles as she places her box near the back wall.

I empty my arms and pull her into an embrace. My hands caress her back, moving up into the hair at the nape of her neck. When her shoulders begin to relax under my arms, I spin her around and hold her back to me. One hand splays across her front, holding her in place. Her breath hitches.

"This is all yours," I whisper in her ear. "Look what you created."

Cassidy scoffs, but her breaths are forced. Slow and long. Pulling away, she turns to face me.

"If I can keep it." Her whole body drops, shoulders curling inward as she hangs her arms by her sides and stares at her feet. "I don't think I'll be able to afford the rent with no winter weddings booked."

My chest cracks. This place is perfect for her, it physically hurts she might have to give it up. "It'll work out," I promise her. I'll make sure of it.

She shakes her head as she turns away, and I think I hear her say, "You don't know that." But the words are so mumbled I can't be sure, so I keep quiet.

We unload the rest of the boxes in an uneasy silence. Cassidy is mulling over her struggling business and I'm busy trying to figure out a way to help solve her problem.

"Do you need help unpacking them?" I ask, as I place the last box on the pile. My phone has been buzzing in my pocket all morning, but it's been a pleasant change to not thinking about work for a few hours. I'm not ready for the break to end.

"No." Cassidy's answer is sharp, forcing me to take a step back.

"Okay," I say, preparing to leave. I feel bad my praise earlier set her on a path of worry, but nothing I can say will make her feel any better.

She barely looks up as I call goodbye.

Chapter Twelve

CASSIDY

Normally, a lack of walk-in customers concerns me. But after this morning's complete fuck around, I'm almost thankful I haven't had to be social today. Plus, I've been busy assembling Betty Blooms' latest masterpiece, so I'm glad I haven't been constantly interrupted.

I'm also, admittedly, still sour about kissing Callum, his blatant rejection, and the way he acted like none of it happened when he ran around the corner this morning. Although I was beyond grateful for the help, his flip flopping mood is confusing. Especially when it sits on top of my own messed up feelings.

I really, badly, wanted that kiss. Just like I really, quite badly, want Callum. I feel like my teenage self all over again, with an added layer of desire I was too innocent for back then. I can't forget how his cock felt pressed against me this morning. Standing on the ladder, I squeeze my thighs together at the thought of our bodies colliding.

Sending him packing as soon as the boxes were out of his car was probably cruel. Even more so considering I didn't even thank him. But I needed him to leave so I could start to think straight again. Instead, I'm standing on top of a ladder thinking about him when I should be creating a floral wall.

The bell next to the entrance chimes behind me and I have to hold in a groan.

I stretch, further than I should when I'm standing on the top rung of a ladder, to position another silky flower to the expanse of greenery. Once I feel the magnet click into place, I descend the ladder and spin to face my customer.

When I see her, my smile stretches across my face, puffing out my cheeks so they squeeze my eyes.

"Madison!" I brush my hands on my apron as I walk towards her.

She skips further into the small shop before throwing her arms around my neck.

Wrapping my own arms around her back, I squeeze my younger sister.

We've always been close. 'Irish twins' we would get called. She is younger than me by less than a year and has been my best friend from the day she was born. We might not have shared a womb the way twins do, but we shared everything else, and the bond between us is unmatched.

It's been too long since I've seen her. So, I squeeze her harder as we sway back and forth, losing our balance in the centre of the boutique.

"How was the trip?"

She looks incredible. Exactly how you would expect a woman to look after her belated honeymoon. There's a light caramel glow to her skin, and her blonde hair looks lighter. My sister has always been naturally beautiful, but something about her sun kissed look is mesmerising.

It was too hard for her and her husband to travel right after their wedding, so they waited. Two years into their marriage, Madison and Oliver were finally able to travel to southern Italy like they had always wanted.

For a while, their relationship was a bit of a sore spot. My sister met Oliver not long after I left Melbourne with Blake. While their love grew and blossomed, mine slowly started to crumble. They made it through everything, despite the situations trying to hold them apart. I'm not proud of the way I acted towards their relationship when I first returned to Melbourne.

I resisted Amira's gentle urges to see a therapist, but when I finally did, I learnt my issues laid far deeper than just being jealous of my sister's relationship. I was able to process the sharp drop off of my own engagement and everything that had caused it. Now, I couldn't be happier for them. I love that my sister has found her great love.

"It was great!" She steps back with a laugh, grabbing her tote bag with both hands so it sits across her front.

"That's all I get? You go to southern-freaking-Italy and all you can say is 'it was great'? Come on Madison, you're supposed to be the writer of the family."

Her hands relax on the tote a fraction, and a tension I didn't realise she was holding starts to release. She winks, before digging one hand into the bag and pulling out a small parcel.

"You get 'it was great' and *this*." She beams as she hands it over.

I greedily grab the gift, pulling at the brown paper. It's heavy in my hands.

"My sister went to Southern Italy and all I got was this lousy mug." I pretend to read.

Madison feigns shock.

"Thank you," I say. "It's perfect."

Because it is. The porcelain mug is painted in delicate swirls of blue, with bright yellow lemons creating a stunning focal point to the pattern. I've always loved collecting beautiful and unique homewares, and mugs are my favourite thing to have.

"You didn't need to get me anything," I tell her.

"I know. I wanted to."

I reach out to hug my sister again, breathing in the fresh outdoorsy aroma of her familiar, signature scent. Her long green dress flows around her as she spins to the wall I've spent all day creating. Glancing down at my dusty black jeans and loose grey shirt, I wonder how two women, grown from the same circumstances, can end up so wildly different.

Madison always cares about her appearance. She's always done up, hair perfect. Her natural beauty leads the way so she doesn't have to put much effort into looking put together. But no matter how many times I tried to be like her, I've always felt the opposite. Dressing for anything more than comfort has always been trying for me, and at some point over the years, I gave up. Comfort over style became my motto.

I suppose it works better in this industry anyway.

"This is new," she says, gesturing at the wall.

"It's my winter project. I need to entice more people into the shop when I don't have weddings to fall back on."

Madison nods, and I can see she isn't convinced it will work.

"It's a selfie wall. I saw one at a coffee shop and people were literally lining up to take a photo."

Her mouth presses into a thin line, far from the enthusiasm I was hoping for.

Sucking in a deep breath, she lets it out as she controls her words. "Yes but, at a coffee shop people will go to take a photo and walk out with a coffee. It makes sense."

"Exactly!"

"What will they walk out with here? I can't make coffee."

In between writing her best-selling novels, Madison works for me at the shop. Thanks to her basic floristry skills, I don't have to close on the days I secure events. The past couple of months without her was a juggle. I made it work, but I don't think closing the shop most weekends was good for business. If I can't somehow fill my winter calendar with events though, I won't be able to offer her the shifts.

"Flowers, hopefully."

This time, her nod is short.

"Cassidy." Her tone is harsh, and I brace myself for the berating I sense is coming. "Dad can't afford to bail you out of another winter."

I clasp my hands together, twisting my ring. Her words hit a bruise I've been carrying for the past year, and it hurts. I never wanted my dad to bail me out, but when I'd mentioned I might have to close the shop, he paid the rent without question. My skin crawls at the way he jumped in to save me. After so many years of barely being around to support me when I needed him, it's like he was trying to make up for lost time.

Acid fills my throat as I try to snap back at Madison, the words melting away before I can get them out. Instead, I turn back to my luscious selfie wall.

It cost more than I care to admit. Definitely more than I'll ever admit to Madison. It has to work.

I don't want to think about her comment, but it sticks in my head and even long after we say a strained goodbye, I'm still wondering exactly what all the influencers will walk out with. Because it's one thing to draw them in with a selfie wall, but for it to be worth the thousands of dollars I spent, I need them to buy flowers while they are here.

Returning home after serving no customers all day, my mind races as my conversation with Madison replays in my head. She has always been my biggest supporter, and I'm used to her kind of tough love, but I can't put my finger on what was different today.

My business is struggling, that wasn't news to me. But it felt like she was throwing my financial concerns in my face. When Dad wrote me the cheque last winter, it was Madison who convinced me to use it, so it's odd for her to now be berating me over that choice.

As I trudge up the stairwell, I can't help contemplating how I ended up in this position. There have been a lot of decisions that led me to this point, and I feel like I made the wrong choice at every turn. Even at the times where I felt I had no other option, I'm starting to wonder if that was true.

I pause on the landing, leaning my forehead against the cool brick wall.

My life is a mess. And it was easy enough for me to swear off men as though they were the problem, but look how far that got me. Barely a week later, I was climbing into Callum's lap and getting rejected all over again.

A swift clang sounds above me and I push off the wall. Turning to head up the stairs, I swipe my hands across my face to dry the tears that were starting to pool.

Seeing me, Callum freezes. He reaches an arm behind his back and I glance up to see a second pair of dainty feet behind him.

My heart sinks as I realise why he rejected me. Putting the pieces together, I keep my head down as I continue up the stairs. Towards him. Towards them. Callum and ... her.

He coughs and shuffles his feet, like he is unsure what to do or say.

A tiny giggle sounds from behind Callum's back, and now I'm closer, I realise how tiny the feet are. The blue sandals shuffle around, glitter catching the light and reflecting it back in a rainbow of sparkles. The owner tries to push past Callum.

"Daddy, *move*."

Wait ... Daddy?

I thought my heart had sunk as far as it possibly could, but somehow it tumbles lower. It's dropped out of my abdomen and straight through the floor. I imagine it resting, bloody, bruised and barely beating on the lobby floor.

My head spins. I close my eyes, trying to steady myself. When I no longer feel like I'm on a cruise in rough waters, I bring my gaze up to meet Callum's.

He hasn't said anything, and the look on his face tells me he has no idea what to say. I attempt to raise an eyebrow, keeping my mouth tight, not trusting myself with words.

He steps to the side. Beside him stands a much younger, female version of him. She's four maybe, or five. I've never been good at guessing kids' ages. Her long dark hair falls over her shoulders in soft waves, pinned off her face in a high ponytail with an obnoxiously oversized pink bow.

"Um, hi, I—" I stutter, incapable of forming a complete word, let alone a sentence.

"Cassidy, this is Maisie." Callum places a hand on his child's shoulder before looking down at her. "Maisie, this is my neighbour, Cassidy."

"Do you live behind the number thirty-three door?" the little girl asks.

I nod slowly, my mind still processing what I'm seeing and putting the pieces together.

I do a mental search for clues, signs I should have picked up that would have made this less of a shock. I've only been in Callum's apartment twice. The first time was the day he moved into the building. There was no sign of the little girl that day. The second was after his panic attack in the hall. I hadn't noticed anything that screamed 'a child lives here', but I wasn't exactly searching the room either.

"Is she—" I start, but I can't force the words out.

"Mine."

Callum's protective tone forces any remaining resolve I was holding onto, to trickle to the floor. I choke back a whimper.

"My dad lives at number thirty-two, did you know? I remember because that's how old my mummy is." Maisie smiles up at me, one hand clinging on to Callum's pocket and the other twirling in her hair.

Her mother. I hadn't even contemplated her mother. But she obviously has one, and everything feels like too much information, and not enough, all at once.

I shift my gaze back up to Callum, seeking guidance, answers.

He stumbles over his words, sounding every bit as flustered as I feel. "I … we were … just on our way to swimming class."

Well, that answered absolutely none of my questions. Words are still stuck in my throat. My vision blurs as I feel tears forming, but I hold my breath and blink them away. I try to tell myself the only reason this feels so unnatural is because I still feel off balance after losing Madison's support this afternoon.

"I have to go," I blurt out.

As I step forward, Callum guides his daughter out of my way.

"Rogue," he whispers as I pass him.

I don't look back. I can't look back. Instead, I storm down the hall, not stopping until I reach my apartment. Fishing around in my bag for my key, the tears start to fall.

When I finally find the keys, I head straight for my bedroom, collapsing on my unmade bed. Today was, quite frankly, shit. All I want to do is sleep the rest of it away.

The sound of the front door slamming closed shocks me out of whatever emotional slumber I had fallen into. There's a greyish haze to the light filtering into the room, and I realise I must have slept away the whole afternoon. The light makes it *feel* later than I'm sure it is, but I still haven't adjusted to daylight savings ending.

"Argh," I hear from the hallway.

I sink further into the bed, knowing whatever silly dating mess Amira is caught up with, my day was worse.

"I said argh," she yells down the hall when I don't answer.

"Yes, and when I did that you told me to suck it up," I yell back.

"Fair," Amira says with a groan as she makes her way down the hall. Her footsteps are long and slow, I can hear her slippers dragging on the hybrid flooring.

I meet her in the lounge. She must see my aching heart through my eyes because she stretches her arms out and pulls me to the couch. Curling up together, Amira rests her head on my lap. I twist until my head is resting on her shoulder.

"Callum," I choke out behind a sob.

Amira sits up straighter, "Tell me he didn't reject you again?"

My whole body shudders.

"He has a daughter. Five maybe, or four, I didn't ask."

"Oh," is all that escapes Amira as she sits back in contemplation.

"Oh," she repeats. She looks to be in the same sort of shock I was in.

We sit, processing the news, Amira realises what I've been trying to convince myself of since I found out the news.

"It doesn't change anything though, does it?"

"I suppose it shouldn't."

I rub my hands over my face, and up through my hair, sweeping it to one side and over my shoulder. Twirling a thick piece around my finger, I bite at the inside of my cheek while I try to find the words to express how I feel.

"I think mostly it took me by surprise," I finally get out.

"But I also don't understand why it *was* such a surprise. Like, why hadn't he said anything before?"

Amira curls her knees underneath her, pulling a blanket over her dress.

"And what about her mum?" I continue, spitting out all the questions in my head. Amira won't know the answers, but it feels good to get them out in the air. "Are they still together, why have we never seen her? God, did I kiss him the other week and that was him cheating on the mother of his child? Am I a homewrecker? An attempted homewrecker? Maybe that's why he threw me off him?"

Laughing softly, Amira places a calming hand on my shoulder.

"I doubt they are still together. He clearly lives alone and if they have a kid, they wouldn't live apart if they weren't."

"Okay, fine," I admit. "But what does this even mean for us? I keep telling myself we are just friends, but I can't shake this feeling he wants more. I see it in the way he looks at me, I feel it every time his hands linger after a hug."

I stop, not wanting to acknowledge the aching that ploughs through me every time I think the words 'friend' and 'Callum' in the same sentence. I feel the electricity in the room when we are together. The attraction between us still lingers, and I doubt the part of me that wonders what more we could be will ever go away.

"If he did want more, could you be with him, now you know he has a daughter?" Amira asks, feeding my fantasy with a side of salt.

"No. It sounds terrible, but I couldn't. Not now. Not after how final I made my decision with Blake. We tried. We tried *so hard* to have a baby, and when we couldn't, I made peace with that. How can I even consider becoming a step-mother after that? No matter how perfect the guy is."

It feels heavy, like it should have been harder to come

to that conclusion. The answers flew out of my mouth without hesitation, but now the words are in the open, they feel harsh. Even with my certainty about our future, the part of me that longs for Callum still festers in my heart. And it hurts.

"I'd never be enough for him. And that little girl will always come before me. I don't want to have to fight for his attention."

Amira curls herself back into my lap.

"You're fucked," she says.

I laugh in response.

A beat passes before Amira adds, "But not as fucked as me."

"What do you mean?"

Her shoulders droop as she squeezes my waist a little tighter before answering.

"I have to go have dinner with my parents."

I pull back to look at her.

"Yeah, you're fucked." I laugh.

Chapter Thirteen

CALLUM

Gravel crunches under the weight of the car as I pull into the driveway. Audrey's house, my old home, is the last place I want to be.

Maisie yawns from the backseat, her hair still wet from the shower after her swimming class, twisted into a bun so it doesn't drip onto her pyjamas.

"Sorry, Daddy."

Scooping her out of her car seat, I pull her pyjamas tight around her and carry her up to the house.

"Don't be. I know you can't sleep without Pavlova."

Of course, the bloody ballerina doll is the crux of this whole custody agreement. I thought we had covered all the bases after we went shopping last weekend, but no number of new toys can make up for missing her favourite. I don't blame her. We noticed it was missing when we first got to swimming, and rather than attempt the night without her comfort toy, I called Audrey.

It hurt, but it was necessary.

My ex-wife appears on the doorstep, her own sweater pulled tight around her middle in protection from the cool autumn breeze.

"Her dinner is on the table."

She was surprisingly understanding when I told her we would need to stop past. She didn't place blame or get upset I was depending on her, she just agreed to do what our daughter needed. Maybe she realised it was her that never packed the special toy in the first place. But I choose not to bring it up, opting for peace instead. Sitting down at the table together, it's comforting knowing despite it all, we can get along when we need to.

Maisie tucks into the small meal of sausages and vegetables Audrey whipped up. Too exhausted to put up a fight, she doesn't complain about the carrot, or demand more tomato sauce. I forgot how much swimming takes it out of her. By the time her plate has cleared, her eyes droop and her head wobbles to the side.

"Daddy," her voice is a tiny whisper, "can I go to bed here?"

The words hit my windpipe. It was supposed to be the first night of our first week together, but everything has gone wrong. Looking to Audrey for guidance, my lungs burn.

"I could bring her back tomorrow? I'll remember to pack Pavlova this time."

It's not an ideal plan, but it could work.

"Does that sound okay, Maisie?"

Her head has fallen into her arms, and she looks ready to fall asleep right here at the kitchen table. Through a yawn, she nods, looking up at me.

"Can you read my story before you go?"

The air in the hallway is wrong. I can feel it as soon as I step out of the stairwell. My feet drag, heavy with the disappointing end to the day. The silence is too loud, it's five degrees too cool, and it feels thick, suffocating and sticky. Whatever is causing the anomaly guides my legs towards Cassidy's apartment, until I find myself standing in front of it, unsure if I should knock.

I messed up. For weeks I've known I need to tell her

about Maisie. Before I started carving something between us. But I didn't, and now it's too late. I should have been honest with her.

An immense sadness hit Cassidy when she saw Maisie. The golden flecks faded away, replaced by a dull shine. I had been afraid that when Cassidy found out about Maisie, it would change the dynamic of our friendship, but I didn't expect the secret to hurt her. My head pounds, knowing it clearly did. Beneath the sadness in her eyes, there was a deep trench of betrayal that wove through her body. As though everything about us changed in an instant.

For so long, for too long, I was trying to keep these two aspects of my life separate. I wasn't ready, but it's too late for that now.

I hold my breath as I tap my knuckles against the doorframe, flexing my other hand at my side. My mind races through sentence after sentence as I work out what I'm going to say, hopeful Cassidy will at least answer.

As I rise my fist to knock again, it swings open.

Wearing nothing but a baggy, faded black shirt and a pair of green fluffy socks, the sight of Cassidy steals the sticky air from my lungs. Her hair has been swept up from its ponytail, a giant black clip holding it in a messy bun.

Without speaking, she steps back and gestures for me to come into her apartment. I pause. I came to her, and I'm not sure what I expected, but her invitation has left me feeling unsettled. Walking in, I don't sit down, instead, opting to lean against the island bench to watch her make her way back up the hall.

The thick air from the hallway has wafted through to Cassidy's apartment, sucking the final sliver of warmth from my lungs.

I don't know how to start. None of the phrases that rattle through my head seem like enough to smooth things over.

Now that everything is all out in the open, it's like I want to throw myself in headfirst. But, I don't think I can do that without scaring Cassidy off.

And there is something about her demeanour that tells me she isn't ready for me to throw myself at her. I just can't figure out what it is.

Cassidy's fingers twitch by her sides, playing with the ring she always wears. Her breath wavers. Fidgeting, she straightens all the cushions before collapsing into the nest she created, covering herself with the scrappy pink blanket that had been draped along the back of the couch.

We've shared quiet moments before, but they have never felt as awkward as this one. The urge to fill the void overwhelms me.

"I was going to order pizza," I finally say.

She turns to face me, wrapped in the blanket like it can protect her from the uncomfortable air. She reaches for the table and picks up her phone, checking the notification on the screen.

"I've got one coming. Gregory is six minutes away."

I push off the bench. "Right, sorry, I'll go."

"Ha." Her breath comes out as a quick, loud laugh. "Gregory is the Uber driver. You can stay."

Cassidy turns towards the hall, her eyebrows crooked. "Your daughter?"

"Maisie is back with her mum for the night."

She nods, short and sharp, as a puff of air escapes her lips.

The tension that had sprung to my shoulders eases, and I sit myself down on one of the mismatched dining chairs.

Cassidy and Amira's apartment is intimate and welcoming, nothing like the clinical feel my own still holds. My furniture came direct from the online catalogue, picked in such a rush I'm not even sure I like it. But here? Nothing matches, and everything oozes comfort. The odd chairs, the bright blanket, the absurd bird paintings behind the couch. Every piece tells a story of their friendship and I want to learn them all.

"About the other night—" I start at the same time she says, "No booze tonight."

Her body slackens as she collapses onto the couch, pulling her legs underneath her, still wrapped in the blanket.

"I took it too far," she speaks into the blanket. Blush rises to her cheeks. "The vodka went to my head and, honestly, I was horny."

I can't hold in my laugh and her features soften as she leans back on the pillow.

"Same," I reply, deciding to be honest. "I'm sorry I freaked out. Again."

Cassidy stares wide eyed.

"Mm hmm." Tight lipped, she jerks her head, encouraging me to continue.

"I wouldn't have kissed you if I didn't want to," I say, "but when you, you know ..." I gesture to my lap, hoping she knows what I'm talking about without me having to say it.

Shuffling my feet underneath me, I wring my hands in my lap. I haven't been this nervous since high school.

Cassidy stands up. "I've changed my mind. We need wine."

The irony is not lost on me that alcohol got us into this awkwardness, and I'm pretty sure the liquid courage will help get us out of it. I force myself to look away when she leans down to choose a bottle from the bottom of the wine rack.

"It's embarrassing," I start, "but when we worked together, I had the biggest crush on you."

Cassidy freezes, wine keeps pouring into the glass she placed in front of me. When it gets dangerously close to the top of the glass, I reach out to touch her arm, encouraging her to lift the bottle upright.

I let out a whoosh of air before taking the wine from her. I bring my head down to take a sip so it doesn't spill over the edge as I place it on the table.

"The last time you climbed onto my lap," I whisper, leaning toward her to speak into her ear. "It nearly killed me. I was an anxious wreck for days and I hated how I'd taken the slightest of interruptions as an excuse to stop. I was so scared I was going to lose you."

The tropical scent of her hair blends with the strong fruity smell of the wine. I want to wrap it around my hands and bury my face in her neck, but I hold back.

She lets out a small, almost silent laugh.

"Exactly," I continue. "It wasn't your fault, but I did. I lost you."

I pause, leaning away from Cassidy to look her in the face. My hands are on her shoulders and our eyes lock. The moment is too intimate for this talk about why we shouldn't have kissed.

It feels like instead of convincing her we should never done it, I'm convincing myself to do it again.

My cheek puffs with air and I roll my shoulders back as I gather my thoughts.

"I can't shake this feeling that the universe threw us back together for a reason." I tell her what I've been struggling to admit to myself. "But everything is so messy and I don't want to lose you again."

She leans her head to the side to brush her cheek against the back of my hand. Looking up at me through her lashes, she whispers, "Neither do I."

The intercom buzzes through the apartment, breaking the spell and causing us to jolt apart.

"Pizza!" Cassidy announces as she jogs down the hall.

She pushes the button to let Gregory know she is on her way down.

While I wait for her to return with dinner, I attempt to reorder my thoughts. We were supposed to be talking about why we shouldn't be hooking up, so why did it feel like we were about to hook up again?

I sit on the couch, but when she shuffles back into the apartment with two large pizza boxes I change my mind. Jumping up to get plates from the kitchen, I rush to set the table before she can put the boxes down. Playing house, making myself feel useful, but all the while wondering how to start the conversation we need to have.

Conversation stalls while we eat, the air still holding a dry electric quality I can't seem to escape.

It's not until Cassidy is placing our used plates in the sink that she breaks the silence floating between us.

"So you have a daughter."

Maisie. The reason I came over tonight in the first place.

"I do. I should have told you about Maisie. And her mum. I'm sorry you found out that way."

"Why didn't you tell me?" She walks over to the couch and curls herself up in the blanket again.

I choose to be honest. "I was scared."

Walking to the couch, I sit down beside her. We aren't touching, but the closeness offers a comfort I don't feel.

"Everything changed when I had her. My career, my relationship with her mother, my life, my friendships. It was nice for a while to have an inch of my old life back."

"That makes sense."

Her body shifts until her head rests across my chest. Taking the clip out of her hair, I brush through the lengths with my fingers, listening to the steady sounds of her breathing against me. My heart beats so furiously I'm sure she can feel it. We're dangerously close to the same cuddled up position that led to us kissing.

I stretch my fingers around the back of her neck, tilting her face up towards mine. Moisture pools through her lashes.

"It shouldn't change anything, but I'm sorry it came as such a shock."

Cassidy pulls herself away from me to sink back into the couch. Her eyes are closed as she tucks herself into a ball. "You're right. It shouldn't change anything."

She looks tired, deflated, so I stand to leave.

"Thanks for dinner, Cassidy."

She hums a smile as I leave.

It's not until I have one foot in the hallway that she calls out a goodbye.

"I don't know if I ever said this, and I know I haven't said it recently, but you're a great friend. Your daughter doesn't change that."

Friend. The word shouldn't hurt, but it feels like a knife. No matter how much it hurts, I'll stab myself with it over and over until I can convince Cass we can be more.

Chapter Fourteen

CASSIDY

"I can't believe you pulled this off at such short notice." Making a final adjustment to a stray petal, I glance over my shoulder. I smile at Noah as I count my blessings my cousin is the events manager at such an incredible winery. He called me in a desperate state this morning, needing floral arrangements for a boujee proposal picnic. I jumped at the chance to get creative and spread love. I need the money, but more than that, I need something to take my mind off Callum. For weeks now, I can't stop thinking about him, about us. And now I can't stop thinking about what we could have been if he didn't have a daughter. About what we might be now I know he does.

Trying to make sense of all the thoughts and emotions in my head is like trying to unblend a smoothie. Impossible, and honestly a little unneeded.

Kissing Callum was … amazing.

And now I know why he freaked out, I don't feel so bad about it anymore.

But things are bound to get messy when two friends step across the platonic line. Add a child, a divorce, and my infertility into the mix and the whole thing is a recipe for disaster. I have no idea where to go from here.

I close my eyes, inhaling the sweet aroma from the roses, before shaking loose the tension in my shoulders and turning back to Noah.

"Thank you," he offers, "this looks amazing."

I grab his hand to pull myself up and start stacking my now empty buckets.

"I need to ask you something." Noah wrings his hands, scuffing his black sneakers in the grass.

"What?"

"Can you be our florist?"

I turn back to the mass of flowers I've laid out meticulously, throwing my arms out to twirl.

"Is that not what I am?"

Walking forward to stand next to me, Noah drops his arm over my shoulder. He deposits more weight than is comfortable and I wriggle to break free from my cousin's overt friendliness. He's up to something, I'm just not sure what.

"I'm not good at this," he admits. "Running everything. *Planning* everything. It's exhausting. But if you were like, the winery's florist, you could do every event. I wouldn't have to worry about linking customers with vendors. I'll add you to the calendar so you can see what we have coming up. And do your flower thing without me having to act as a middleman."

I blink away the sun, contemplating his words. If I was the winery's sole florist my calendar would end up completely booked. I wouldn't have to stress about finding events, they would come to me. A tingle starts in my throat, forcing its way down to my heart. My fingers twitch with excitement.

"I'll pay you," Noah adds when I take too long to reply.

Turning to face him, my cheeks puff with my broad grin.

"I think you just saved my business."

Although it took me a while to find floristry as my preferred outlet, creativity has been in my bones for as long as I can remember. As a child, I played with my Barbies by hand sewing new clothes for them, or painting the doll house an array of colours. My best subject at school was always Art, and I went through a portrait phase that saw my final high school submission on display in the National Gallery of Victoria.

Until, in my final year of school, my aunt got married.

My sister and I had been called in as 'junior bridesmaids' and set with the task of helping set up the venue. I was fascinated watching the florist work. The way she had twisted the flower stems around one another to hold them in place, the careful consideration while filling mason jars with blooms. To see how the colours came together, how the arrangements on the wine barrels coordinated with the posies tied to chairs, and how the flowers transformed the look of the whole venue.

It was a life changing experience, standing there, deciding that this, *this,* was what I wanted to do with my life. I enrolled into a Cert 3 in floristry the following day and started approaching companies that week.

It only took a few weeks to find a storefront florist willing to take me on as an apprentice, and once I had learnt the basics I started growing our business by providing bespoke arrangements for events. When I moved interstate, I started my own floristry business, specialising in events, and eventually weddings.

It wasn't until I moved back to Melbourne that I opened Betty Blooms Boutique. It was a slow start to the business, and it still hasn't exploded in the way I had hoped. But I love what I do, and deep in my soul, I always knew I'd find a way to keep my business afloat. I'll never let my cousin know how much I appreciate him, but thanks to Noah, I'm about to become the go to florist, the only florist, at one of Melbourne's most exclusive wineries. It's a business saver, and if I'm lucky, we'll have a mild winter, with more sunny days than rainy ones. The countless micro events sure to take over the outdoor spaces through the season will all require a little floral touch.

Since being a small business owner also equates to being a content creator and social media manager, I pull out my phone to take a few photos of the picnic setup. Alongside the muted pink and white florals, today I included a small posy of dried blooms for the couple to, hopefully, keep forever. It's a small addition in an attempt to boost my reach even further.

Once I have filled my camera with shots from every angle, I linger. Lost in a daydream, imagining what it would feel like to have someone set something like this up for me.

When my thoughts find their way back to Callum, I pinch the bridge of my nose and try to force them away.

Every time I see Callum, I fall, harder and deeper into something that feels like love, *only love shouldn't be this hard, right?* Love shouldn't make me question everything I thought I knew about myself. Love shouldn't feel like a knife to my heart.

And yet, no one else can make me laugh, roll my eyes, scoff, joke, the way Callum can. And every time I see him, I feel warm and cosy, and a smile spreads across my face. I haven't felt this way since I first met Blake, and even then it didn't feel quite this intense.

I'm in this way too deep, and I'm scared.

"Thinking of someone?"

My cousin's voice shocks me out of my head.

"I'm so fucked," is all I can manage to say.

"Your neighbour?"

"He has a *kid*."

"And?"

"*And?*" I throw a stray stem at Noah's face, scowling when he bats it away with ease.

"You don't know he would want more kids. You have to talk to the man instead of avoiding him."

I sigh, because although I'm not avoiding Callum, Noah is right. I do need to talk to Callum about this, but I refuse to admit it out loud. I also cringe at the thought of being the one to reach out about something so big. Single gal dignity, or something like that.

"What if Maisie wants a sibling? Even if I can get on

board with his family situation—which I'm still not sure about—I can't take away his choice to give her that."

I keep the extent of my feelings to myself. Because in reality, it doesn't matter how deep my feelings for Callum run through my veins. He comes as part of a package, and I still don't know if I can take it all on.

"She has another parent you know."

I step back, planting my hands on my waist and popping my hip. "And?"

"And it took two to tango. And you have no idea what Callum and his ex's plans were before they split. You have no idea if either of them ever wanted to have another child and you have no idea if either of them want that now."

I fold my arms across my middle, trying to find the right words to rebut what he is saying.

"No, stop." He holds his hand up to my face. "Stop beating yourself up with the what-ifs and the imagined scenarios. Stop turning your life into one big miscommunication trope and just talk. To. Him." He claps with each word, emphasising his point.

"I can't," I choke out between breaths. My eyes sting and I blink away the liquid pooling in them.

"You have no idea," I'm aware I'm yell-crying now, but I don't care. "I spent my whole life wanting to be a mother. Wanting to prove to the world I could do a better job than the incompetent woman who birthed me and Mads. Only for the world to rip that one dream away from me."

Tears are streaming down my face. I'm vaguely aware I need to stop. That Noah is working and technically I am, too. That customers will start arriving at the winery soon, and that I need to finish tidying up my empty buckets ready for the lucky bitch who's about to get engaged.

I'm aware of all of that, but I can't stop.

"I've lost everything," I sob. "I lost the picture of my

future I always had in my head. I lost my ability to choose. I lost the man I thought I was going to be with for the rest of my life because I couldn't give him what he wanted. And you," I shove my finger into my cousin's chest, "you just want me to talk to the guy I like now and beg him to be with me, even though I can't help him grow his perfect little family. You want me to tell him I will always struggle to be a parental figure to his daughter, but I hope he picks me anyway."

Noah stands back, arms by his sides, his mouth drops open before closing into a lopsided smirk.

"What?" I scream.

"You love him."

"I don't love him."

I say the words, but they aren't the full truth. From the look on his face, I'd say Noah can see through the lie. I hadn't acknowledged it to myself before now. Even though I knew what the feeling was, and I was still trying to shove it down, pretend it was something else. But it's not.

I'm head over fucking heels for Callum, but my shitty broken uterus and my aching heart will never let me have him.

The realisation is swifter than a slap to the face, and with it comes a flood of emotion I thought I had moved past. I thought I was healed, that my goals had realigned and I knew what I couldn't have, and what I didn't want. And then Callum showed up across the hall. In the space of a few months he weaselled his way into my life, gnawing a deep pit in my chest. At first, I was torn between needing a friend and having a crush, until I found out about Maisie.

Now I'm torn between being with the guy I've grown to love, and being the adult I thought I was happy to be for the rest of my life.

I don't know if I could ever be the kind of person to put the needs of a child above my own. And I'll never get used to the idea someone else will come before me in my partner's eyes. Even if that person is his child. But I also don't think I'll ever get over the vision of Callum in my head.

The one where we are together.

Tears pool, spilling onto my cheeks.

"I can't do that to him."

Collecting my buckets, I storm past Noah, and up the sloping winery towards the back parking lot where I left the van.

That saying replays in my head as I walk, the one about loving someone and setting them free. I never liked it, because I always felt that if you loved someone you would never trap them in a cage in the first place.

Maybe it would be best to talk to Callum first. But I can't stand the thought of my heart shattering every time I'm around him. I hate the thought of losing Callum as a friend, and to ensure that never happens I need to set a boundary to protect us both.

Cassidy: I'm sorry about freaking out. Friends still?

I finish loading the van and pull out of the car park without waiting for a response. It's waiting for me when I get home.

Callum: Friends always.

Chapter Fifteen

CASSIDY

Callum: No pressure, AT ALL, but do you want to come hang out today?

The message lights up my phone screen when I step out of the steaming bathroom. My water wrinkled fingers catch on the screen as I stare at it, still wrapped in my towel with my hair dropping water down my back. Undecided if I want to hang out today, or any day.

While it changes everything about the future I kept imagining, Callum having a child doesn't necessarily have to change the friendship we have. *Isn't that what I told myself?* I put aside the lust that crawls through me once before, I should be able to do it again. And I'll just ignore the other 'L' word that creeps into my thoughts next to Callum's name. Shouldn't be too hard.

It's not even been a week since I ran into Callum and Maisie in the hall, and although it was jarring at first, I've settled into the idea of Callum as a father. I'm not bitter. At least not anymore. I'm coming to terms with where our relationship can go from here, and it's strictly platonic. No matter how hard I'm still crushing on the man.

Having wrapped my hair in the towel, I pull on a pair of leggings and an oversized sweatshirt. Drafting a response in my head, I want to come across as casual, laid back, easy breezy. But I feel anything but.

Cassidy: Why would there be pressure?

Cassidy: Are we monkeys now?

Cassidy: What are you planning?

I delete them all, hating myself for allowing this unwelcome vein of anxiety. I throw my phone on my bed to unwrap my hair when it vibrates again. The anxiety bursts through me and I rush over, panicked I accidentally sent one of the messages I thought I deleted. But I didn't.

> **Callum: I have Maisie with me, I thought you should know. But we are going to the ballet exhibit at the Light and Sound Museum, and I thought of you. Leaving in fifteen, if you're home and want to come. NO PRESSURE.**

Fuck. I really want to go. But I'm not sure I can.

The Light and Sound Museum puts on incredible displays, showcasing artists or artistic styles in a way they aren't shown anywhere else. I've never been, but I've seen footage of the way animated light shows are projected all over the walls and floor, immersing patrons within the paintings and videos.

Ballet dancing and art were my two great loves through school. I heard about the ballet exhibit and have thought about going. It felt awkward taking myself though, and Amira's not interested. I don't blame her, art isn't for everyone, but it means the exhibit is still on my to do list.

I'm torn between wanting to go, and not being ready to spend time with Callum, let alone his daughter. As I collapse on the bed, I try to weigh up the pros and cons, but find my mind blank. I need to reply, to let Callum know either way, but I get stuck, lying on the bed. Time escapes me as I allow myself to feel every battling emotion.

A knock sounds, jolting me out of my trance. I stand up too quickly, blood rushes from my head and my vision goes black.

"Coming," I call out while I wait for the stars to fall so I can regain my balance.

When I throw open the door, my vision darkens again and I have to lean on the wall to keep my balance.

"Hi," a tiny voice calls out.

I stare down at Maisie, incapable of forming words. She's wearing a grey, hooded jumper over a dress with a rainbow tutu skirt and black leggings. The huge pink bow is still attached to the side of her head, and I wonder if she sleeps with it in.

"My daddy said you like ballerinas, too." She swings her arms as she talks, and I notice the soft ballerina doll in one hand. It's cute, and only a little bit daunting.

I glance up at Callum standing behind her, unsure how to interact with a child. He folds his arms across his chest, a small smile on his lips.

"I ... ah ..." I start, but Callum interrupts me.

"Come on, Maisie," he says, catching hold of her free hand and tugging gently. "We should go to the museum."

She plants her feet, refusing to move.

"Wait," she says to her dad before turning up to me. "Do you like ballerinas? Because you can come with us if you do."

Her arm stops swinging as she cuddles her doll close.

She's cute, and somehow convincing. I look to Callum for confirmation.

"As long as I'm welcome?"

He nods as Maisie starts jumping and cheering.

"I need five minutes, okay?"

"Go." Callum gestures back into the apartment, and I rush back towards my room.

Pulling my hoodie off, I grab a baggy knit sweater instead. The quickest fix for my still wet hair is a messy bun, so I assemble it with a claw clip before swiping some concealer under my eyes. It does little to hide the purple tone that has settled over the past few days, but allows me a hint of confidence.

I glance at the mirror, ready to head back out, when I hear laughter from the hallway. Maisie's high pitched giggle blends with Callum's deeper rumble. The sound exudes joy, but to me, it serves only as a reminder of the situation.

As anxious butterflies settle in my stomach, I grab a lavender oil roller and slip on my spin ring before rushing out to meet them.

We spend the car ride listening to Taylor Swift and I swallow down the pit growing in my throat. My mind racing between worst case scenarios and reminding myself that Callum and I are just friends. Callum either appreciates I need the time, or is too busy juggling his focus between the road and his daughter to talk. He reaches to the back seat often, to pass snacks, pick up the dropped ballerina and collect rubbish.

I'm starting to think this whole excursion was a mistake when we pull into the museum car park. Huge posters of the display light up the dim underground garage, reminding me of how much I wanted to come. It's not the place that's the issue, it's the company. Half of the company. The tiny half.

Still unsure how to act around a five year old I've barely met, I remain silent as we enter the building.

Callum leans across his daughter's head, speaking softly. "You can go do your own thing if it's too much."

"Thank you," I reply, certain I'll take him up on the offer as soon as we get inside the exhibit.

I lag behind Callum and his daughter as we walk through the dark entrance corridor. She wraps her arm around his leg as the lighting dims and I notice he slows his pace so she can keep up.

It's subtle, but sweet. Leaning down, he stretches his arm behind her head to place a hand on her shoulder. I rub my palm over my sternum, willing away the unusual, molten feeling rising towards my throat.

I linger, watching as they walk, linked together, further down the corridor, imagining how I would look as part of the picture before me.

As they make their way through the final corridor, I shake the daydream away, because I don't fit, and it wouldn't be fair to either of them if I tried to squeeze myself into the frame.

My fingers find my ring, spinning it furiously. Pressing the spikes against my thumb, I focus on the mild pain it causes to distract me from the icy pressure building in my chest.

I lean against the wall, enveloped in shadows.

"Cassidy?"

I feel a gentle tug on the bottom of my sweater and look down to see Maisie smiling up at me.

"Are you okay?" she whispers.

Her gentle voice is calming in a way I never expected from a child. The pressure inside me eases, a sliver of warmth spreading from the centre to melt the ice away.

I smile down at Maisie as I push off the wall. She reaches to grab my hand, and we walk together.

Callum stands at the end of the corridor, just before the bend. One shoulder rests on the wall beside him, his arms hang loose by his sides with his thumbs in the pockets of his dark jeans.

I can't make out his face in the lighting, but I can sense the way his face lights up as Maisie drags me along beside her.

"Wait until you see it." Maisie bounces down the hallway, tugging me behind her.

145

As we turn the corner, soft, classical music plays and a rush of calm energy brushes over me. It's not cold, but goosebumps erupt under my sweater, the anxiety and grief and longing making way for a subtle excitement.

The exhibit itself is a wide, dimly lit room. Bench seats are scattered throughout, with a petite café in the corner offering extra seating. The walls and floor are projected with bright impressionist style paintings with swirling lights. I can hear the classical music building to a crescendo that awakens the young ballerina inside me.

We pause, midway into the room, taking in the sight. It's like no art exhibit I've ever been to. The giant room is immersive in a way that feels like it should be overwhelming, but it's not. The calm that rushed over me as I turned the corner sticks, and I feel at peace for the first time in weeks.

The music softens, fading to a few notes that sound vaguely familiar. Paintings of ballerinas appear on the walls, and the swirling lights on the floor fade. Scattered through the projections come videos of ballet dancers performing.

Dance of the Four Swans plays through the speakers, and like they always do when confronted with classical music, my feet turn out. I keep the movements small, but allow myself to enjoy the music and reminisce on my days as a dancer. I can't help but move with the music, my arms and legs gliding around me until I finish with a low and very off balance pirouette. Out of the corner of my eye, I spot Maisie. Eyes wide and mouth open, her face is full of awe.

I reach out a hand. It's a gentle invitation, and she takes it, grabbing my hand and kissing the back of it. She stumbles as she curtsies, but I steady her.

"Are you a real ballerina?"

"Not anymore."

Maisie's face twists in confusion before I deflect away from the painful truth. That I stopped when I moved

146

interstate, that I should have found a class in my new area so I could continue. That by the time I came back to Melbourne, I felt too broken to start again.

"I can show you some moves, if you like."

I can see Callum in my peripheral, the lights reflect in his eyes, making them twinkle. His smile widens when Maisie jumps in agreement. He steps towards us, his arms still crossed.

"Yes please, yes please," Maisie squeals.

"Wait," Callum interrupts.

My heart sinks, and I wonder, not for the first time today, if I've done something wrong. I hadn't thought it would be an issue to show the girl a few pointed toes and arm positions, but now I'm second guessing my viewpoint.

"Sor—" I start to apologise but Callum shakes his head at me.

Bending down towards Maisie, he reaches out a hand.

"Let me take Pavlova."

"Pavlova?" My brow furrows and my lips turn up, determined to work out the doll's name without asking.

"Anna Pavlova," Maisie's little voice pipes up. "But one of my friends at kinder is Anna so we have to call her Pavlova."

"A ballerina had to have a ballerina's name," Callum adds with a gentle shrug.

He tucks the doll into the neck of his tee. It nestles against the soft skin of his neck, and I'm reminded of how comforting it felt to be so close to him. To feel his pulse against my cheek.

"Ready?"

Maisie's voice shakes off my inappropriate thoughts.

Taking both her hands in mine, I stand in first position.

"Wait!" she squeals, turning back to her dad. "I need a ballerina bun."

Callum nods, and kneels down. Placing Pavlova the

ballerina doll in his lap, he pulls a hair tie off his wrist. Maisie walks over, and before I have time to blink, Callum has whipped her hair into a bun that rests halfway between a messy up do, and a perfect ballerina donut bun.

After fixing the pink bow to the front of the bun, he places both hands on Maisie's shoulders to spin her around.

"You ready now?" he asks, and she bounces in excitement.

I hold back the absurdity of it. Needing the perfect bun before having a silly dance with the lady who lives across the hall from her dad. But seeing Callum help her without hesitation makes the warm patch in my chest spread even further. When Maisie turns back to me, her ecstatic grin reaches her ears and I know the quick hair change was worth it.

I take her tiny hands in mine. "Okay, first position. Stand up tall, put your heels together, and point your toes out to the sides."

She loses balance slightly, but settles into a semi turned out position, the natural flexibility in her hips helping stretch her toes out wide.

Together, we go through some simple moves. A plie, some pointing, a little sauté jump. Maisie's grin continues to grow with each move, her little arms shaking in excitement at her sides. When the music ends and the exhibit lights fade, her shoulders start to slump. I'm unsure what this pull at my heart is, but I bend down on my knees to comfort her.

"It's okay." I place my hands on her shoulders to comfort her. "We can dance again another time."

She looks up at me, hope glittering in her eyes.

"How did you learn to be a ballerina?"

"I went to ballet class."

Maisie stares at her feet, tapping her heels together as she asks, "Daddy, can I go to ballet class?"

I hold my breath, wondering if I said something I shouldn't have.

"I can look for a class," Callum answers. "Last time we looked you were too little, but maybe now we'll find one for you."

I release the air I was holding, stretching my lips into a smile as I catch Callum's eye. He smiles back at me with a nod, before turning to Maisie and announcing it's time to go.

We walk through the exit in a row. Callum and I each holding one of Maisie's hands. She dangles between the two of us, pulling her feet off the ground to swing in our arms.

It feels natural. It feels right. It feels ... doable.

Like, maybe I was never destined to be a biological mum because I was always meant to find my way here. With Callum and Maisie. And I'm lost in the daydream while we walk out.

Until we walk past a lady pushing a pram. The future I had started picturing in my head crashes to a million tiny pieces, each one a shard of glass to my heart.

"Oh, is there a baby in the pram?" Maisie looks up to her dad, full of wonder.

He coughs, stutters a little bit before answering, "probably."

She looks up at me, and breaks my heart without meaning to.

"Will you have a baby one day?"

I hear Callum's swift inhale, while I struggle to find my own. I can't find words, instead shaking my head in quick jerky movements. I turn away so she won't see the tears welling in my eyes.

Oddly, it's not the fact I won't have a baby one day that hurts anymore. It's the realisation that no matter how many nice moments the three of us share, no matter how much it feels like I might be starting to fit, I can't be what they deserve.

I'm furious at myself for getting swept away in the

illusion of the day and imagining the three of us as something more.

The ride home is better than the ride in, but I can't shake the hollow pit in my stomach. Maisie is still living the high of the day, asking hundreds of questions about my previous life as a ballerina. I stretch the truth only a little to keep her entertained, and to keep the topic away from babies.

The three of us feel in sync in a way I have never felt with another person, let alone with a kid. It's heartwarming and heartbreaking all at once, feeling like I fit in with Callum's mini family, but knowing deeply that I never will.

Today was a lot of fun, and it reminded me of all the daydreams I used to have about Callum and me. But so much has changed since then, and while it was nice to forget for a while, the little chatterbox in the back seat is a stark reminder. Seeing how Callum interacted with her all day, seeing how he looked out for her, there's no way he is finished having kids. And even though I never started, I've accepted I am. That I have to be.

Even if a tiny part of me felt, *feels*, like we could make it work with Maisie around, I can't give Callum what he deserves. I couldn't give Maisie what *she* deserves. A child, a sibling. Their mini family deserves to grow, and I can't give them that. I made my decision long ago, it's too late to change it now.

Chapter Sixteen

CALLUM

Cassidy and Maisie walk up the stairs ahead of me, and I fight every bone in my body not to stare at Cassidy's ass as they do. There are a million reasons it shouldn't even be on my radar, but those damn leggings hug her gentle curves so well I can't resist.

I never expected her to come today, even if I had conveniently planned an activity I knew she would love. Heck, it was her idea to go there in the first place. She'd mentioned the ballet exhibit no less than five times in the past month. I'd been torn between taking Maisie, or taking Cassidy, and I'm feeling pretty incredible I managed to get both my girls there at the same time.

My girls. The acknowledgement sits in my throat as I watch them. The three of us were perfect together today, and although Cassidy is still insistent on calling me her friend, I can feel the attraction between us growing. There's only so long we can fight it for.

As we make the final U-turn up the stairs, Maisie begins to drag her heels. It's been a long day for her.

"Daddy I'm tired," she announces, stopping mid-step and yanking Cassidy's hand back. "And hungry."

"I know, chicka," I respond. "We are nearly home okay."

She nods a little, but keeps her eyes pointed to her feet; they shuffle, knocking against the step ahead of her.

"It's been a lot of walking for my little legs."

I hold back a grin. She's not wrong, my legs are tired, too, and she's taken twice as many steps as I have.

I squat down, a few steps below the girls, turning my back on them.

"Up we go." I pat my shoulders before holding my hands behind my head.

Maisie leaps onto my shoulders, and once I've got a firm grip on her legs with one hand, I use the handrail to pull myself back to standing with the other. She's getting too big for this, and I'll probably feel it tomorrow, but I can't help savouring these moments. These little snippets of time that won't be around forever.

"Is that safe, up the stairs?"

Cassidy's question isn't accusatory, but is laced with concern.

"We'll be alright," I say as I start walking up the stairs, a little slower than before. "Maybe just walk behind me in case I drop her."

Maisie leans forward squealing, grabbing on to my head in fear.

"I'm joking!" I force out between laughs.

We walk up the final flight of stairs, and when we enter the third floor hallway, Maisie's stomach rumbles behind my head.

"You really are hungry, hey?" I laugh.

"Can we have sweet n chicken tonight, Daddy? Can Cassidy stay for dinner, too?"

Amira's cooking, the smell of a roasting lamb blended with spices wafts through the building. My mouth waters. I might have only had a couple of her meals, but the woman is a master cook, and it's sure to be delicious. I doubt Cass would want cheap jar sauce over whatever creation Amira is cooking. Besides, I don't think extending our time together is the best idea.

"I think Cassidy probably has better plans than a jar of sweet and sour sauce and some overcooked chicken." I glance at Cassidy with an upturned lip. "Plus, she looks pretty tired. I think we're all just about ready for bed."

I wink, hoping she gets the hint. It's not that I don't want her with us, it's that I'm worried more time with Maisie will be too much for Cassidy. And equally so, that Maisie is getting too attached to Cassidy. I can't have her latching on to something that is still too unstable.

"What could be better than my favourite meal?" she says with a giant grin, but when she sees my wide eyes and subtle headshake she stretches her arms out wide in what is clearly a fake hug. "But, I am pretty tired."

Maisie kicks her feet against me in protest.

"No, Maisie."

A puff of air hits my head as she gives in.

As if she senses the changing mood, Cassidy races off ahead, calling out a goodbye before she ducks into her apartment.

Whatever reservations she had about Maisie, the demons she still holds, I'm glad Cassidy has been able to relax and have fun today. And I hope she realises we can still be 'us', even though I have a child.

Going through the motions of cooking dinner, and helping Maisie to bed, I'm stuck replaying Cassidy's comment about sweet and sour chicken in my head. Wondering if it is her favourite meal or if she was making excuses because she wanted to spend more time with us.

The idea she wasn't quite ready to leave warms my heart, until I remember the many lunch breaks we shared.

The slightly sour, pineapple smell of her left over dinner filling the tiny break room, and the way it stained the microwave orange. The time a carton of sauce came in with damaged lids and she took them all home. I never asked what it was she liked about it, never thought anything of it. But for her to consider choosing it over Amira's cooking, there must be something special about it.

With Maisie finally sleeping, I creep into the hallway. Keeping the doors open so I can hear her just in case.

I lift my hand to knock, but Amira appears in the hallway before I get a chance.

"Cassidy," she calls as she walks towards the stairwell.

Tapping my knuckle against my chest, I try to remember why I'm here. Cassidy comes out of her room wearing the baggy oversized tee she loves, and I can't take my eyes off her.

"Do you really love sweet and sour chicken?"

Of all the things I could have said, *that* was what I led with. I cringe at myself, hoping I haven't blown my chances at spending the evening with her.

"Oh," she whispers.

Her whole demeanour changes and I instantly regret bringing it up. Cassidy's lips tremble and she plays with the ring on her forefinger. Her shoulders round down as she folds into herself, but she shuffles forward.

"I'm sorry." I rush to take back the question. "It doesn't matter, you don't have to answer."

She shakes her head, looking up with glistening eyes.

"No, it's okay," she says slowly. "It's the only meal I can remember my mum cooking. When she left, I started making it for Madison. It reminds me of the good times."

I know enough of her family history to know I hit a sore spot. Reaching out, I take her hands in mine, allowing her enough freedom to keep playing with the ring. Instead, she loops her fingers through mine and squeezes.

"It's okay."

I step closer, wondering if I can envelop her in a hug. I want to. I want to do more than that, but I won't. Not again. Not until we are both ready. She steps in, too, and I take my chance, wrapping my arms around her and pulling her into me. Squeezing tight, I'm reminded of all the times I used to comfort her. All the times she needed a parent and never had one. Her runaway mother and her deadbeat dad let her down far too many times.

"Maisie is in bed. Do you want to come watch a movie?"

Cassidy steps back, her face going bright red. I cringe, remembering the last time we did that. For the second time tonight, I want to take back the words right after they have left my mouth. I stutter, not knowing what to say to turn this around. Instead of retreating, Cassidy slaps me on the shoulder with a laugh before leaning into my ear.

"I promise I won't climb into your lap this time," she whispers, just loud enough for me to hear.

Her breath hits my pulse point and sends sparks down my back. Blood rushes south at the reminder of the last time we were this close.

"I wouldn't hate it if you did, Rogue."

Cassidy follows close behind me, and there is nothing stopping my erection when she makes herself comfortable on my couch. The faded fabric of her dress stretches over her breasts and gathers around her legs. My fingers tingle, daring to imagine how delicate the skin of her inner thighs would be.

This is exactly how we should be. Together.

"Thank you, for today," Cassidy starts.

"Of course, I'm glad you came. Maisie, too."

Cassidy looks up. A twinkle lands in her eye. "She is a firecracker, she's great."

The swelling in my chest comes back, loving that Cassidy *gets* Maisie the way I do. She can be a lot for a five-year-old. A lot.

I want to express how much it means that Cassidy hasn't brushed my daughter off, but I can't think of the words. And I'm worried I'll put my foot in it, *again*.

"I'm glad you like her," is all I can think of.

"Of course." Cassidy brushes off the comment as we settle in. She snatches a pillow from behind me, cuddling it on her lap.

"You know I was always great with children." Her voice is soft as she waves her arm across the pillow. Sucking in a deep breath before continuing, her fingers trail patterns on the fabric. "Lately though I've started avoided them. I stopped running past the playground, I distanced myself from the few friends who already had kids, I stopped visiting the library ..."

Her voice trails off as she continues to list all the things she stopped doing.

"It was too hard," she says, surprising me when she leans down to rest her head on my shoulder. She lets out a whispered breath that sounds a little 'until today'.

"Why did you stop doing those things, Cass?" I lean my head against hers and wrap my arm around her.

She hiccups, and a tiny wet pearl forms on my shirt as she cries into my shoulder.

"I'm sorry," I add, unsure what else to say.

My hand itches to trace patterns up and down Cassidy's arm, to spin her towards me and pull her lips towards mine. But I can't. I won't.

"I can't have kids."

I barely hear her, and she offers no further explanation,

but a knife drives through my lungs when I realise why she is so upset.

There are no words I can say to offer even an ounce of comfort. Instead, I hold her close, letting her cry into my shoulder.

"I don't want kids." After minutes of silent crying, she sounds sure when she utters the words. Sitting herself up, she pulls away from my shoulder to look straight back at the blank TV. "I mean, I used to, but not anymore."

There's a hole left in my heart where our future once lived. Even after we grew apart, even while I was happily married, there was always a piece of my future I'm now realising I kept safe in case Cassidy wanted it. Only now, it feels like she won't ever want it. And it kills me the reason is the only thing I can't change.

Maisie is as much a piece of me as my head. We are a package deal whether Cassidy likes it or not. Which she doesn't.

"Thank you for coming today."

The silence that had spread between us wasn't uncomfortable in the way some are. It was contemplative and oddly calm, but I couldn't stand it any longer.

"Of course."

Cassidy wriggles against my shoulder when she answers.

"No I mean it," I clarify. "I know it must have been hard on you."

Her hand rests on my knee as Cassidy turns to face me, staring straight into my soul. Curling her legs onto the couch, she pulls her baggy knit over her knees.

"You're my best friend. Which seems silly since we didn't see each other for so long and I barely know you now. But it's true."

I wonder if she can see everything about how I feel for

her. I hope she can't. She just made it more than clear we will never amount to anything more than what we are already are. Friends.

The word has never hurt more, but I'll take whatever amount of her that Cassidy allows me.

When she rests her palm on my cheek I lean into her touch, allowing the warmth of her hand to spread through me.

"You're my best friend, too," I tell her. *Even though I want more.*

I shove all the inappropriate thoughts and the dreams of the future down. Way down, without a ladder.

And I hope if I trap them down there long enough, they'll go away.

Chapter Seventeen

CASSIDY

Sitting in the office of my boutique, I wonder why I bothered putting in any effort this morning. Amira did my hair before rushing off for her morning shift, and I put on a floral summer dress instead of my usual jeans and plain shirt.

Giggles float across the space from the small group of women crowded around a camera that points towards my gorgeous floral wall. They all must be at least ten years younger than me, but their designer bags are a blinding indicator of how different our lives are.

"I need to try that again."

The blonde bombshell skips in front of the camera, her pink skirt floating around her. She puffs air in and out of her cheeks. Someone waves for her to start, and she pastes on the fakest of smiles.

I tune out the words, not needing to hear the fifteenth take of her skin care commercial. No, not commercial. 'Gifted content' was the phrase she used. Although I'm pretty sure the skincare company is paying her.

This is not what I had in mind when the influencer said she wanted to hire my space for a photoshoot. She came in last week and fell in love.

"I just *have* to film here!" She had all but squealed as she took a hundred photos of the floral wall.

Every short format video and photo filmed this morning has been meticulously staged in front of the wall I spent hours creating, but not once has it been a focus. She promised to tag the location in the videos, so at least there's that.

And the money she paid to rent the space. I may have overexaggerated my average daily sales when working out how much to charge her, but she never questioned the amount. And it will be a good boost to my bank account. With the events at Noah's winery, the winter might not be as tight as I thought, but we are still a fair way out from wedding season. I need to bank as much money as I can.

"Did you want to shoot some videos together?"

I look up from the endless scroll of videos I'm flicking past on my phone. Fumbling as I lock the screen, I drop it on the desk.

Blondie has poked her head into the office, smile still plastered on but the rest of her face is frozen in place. Her laminated brows and thick lashes frame her perfect features. It's sickening someone can be so, perfect. She looks like a Barbie, and I can't blink away the spots in my peripheral vision. I thought by the time I was thirty, I'd stop being jealous of perfect women. How wrong I was.

Despite how insignificant I feel next to her, I can't turn down the offer to film some content together. She has over 500 thousand followers, and this is what I had in mind when I hired her the space.

To her credit, she knows social media well. Under her instruction, I film some 'behind the scenes' videos while she goes through yet another take on the skincare ad. We take videos together and record me handing her a bouquet of flowers from behind the counter. Her photographer—who I suspect is just a friend, given the phone she uses as a camera—takes some stylised headshots of me. Some in front of the wall, others behind the counter, and even some 'at work' shots cutting stems. I never could have afforded this kind of photo shoot, but my email pings almost instantly with the files.

"I need coffee." Blondie stretches with a yawn as we start to pack up her giant lights.

I point down the street. "The nearest café is about ten minutes that way."

It's ridiculous, for Melbourne. She groans and a light-bulb above my head flickers on. Coffee. I hold on to it, finding a marker to write the word on my hand so I don't forget.

With everything packed up, the women invite me into a group hug.

"Thank you *so much*." Blondie tucks a stray piece of hair behind my ear and taps me on the shoulder. "I will tag you in everything. And please tag me in your posts, too."

I promise her I will, flicking the sign to 'open' as they leave in the direction of the café down the road.

The storefront is quiet for the rest of the afternoon, and although that's typical for early in the week, on a Friday afternoon, it's still concerning.

Light floods in from the street windows. Dust sparkles in the rays and I take a second to stand in the glimmer and appreciate the moment. The floral wall creates a bright backdrop to the boutique. My initial worries, that the buckets of available blooms and bouquets would get lost amidst the extra colour in the space, were unnecessary. Instead, they somehow stand out in the foreground. I'm grateful that today my creation had its time to shine.

Purples, pinks, yellows, oranges, they all stand out against the green of the wall and the scattering of white flowers spread along it. Thanks to today, I've got some incredible shots for our socials, and hopefully the online response brings customers into the store.

My sister was right though, they need something to buy once they are here, and not everyone needs, or wants flowers. All the little nuggets of gold the universe has been dropping me start to fall into place.

People don't come to a florist for a wall they can't buy. The concept worked in the café because so many people buy coffee almost every day. Flowers don't have the same impulse appeal.

Coffee. This strip of shops has needed a café since before I moved in. Most shop owners tell me they had hoped I was opening one when I first took over the space. The coffee van that drives past every morning always ends up crowded with customers.

But if I had coffee available here ...

I'd need Amira's help. More than that, I'd need her to be fully on board.

After tidying the display area, marking down some two-day old blooms and carting all the flowers back into the refrigerated storage room in the back, I lock the front doors and flip the sign to closed.

Often after closing the shop, I stay back to share some posts on our socials, and catch up on some admin. But today I'm on a mission. I throw my laptop into my tote, deciding to do all the remaining admin stuff at home.

Cassidy: On my way home for dinner— are you cooking?

I send the message to Amira, craving a home cooked meal. It'll be easier to convince her to jump on board with my plan if I'm complimenting her skills in the kitchen. It's not until I'm climbing the stairs of the apartment building that she messages back.

Amira: We have leftovers, but I'm making dessert.

Even better.

Inside the apartment, the sweet smell of cookies baking makes my mouth water. Fidgeting with my ring, I creep into the kitchen. There's no good way to ask my roommate to quit her job, so I decide to blurt out the idea before I can convince myself it's a bad idea.

"I want to open a coffee cart in the boutique."

Amira spins to face me, turning the electric mixer off. Her bright yellow apron is scattered with flour, and a tiny piece of the icing has flicked up onto her cheek. One of her eyebrows rises toward her hairline as she wipes off the sticky sweet goo, licking it off her finger slowly.

"But you make coffee that tastes like dirt."

True. And also why I need her help.

"I had an idea."

She holds her hand up to stop me.

"I need a full stomach for this kind of conversation."

So I hold on to my thought. Glancing down through dinner at the note I left on my hand, I drop my fork over and over again. My muscles feel twitchy until I can't sit still. This is a brilliant idea. It's perfect, I need to share it. And I need Amira to go all in with me.

The second she drops her fork on her empty plate, I scoop it off the table and run it to the kitchen sink.

"You're right, I can't make coffee. I also can't make flowers and serve coffee to customers. But the boutique needs both. The whole strip needs both. The nearest coffee shop is a ten-minute walk away."

Amira allows her head to bob in a gentle nod.

I'm still pacing the kitchen, working off the adrenaline surging through my muscles.

"If I open a little coffee cart in the boutique, I could cater to every customer from every shop on the street. And while they are there, maybe they will also buy some flowers. But who would make the coffee?"

Pushing to stand, Amira does a little hop before planting her butt firmly back in her chair. I love the way she can read me like a book.

"Who would make coffee, Cass?"

I grab an un-iced cookie from the cooling rack, taking my time to savour the way it crumbles in my mouth.

"I was hoping you would." Amira jumps from her seat, swatting the treat from my hand. I quickly follow with, "I don't want to be your boss. I want us be business partners."

"You want me to use my grandma's inheritance."

I wince. She's right, I was hoping she could use it to cover some of the costs. No doubt they'll be exorbitant.

Amira stares me down, and tiny beads of sweat form on my temples.

"I'm in, but I have one condition."

My lungs release the air I'd held in. Knowing Amira, there's every chance she is going to say something ridiculous. And she does.

"You have to find me a date."

She holds her hand over my mouth so I can't ask questions.

Chapter Eighteen

CASSIDY

Manning the shop has never felt so lonely. It's late afternoon, and although I had some customers early in the morning, they've become few and far between since lunch. In between fixing together the few bouquets and posies, I've been pushing around the low tables, rearranging the space to find where a coffee cart would fit.

My cheeks still hurt from how wide my grin was last night when Amira told me she was interested. When I woke up this morning, she was already working on her laptop, looking at how to register our kitchen to make the sweet treats we could sell. We'd need one certification for home, and one for here in the shop. But it feels worth it.

I haven't been this excited about my business since I first opened.

Since today was so quiet, I contemplate staying open later to see if I can catch some commuters on their way home. Despite becoming the winery's florist, it hasn't been easy to secure events. I had to cut my sister's hours even more and reduce my fresh flower deliveries. I'm not even paying myself a proper wage anymore, only pulling out just enough to pay my share of rent to Amira.

I'm tired, and all I want to do is curl up on the couch under my grandma's blanket and read my book. But I need to scrape together as much spare change as possible to invest in the coffee cart. I can't wait for yesterday's content creation to bring in a hoard of customers.

The bell by the door chimes and I force a smile before I greet the customer.

Seeing who walked in, it immediately drops off my face.

Callum stands in the entry, admiring the space.

I don't know how to act around him anymore. Part of me aches to leap into his arms, but an even bigger part wants to run and hide in the office. I still remember the first time he was here, helping me unload the boxes for the green wall. The way he was so proud of me had swirled something in my core. It was embarrassing, having to tell him how my business was struggling. Especially considering he is so ... wealthy. I'll never get over the fact he owns the entire building we live in and drives a Mercedes.

All of that sits on top of the memory of sitting on his lap. Of how our bodies rocked in time, if only for a short moment. My core aches, wanting more. Always.

Heat swirls inside me as I force the memory from my mind.

"Is this from the boxes?" Callum *strides* into the space. He moves as though he owns this building, as well. His confidence is sexy, without being overbearing, doing nothing to help cool the fire burning through me.

I nod, meekly, fearing what will come out of my mouth if I attempt words.

"It's incredible," he mutters, before turning to me. "Rogue, you're incredible."

I can't help but smile at his words.

"I'd still be transporting boxes if it wasn't for your help."

"True." He laughs, the low rumble filling the room.

Leaning against the counter, I can't help but wonder why he is here. His dark slacks and white shirt imply he has been working, but it's too early in the afternoon for him to be finished for the day.

"Do you ... need flowers?"

There is a thickness in the air between us.

Although I should have been expecting it, the admission in his nod hits me with a force I was not ready for. *Who does he need flowers for?*

Typically, there are very few reasons men buy flowers. Anniversaries, apologies, occasionally a first date. Usually almost always for their wives or girlfriends.

My face must twist into an unnatural expression because he raises an eyebrow in my direction.

"Roses," he states, and my heart drops to my knees. On the very rare occasion a man buys flowers for someone other than his partner, they are never roses.

Roses are the flower of love, everyone knows that. The men buying them know that, the women receiving them know that, and I especially know that.

I hold in a cough as I push off the counter.

"What colour?"

"Pink, if you have them."

I do, so I stroll to a far table to grab the flowers.

"How many?" Despite my need to know more, I hold back my questions. Restricting myself to only the essential questions I need to get the bouquet complete means I'm less likely to burst into tears.

It shouldn't feel this way, him buying flowers for a woman that isn't me. After all, I'm the one who ran out after our night together. The weirdness between us is all on me.

"A dozen?" His answer is a question. There's a hesitation in his voice.

After grabbing the flowers, I collect some greenery and wax flowers to fill out the bouquet. When I get back to the bench I lay everything out and get to work.

I focus on my work, trimming and assembling the flowers without making the empty small talk I would with any other customer. Callum wanders the store, admiring the produce, sneaking glances over to where I'm trying to focus.

"Stop watching me," I groan.

Callum tucks his hands under his armpits, turning to face me. "Stop watching me."

I huff, returning to my work, determined not to look up again.

When the bouquet is finally finished, I go to stand tall but find I can't. Callum is hovering over me. His lips linger on my neck, but there is a gap between the rest of our bodies.

I suck in air, debating between squirming away, or pushing myself into him. His exhale is hot on my neck, spreading goosebumps down my back.

"Are you jealous, Rogue?" he whispers into my ear.

I freeze, unaware I had been so obvious.

He laughs, stepping back from me.

"They are for my sister. It's her birthday tomorrow."

Relief washes over me. My shoulders drop from beside my ears and my fists unclench.

There's a cheekiness to his expression, and I want to claim it as my own. When he catches me staring, he steps into me. I look up to see his face, and he gazes down at me with a twinkle in his eye.

"I think I'll have to buy flowers more often," he chuckles. "I like seeing you like this."

I scoff, placing my hands on his chest to push him away. He doesn't even flinch at the touch. Grabbing my hands, he holds them tight as he leans down and plants a kiss on my forehead. My toes tingle as I relax into his kiss. I hold back a moan when he pulls away, but before I can protest, one of his hands is under my chin, tilting my head up towards his.

Our mouths press together in what feels like a loving embrace. But it's too intimate, and there is still so much left unsaid between us. Still so much uncertainty, and too much baggage.

Hesitation has me falling back to flat feet, but Callum's mouth follows mine. He walks me back until I'm leaning against the bench, and I give in to desire. I boost myself onto the counter, spreading my knees so he can stand between them.

Callum kisses me like his life depends on it. He is hungry and consuming, but kind and gentle. His large hands roam my back, squeeze my hips, tug my hair. I'm lost in the moment and all my concerns and worries melt away under the fire that always burns when we are together.

I kiss him back, sucking at his lips and pulling his body closer. He brings a hand between us, groping at my breast. He pinches my nipple through my clothes, sending a zap of electricity through my veins.

Wrapping my legs around his waist, I pull at his hair. He presses himself into me and I can feel just how turned on he is. His hard length presses against the zipper of my tight pants and into my core. The friction through my jeans is tantalising yet infuriating. I want more.

Leaning back on my hands, I push against him. My hand catches the ribbon of the bouquet I made, and I'm thrown out of my feelings and back into my head. We are in my shop. My open shop with full front windows. Anyone could have seen. Anyone could have walked in.

But I was so lost in the moment I forgot where we are. Or didn't realise. Or didn't care.

I push Callum back and clamber down from the bench. He runs a hand through his hair as I straighten my top.

"Sorry, I—" He breathes heavily, but so do I. My heart is racing, and his cock is still strained under his pants.

Seeing me staring at it, he adjusts himself into a position that looks marginally more comfortable.

"It's okay," I say with a smile, running both hands over my face as I try to calm my body down. It does nothing for the aching between my legs.

Reaching behind me, I grab the roses and hand them over. "Your flowers."

He laughs as he grabs them. The rumble sends a shiver down my spine. Pulling his phone from his back pocket, he hits the button to pull up his card.

I hate charging him for flowers, but at this stage I can't afford not to. His $60 bouquet isn't even 10% of what Amira and I need to pull together.

Speaking of . . .

"Do you have any single friends?"

Callum folds his arms, the flowers dangling by his hip.

"For Amira," I clarify. "I have an . . . idea . . . but she wants me to find her a date."

Dropping his hands to his sides, Callum's shoulder's tremble as he puffs out a breath.

"No one who could handle her."

I thought as much. The only person I know with a strong enough personality to handle her and her family, is my cousin. But he would never go for it. She never told me why she needs a date, but if it means I can expand Betty Blooms in the way I hope, I won't question it.

Callum steps back towards me, planting another soft kiss on my forehead before he turns to leave. "If you need, I'll find someone. I'll round up every single guy on this side of the city if it gets you what you need. As long as they aren't there for you."

There's no hiding the blush that forms at his words. After today, I don't think I'd want them there for me anyway. The man I want is already here.

Chapter Nineteeen

CASSIDY

Bass beats in my ears and my eyes strain to see around the flashing lights and dim tables.

The thought of dinner and dancing with Amira, and the girls from her work, felt draining, but I couldn't say no to celebrating with Amira. I'm only here because it's her birthday. Noah is only sitting next to me because I called him at the last minute, demanding he come with me as a social buffer. The two of them have been bickering all evening. I plan to slip out after dinner and avoid the crossover as the trendy restaurant fills with club-goers.

"Here's to thirty," Amira cheers as we all hold up our tequila shots, "And to being forced into marriage."

Unsure what to say, we throw back our shots in sync. Her birthday isn't technically until next week, but her parents always steal her away for family gatherings, so we are celebrating tonight instead. Although with that news, celebrating doesn't feel like the right word. No wonder she wanted me to find her a date.

Noah chases his shot with a long draw of his beer, slamming the now empty glasses back on the table. I spin my margarita straw around the fancy glass. No one speaks, as we all look to Amira for clarification. Because I'm sure she said she was being forced into marriage, but even for her parents, that feels intense.

Amira pulls her own drink toward her, tapping her fingers on the stem of the glass. The clique of barristers and waitresses from Amira's work start to ignore the awkwardness, chatting and giggling at the other end of the table.

"What do you mean?" I lean in, but still have to raise my voice to be heard over the music.

"My father thinks thirty is too old for a woman to be single," Amira groans. "So if I'm not in a serious relationship before my cousin's wedding, he is going to find one for me."

Her face scrunches up.

"When's the wedding?" Noah asks, leaning into my personal space to join the conversation.

Amira leans over her margarita, her face in her hands as she takes a long sip.

"Three months."

My brain stops functioning, because even with all I know about her father, I can't comprehend him giving her a few months to find a serious relationship.

"If only my life was a romance novel," Amira mumbles after taking another long sip.

"How so?"

"Some man could come in and pretend to be my boyfriend just to shut my father up." After finishing her drink, she leans back in her chair. "Who knows, maybe we'd even fall in love."

Noah tenses at the words. He reaches across to grab Amira's arm. "I'll do it."

Amira pushes in front of me. The two of them crush my sides as they stare each other down.

"Really?" Amira asks.

"Yeah," Noah replies with a shrug. As though this conversation is the most everyday occurrence. "Can't promise the falling in love bit. But you can tell him we're together. I'll go to the wedding with you."

His knee knocks against mine under the table, but he

beams at Amira, letting go of her arm. I look at him, wide eyed, but he kicks my shin under the table.

Amira's spirits rise, the sparkle returning to her expression. When another round of shots arrives for the table, she downs her own before quickly pinching mine.

When the shots have been cleared, most of the table heads for the dance floor.

"I think I'm going to go," I yell over the music.

When Noah mimes he can't hear me, I lean in closer to his ear to repeat myself.

We walk through the dance floor on our way out, finding Amira, and saying our goodbyes. She clings to Noah longer than normal, hugging him close and talking directly in his ear. He pulls back to smile at her, giving her a final squeeze before we leave.

"I think I'll crash on your couch," he says as we exit the club.

His phone lights up with the Uber app as he books our ride.

"Cheaper than getting a ride out your way," I agree.

Back at my apartment building, I trip, multiple times, up the stairs. But in my defence, so does Noah. I only drank one margarita with dinner, and the tequila shot Amira demanded we all partake in. But the combination of stairs, and the heels I've been wearing for hours, and the drain on my already flat social battery, is not great for my balance.

By the time we finally reach my apartment, I'm out of breath from wheezing so much. I rifle through my bag searching for my key, cursing myself for every useless thing

I continue to bring no matter how many times I've never needed them.

When I can't find them, I start to panic. I don't want to wake Callum in the middle of the night and ask for the spare I left him. *What if he has Maisie tonight? What if I wake her up?*

Every time I come and go from my apartment, I stare at his door for a moment too long. After we lost ourselves to our feelings in the boutique, I'm still stuck wondering if there is hope for me and Callum. Until I hear a ghost of a giggle from inside his apartment and remind myself of why I decided being with Callum would be a bad idea. I even hear it when I know she isn't there.

When Noah coughs, I realise I'm doing it again. The staring.

"You look," I cry as I heft my bag at Noah.

He's too calm, leaning against the wall and staring at the door across from mine. While he searches through my bag, I sit on the floor and unbuckle my heels. Pulling them off my feet, I moan as I massage my arches and calves.

"What the fuck, Cass," Noah throws the bag on the floor before dropping down beside me. "How much crap do you have in here?"

He's not wrong, but I cringe as he upends the contents onto the floor. Looking at everything strewn about, I wonder how it all fits in the small crossbody.

Two sticks of lipstick I never wear, two lip balms I do.

An unopened travel pack of tissues, a tampon despite the IUD that regulates my hormones and stops me getting a period.

My wallet, and my sunglasses even though we left after the sun had started to set.

Seven hair ties in various states of distress, and countless bobby pins—so *that's* where they all end up.

A pack of gum that is lord only knows how old.

And, a lone matte silver key.

"I'm buying you a key ring," Noah scoffs as he picks it up.

The door opens while I attempt to shove everything back in the bag, collect my shoes, and stand without falling over. Which of course, I do.

Toppling over as I get myself upright, I reach out to grab Noah's arm to steady myself. But it's not Noah's arm. Noah had a shirt on and this arm is bare. And I've never really *felt* Noah's arm before, but I don't think I expected it to be so firm.

I flinch my hand back when I worry I'm feeling up my cousin's arm, but it's not until I hear a low grunt that I register it's not my cousin at all.

"Rogue, are you okay?" Callum's grouchy voice somehow feels like honey in my ears. Soft and sweet and warm.

Although I had removed my hand from his arm, Callum's now holding the small of my back. He stepped somehow between me and Noah and is staring down at my cousin. I'd be scared if that look was directed at me.

"She's all good, mate." Noah reaches a hand out towards me. My door is now open and I can hear my couch calling my name. My feet hurt and I just want to sit down.

I step toward Noah and my apartment, but Callum moves in front of me to block my path.

"I'm Noah—" my cousin starts, but Callum interrupts, apparently not caring who the man in front of my apartment is.

"I don't care, it's time for you to leave. I'll take it from here."

"I'm not an *it*," I protest, but I also melt into the arm Callum holds behind his back to me.

The man is acting like a jealous, overprotective boyfriend. It's frustrating and annoying but, I think I kind of like it, even though I definitely shouldn't.

"What are you doing?" Callum grunts.

"Uh, this is Noah," I say, not sure if he was talking to me or Noah, "and Noah this is Callum. My neighbour."

"He can go home now," Callum says as he turns to face me.

His eyes are dark, but he stares into mine like he sees my soul.

"No," I start to protest, feeling the need to explain the situation.

But instead of helping me, Noah backs down.

"Actually that's a great idea," he rebuts, with a sly smile.

Callum's eyes don't leave mine, so he doesn't see Noah mime that he'll call me. Or, thankfully, the dry humping gestures he makes as he walks backwards down the hall.

Static electricity fills the air as tension builds between us. The line between Callum's brows disappears once we hear the heavy door to the stairwell slam shut. I'm not sure who he thinks he is getting possessive, and I don't know how to handle the way it makes my core throb.

Callum's chest is heaving underneath his signature black t-shirt, and his hair is messier than usual. It takes all the willpower I have not to glance down at his grey sweats. I will not give in. I'm infuriated, and no amount of attractive possessiveness or sexy clothing will change that.

"What the fuck was that?" I demand taking a step closer.

Cal takes a step back into his doorway. His arms are still folded, but he leans to the side, resting a shoulder on the open door. My eyes linger on the way his shirt stretches against his muscles, taking in the intricate dragon tattoo. It's so familiar, but I still can't place it.

I step forward again, "Well?"

His gaze drops to the floor, body vibrating.

"I don't know," he admits.

I can't hold on to the physical aspects of my anger—the stomping, the scowl, the crossed arms—when he isn't matching the mood. I relax my shoulders and tuck my hands into the pockets of my jacket instead.

"Noah is my cousin."

Callum's eyes dart up to mine, and back down to the floor before he rakes them up my body. I feel his gaze lingering all over me.

"So what was it?" I ask again. I'm still angry, but the energy now is weird.

"I don't know," he repeats. His mouth opens and shuts a few times, like he wants to say something but doesn't have the words.

I stare at him, still expecting some kind of explanation. Wondering if it means what I think it could mean. Wondering if his possessive actions meant he wanted more. Because if that's true, he should say it.

I'd been holding on to the idea that I needed to stamp down my feelings because we would never work. Because he has a child and I can never be a mum. Because I'm not the person he needs. I'd pushed back against all his advances, worried I could never be enough. But he hasn't backed down, and this feels bigger than everything that has come before.

I stare him down, waiting for him to explain himself. To say something, anything.

"Goodnight, Cass," he says finally, as he turns into his apartment.

"Wait!"

Before he can close his door, I slam mine shut behind me. Closing the distance between us, I breathe deep into my stomach. I fake a kind of courage I've never possessed as I step closer. So close I can feel the rise and fall of his chest, and I'm sure he can feel mine. My breasts tingle, rubbing against him with the movement.

I look up at Callum and I see the man who takes my breath away. But I also see the boy I used to like. The best friend I had through high school. One of the best friends I have now.

Every swirling emotion inside him rests in his eyes and on his face. From this close, I can see his pulse throbbing in his neck, and the way his Adam's Apple bobs. I can feel his shaky breaths, and the way his arms are stiff at his sides. He is holding himself back. We both are.

Reaching up, I place my hand on his cheek.

Callum's beard, longer now than when he first moved in, tickles my fingertips as I trace the chiselled structure of his jaw. My thumb finds the dimple in his chin when I cup his face, guiding him to look me in the eye.

"Were you jealous, Callum?"

He deflects, tucking a strand of hair behind my ear instead of answering.

"How much did you drink this evening, Cass?" he asks, his hand tracing slow lines from behind my ear, down my neck and over my shoulder.

"Enough," I whisper, before shaking my head to continue. "Enough to have tripped on my way up the stairs and to lose my key in my handbag. Enough to have a little liquid courage. But not so much that I don't know what I'm doing."

Callum's breath catches, stealing mine away as his fingers caress further down my arm. He tilts his head into my hand.

I suck in the thin air between us, trying to steady the fire burning inside me. Callum doesn't speak. He bows his head, urging me to continue, but I have no idea what exactly it is that he wants me to say. I don't know what I want me to say, either, so I let it all come tumbling out.

"I've drank enough that even though I'm angry about what just happened, I don't want you to go back into your apartment. Not enough that I don't know what I'm saying, but enough that I don't care about how messy this whole thing is. Enough that I can finally admit to myself, to you, that I crave you. That no matter how hard I try to stop wanting you, no matter how often I remind myself of how different our futures might be, I can't stop."

The words fly out in a single breath, liquid courage forcing out secrets I thought I would never tell.

"I want this," I end with a whisper. "I want us."

The words haven't fully left my mouth before he traps them. Slamming his lips into mine with enough force to knock the wind out of me.

Chapter Twenty

CALLUM

When you think you've found the love of your life, everything about your world changes. And for a long while with Audrey, I thought that's what I had.

She was, when I met her, a peer from another Supers branch. From one Pantry Manager to another, we bonded over delayed shipments, damaged cereal boxes, and chips nearing their best before dates. We became each other's 'go to', whenever either of us needed to whine, we knew the other would be there.

It didn't take long for our friendship to blossom. The phone calls became less work related and more about our lives outside of work. We would talk for hours, neither of us with enough guts to say how we really felt.

Looking back, I'm not sure who made the move first, or what prompted it. We just fell quietly in love. In the same way our relationship had flowed from colleague to friends, it continued to flow from friends to lovers, to married couple, to parents. My life was no longer just about me, it centred around Audrey and her needs. It was, for all I knew, exactly how love was supposed to feel.

Here and now, though, with Cassidy, everything is … different.

My world hasn't changed, it's brightened. Like putting glasses on after years of living with astigmatism, or finally turning on the lights after dusk. Finally acknowledging the emotion that has been building inside me, a light has switched on in my brain, and every small, or excessively big, reaction makes sense.

And I don't know what to do about it.

For how long were we friends? After how long apart have we finally built that friendship back up?

I doubt she understands the extent of my emotions. If I dive in, there is no turning back. None. There will be no land to save me except her, and if she doesn't feel the same way, I'll drown.

I *am* drowning, knowing what's holding her back from feeling the same way about me as I do about her.

After her barrage of confessions, she looks up. The golden flecks in her irises look like glitter against the mossy green, and her eyes are full of hope.

"I want us," she whispers.

Those words act like a magnet.

I don't care about the red flags in our relationship. I don't care that she has been avoiding her feelings since she met Maisie. I don't care that if we do this, we also have a lot of extras to discuss. She wants there to be an us, and that's enough for now.

I slam my lips against hers to savour the words, the moment.

This kiss with Cassidy is unlike any other kiss I've ever had. Unlike the kisses I've shared with her before. The first one was an awkward mess of teenage lust. The last one a confusing mashup of emotion that neither of us was ready for.

But this one. This kiss feels important. It feels big. It feels like I've been flatlining and Cassidy's mouth is the defibrillator shocking me back to life.

I'm cautious about giving away too much of what I'm feeling, but can't stop myself from devouring her.

Her mouth opens a sliver and I take it as an invitation. Grazing my tongue across her lips, I beg to be let in, and she lets me. Our mouths collide as we taste each other, hastily now because I can't get enough.

I want everything about Cassidy, and from the way she drags her tongue against mine, it feels like she wants the same.

Wrapping my hands around her back, I tug her closer to me. My blood pumping below my waist, my cock hardens, and her breasts rub against my chest. I curse the satin of her simple black dress, the cotton of my tee, the fabric barriers stopping me from feeling her skin.

Every thought in my brain falls silent. The cars on the street below stop revving their engines, the hum from the building's heating system quietens, the clock inside my apartment stops ticking.

It's only me, and Cassidy, and this life altering kiss.

After a while, our foreheads touch, and our lips pull apart.

Cassidy's hand moves from my cheek to grab at the back of my neck. She drops her bag and the other hand reaches up over my shoulder. Her upper body heaves, and my breath hitches with anticipation.

"I—" she starts, but I steal whatever it was she wanted to say by claiming her mouth again.

With a hand on her waist I reach down to pick up her bag. Tugging her closer towards my apartment, she follows me in.

We fall against the wall as I push the door shut behind us. My hands itch to feel every inch of her skin.

Dragging one up her sides, I stop when my thumb grazes the underside of her bra. She smiles into our kiss and arches her back, pushing her breast into my hand. I run my thumb over the peak of her nipples before palming her breast. The other hand lowers down her back to knead her ass, pulling her closer to me until my leg rests between hers.

Cassidy moans into my mouth. Her hands are in my hair,

rubbing down my back, my shoulders. She rocks her pussy against my thigh as my erection grows against her front. I can't think, I can barely breathe, and all the while, our mouths haven't stopped. Teeth crashing against each other, both fighting for more.

It's me who pulls away this time, although at first, I don't know why.

"Callum?"

I can feel the warmth from her mouth as she utters my name. Leaning my forehead to touch hers again, my eyes close as I catch my breath.

"Rogue."

She caresses my sides as she pulls my shirt over my head.

"Cassidy," I call her by her name this time, because I need the moment to slow down. I need to know what it means to her, what it means for us. And I need her to know how much it would mean to me.

"Shh." She silences me with her lips. "I don't want to think right now, I just want to *do*."

And I let her, because part of me also wants to just *do*. It feels like I've been thinking and overthinking my whole life. Maybe I need to let go of all the what-ifs and the maybes and just allow this to happen.

Cassidy is everything to me, I want more than she thinks she can give, but I'll take whatever it is she is offering.

I tease her neck with my tongue as I slip the straps of her dress down her shoulders, revealing the simple black bra she wears underneath. The padding is thin, and I can see the mounds of her taut nipples through the fabric. Pulling the cups down, I take one breast in my mouth while I knead the other. My teeth and tongue catch against her firm nipple while I pinch at the other. She moans as she drags her hands along my torso, tracing the lines of my abdomen and down to the waistband of my pants.

Smiling up at me, she drags the waistband of my sweats down. My cock bounces free, firmer than it's been in years and aching for her touch. The tip glistens in anticipation. As soon as my feet are free, I wrap my arms around Cassidy and lift her up. Her legs wrap around me as I walk her to the bedroom.

I lay her gently on the bed. Her dress bunches at her middle, breasts still bouncing above the cups of her bra, her black lace panties on display.

She's a vision. I stare at her stunning face, her beautiful body, committing every single pixel of this picture to my memory. I will never forget how perfect she looks, lips swollen from our kiss, bare chest heaving, and that wet patch on her panties showing me how much she wants this.

I lean over her to take her breast back into my mouth, grazing my teeth against her nipple. When she gasps in a playful response, I trace my fingers down her front. Kissing my way down, I bunch the dress up further to reveal as much of her to me as possible.

Spreading her legs, I run my tongue along the edge of her panties.

Cassidy whimpers as I kiss her inner thigh and trace a finger along her seam. I can feel how wet she is through the fabric, but I push it to the side to spread the moisture around.

My mouth finds the waist of her underwear, and I drag it down to her ankles. I pause to take in the sight of her, spread out before me, before kissing my way back toward the apex of her thighs.

"Fuck, Rogue." It comes out as a whisper as I plant a kiss behind her knee.

"Please do," she whispers back.

My finger is still rubbing slow circles around her clit, and she groans when I remove it. But when I plant a kiss right on her core, the groan turns into a satisfied whimper. My tongue traces a path along her opening, and I kiss her again before flicking the sensitive bud with the tip of my tongue.

She tastes musky yet sweet, and it only takes one lick for me to become addicted. I want more, need more. I could taste her over and over again for the rest of my life.

Her hands grab at my hair as I gorge on her taste, lapping up the wetness trickling out of her. With my thumb pushing gentle pressure on her clit, and my tongue never giving up, I trace one finger around her opening before slowly inserting it. I curve it up to hit her walls, then ease it out to add a second finger.

"Cal," she calls out between her moans. The shortened version of my name has never sounded so perfect.

I can feel she is close by how her walls are constricting around my fingers, so I pump them harder, faster. As I suck on her clit, she thrusts against me, fucking herself with my fingers. Her moans grow heavy as she reaches her peak, shuddering against me before collapsing back into the mattress. I steal a final taste, licking away her wetness and sucking her juices from my fingers as I bring my body over hers.

I want to soak into her, to feel her wrap around my cock, but the uncertainty between us is holding me back. Leaning down, I claim her mouth again. The musky flavour of her come blends with the fruity remnants on her tongue. My fingers dive through her hair.

Her hips buck up to meet mine, the wetness from her pussy slides along my length in a way that feels effortless and right. That's how this whole evening feels. Right.

Keeping my mouth on hers, I reach for the bedside drawer and pull out a condom. Cassidy reaches between us, palming my firm length.

"Fuck," she whimpers. She bites her lip as she watches me roll on the condom.

Reaching for me again, she grasps firmly. Pumping my

dick a few times, she tugs it closer to her entrance. My balls draw up at the thought of burying myself deep inside her.

Leaning down, I push her hair back to whisper in her ear. "Are you sure?"

"Very."

I ease myself inside her, giving her time to adjust to the size of my cock. When I feel her walls relax, I pull out before thrusting back into her. A groan escapes me. A moan escapes her.

Cassidy pulls my face to hers, devouring my mouth while I pump furiously into her. With one hand, I reach between us to pinch her nipple.

My release comes hard and fast as Cassidy reaches her own climax, and I collapse over her. Foreheads touching, the words are so close to my lips. So close to falling out.

I love you. I keep them to myself. For now.

We fell asleep tangled with each other on my bed, stirred enough while the night was still dark to crawl under the blankets. Cass ended up in one of my tees, and in the morning light, I can feel her bare legs entwined with mine.

My nose brushes the nape of her neck and I breathe her in. I've imagined this moment for years. Decades. But nothing could have prepared me for how perfect waking up next to Cassidy is. How natural it feels.

Stirring awake, I feel Cassidy let out a deep yawn and she leans into me.

"Morning," she whispers. Her voice is husky, awakening a primal need in me. I reach under the shirt she wears, trailing my fingers over her nipples.

One taste of Cassidy will never be enough. I'm hopeful

this could be the moment to change the course of our relationship, but hesitant because there is still so much that needs to be said between us.

She arches her back into me, her arm reaching up to cup the side of my face. I kiss her jawline, sucking on her pulse point.

A loud buzzing sounds from the living room, followed by the shrill sounds of my alarm.

Cassidy groans, pulling her hand back to cover her ears.

"Why do you have an alarm set on a Sunday?" she wails.

"Maisie," I offer in explanation, knowing it's not enough, but climbing out of the bed to switch my alarm off.

Knowing what this moment will mean for Cassidy, I hate that I agreed to pick up Maisie this morning. I could have got her after lunch, or before dinner, or any other time that wouldn't act like a giant red flag in Cassidy's eyes.

When I finally find my phone hidden between the cushions of the couch, I curse myself and silence the scattered tune. Carrying it back to the bedroom to drop it on the charger, I find Cassidy standing, searching the floor.

"My clothes?" she asks when she hears me enter.

I try to tell her she doesn't need to rush out, but a small part of me understands.

"You don't have to go."

"I do."

"Rogue—"

She still wears my shirt, but her clothes and shoes are bundled in her arms as she reaches to pick up her bag from beside the door.

"I do," she repeats, "because—"

"Because of her," I finish for her. "I get it."

I don't get it, at least not completely. When the door closes behind her, I sink back into the couch and crouch my body forward so my head falls between my knees.

I'm fucked. I'm so fucked.

Because I want Cassidy more than anything, but I need Maisie more. And I never want to have to choose between the two. But if she makes me, I'll choose my daughter. A million times. No matter how hard my heart breaks.

Chapter Twenty-One

CASSIDY

Maisie's laughter stretches from her dad's apartment, infiltrating mine with its high pitched giggle. It's infuriating, the constant reminder of why I ran back across the hall Sunday morning.

Saturday evening, after Noah ceremoniously left Callum and I in the hall, still feels a bit like an out of body experience. And I'm certain at some stage, I had the most mind blowing orgasm of my entire life.

I've never done anything that felt so brave, yet equally so messy.

I can't say I regret it, because I don't. Just thinking about it has my insides somersaulting and my thighs clenching.

But it can't happen again. Things get complicated when friends cross the platonic line. With everything between us, Callum and I are too far apart.

It was the worst and best decision of my life.

Thanks to my liquid courage, we'd spent the evening in blissful ignorance, but the alarm that rang out on Callum's phone in the morning was a stark reminder of how complicated our whole situation is. In the same way Maisie's current merriment is a blaring horn, ensuring I don't forget.

I should be at the shop, but by three, I'd had a grand total of one customer, and decided to call it a day. My shoulders are tight as I sit over my laptop at the dining table. Everything that could help us with the opening of the coffee cart either costs more money, or takes too long. Business courses, social media marketers, barista training.

Stretching out my neck, I fire off a direct message to Blondie B. In the two weeks since she filmed her videos, she's shared one every other day. Just like she promised, she tags my Betty Blooms socials in every post and talks nothing but praises about the boutique. It's given our social media pages the boost I was hoping for, but so far, I haven't seen an increase in foot traffic like I'd hoped. After how she craved coffee when the shoot was over, maybe she'll help promote the opening of the coffee cart. If she could come down and rave about how good our coffee is, it might give us the boost we need for this whole idea to work.

The message wooshes away and I slam my laptop shut. The sound cracks through my spine, sending a shiver through my neck.

And Maisie's laughter still won't quit. Which is odd because I never hear Mrs Kelly and our living spaces share a wall. I never heard the previous occupant of apartment thirty two. But Maisie, I hear her every time she is here. And right now, her voice is getting louder.

Callum's is there, too. Gruff and grumpy, broken, cut-off sentences spread across the hall.

"Cassidy!" Maisie's voice calls to me as a sharp rap sounds.

I shake off the unease that was starting to spread through me. Walking up the hall, I step out of my apartment and collide with Callum. Wearing dark suit pants and a tight white shirt, he has one arm stretched above my doorframe. He hangs his weight in the most infuriatingly sexy way. It's unfair. That a man this perfect has a daughter. That nothing comes easy for me. For us.

"I need your help." His voice is low and restrained, as though he is holding back all the tension I heard while I was unintentionally eavesdropping. Although his stance is casual, his fists are clenched and the vein in his pulse point throbs.

"What happened?"

Maisie squishes her way between us. The bright pink bow sits on her head, atop a near perfect ballet bun. Her tutu puffs up as she finds space that doesn't exist against Callum's legs.

"Will you take me to dance class?"

Her face is lit up, eyes sparkling and cheeks puffed up in her trademark grin.

"Huh?" I blink a few times, processing what she asked me.

"I was going to take her, but I'm also supposed to be at work. The board called a last minute meeting. They want me there in person."

"Is everything okay?"

He grunts as he nods, dropping his arm to rest a hand on my shoulder.

"With work, yeah. They pull this all the time and it's nothing. But it's Maisie's first class, it's not fair if she has to miss it."

My ears ring. This feels like too much. I hardly know Maisie. She barely knows me. Callum and I aren't even a couple, no matter how much a part of me might wish we were. It's not right that I should take her to her first class.

"What about Audrey?"

"She's at work. She's too far away to get back on time."

"Please, Cassidy!" Maisie tugs at the hem of my shirt. "It will be so cool. To have a real life ballerina take me to my first class!"

Clasping her hands under one cheek, she tilts her head to the side and pouts her lips. Blinking vigorously, she looks up at me through her lashes. It's impossible to resist.

Shaking my hands at my sides, I shift my attention back to Callum. He has taken a step back, and now holds a laptop satchel at his side.

"Please, Rogue?" His voice is tender, lips tight and eyes a little glassy as he looks between his daughter and me.

"Okay, tell me where we have to go."

If it was anywhere else, I would have said no, but the ballet studio is only two blocks away and we'll walk past my favourite ice cream shop. Plus, I did have fun dancing with Maisie at the ballet exhibit. Knowing I passed my love of dance onto a child fills my heart more than I care to admit.

Maisie walks the whole way to the studio without complaining. She skips along the sidewalk, singing as she goes. When we step inside, she jumps herself onto a chair and starts pulling off her boots.

The reception area is a long room with plenty of couches and chairs scattered along the side wall. A pair of giant pointe shoes hang from the ceiling. Young girls giggle in excitement, gracefully skipping lengths of the space while their tutus bounce behind them.

"Will you help me, Cassidy?"

Maisie holds out two tiny ballet shoes. Just like the ones I still have tucked into my bottom drawer. To this day, I can't bear to get rid of them. I'd always imagined passing them to my daughter one day and when I found out that would never happen it was easier to throw them in the drawer and forget about that dream.

Seeing Maisie's bright new shoes though, I wonder why I thought any child would want my old ones anyway. Where my leather has cracked and the pink has faded to a murky tan, Maisie's are shiny and clean. Much more fitting for a ballerina in training.

I stretch them onto her feet, careful the elastic doesn't pinch her skin.

"We'll need to get you some ballet socks or tights."

Her head bobs in excitement as she pulls off her spotty puffer jacket.

Young girls crowd around the tiny reception, women I can only assume are their mothers hanging back. I'm sure they assume I'm Maisie's mother, too. The thought twists at my insides.

When the teacher calls all the girls into the class, I go to step forward with them. But all the other women hang back and I realise we aren't supposed to go in.

"Are you sure it's okay?" one mum says to another. Her hand rests on a young boy's shoulder.

"Yes, go. Get this guy to soccer. I'll stay here."

"Thank you! I'll be back before they finish."

All around me, the women start chatting. They talk of juggling activities between kids and of the birthday parties they have to attend on the weekend. Of all the toys their children are begging for, and how little Josie needs a whole new wardrobe because she had a growth spurt.

Is this what mothers talk to each other about? It sounds draining, but they beam at each other.

"Is this her first class?" A woman younger than the others sits on the small couch next to me. A baby bounces on her lap, pulling the ends of her bright copper hair.

"Yes."

"She looked very excited."

The twisting in my gut loosens a fraction. "She was. Is. Ever since we went to the ballet exhibit at the Light and Sound Museum with her father."

The woman nods, prying the baby's fingers away from her hair.

"We wanted to go to that, too. Was it good?"

Conversation flows and I find myself enjoying chatting with this woman. Together we coo over her baby, and she tells me about the end of year concert the dance studio is planning.

The music inside the studio dies and the troupe of young dancers skip back into the waiting room.

"Cassidy, I had so much fun!" Maisie calls from across the room.

Next to me, the woman reaches out to hug her own child. "It was nice to meet you, Cassidy. Will you be here next week?"

"Mummy will bring me next week," Maisie answers.

I smile down at her, twirling a stray piece of her hair back around her bun. The twisting in my gut finally gives way, replaced by a swelling from my heart.

"You know what." I crouch down to Maisie's level, tugging on her jacket. "Maybe we can convince Daddy to let me come the week after."

She jumps into my arms. "Yes, please, Cassidy."

Above us, the woman shifts her child to the other hip.

"See you then," she calls out as she leaves, tugging her daughter beside her.

Maisie and I stop for ice cream on the way home. It's probably too late in the day, but the Scoops shop calls to us as we walk past, and I can't resist.

It reminds me of all the times Madison and I would save up our coins for ice cream. Of how *big* I felt reaching over the counter to pay for our cones when I had no business feeling that responsible at such a young age.

I was only a little older than Maisie is now when our father became distant, and our mother left him. But no matter how many years I tried, I never got used to her absence. Until she left for good the year we both turned thirteen, like she'd been waiting for us to become teenagers. For a long time after that, all I felt was anger, but as I sit here with Maisie, it's replaced by something else.

Confusion.

I'm not Maisie's mother. I'm still far from that, but I could never imagine walking out and never seeing her again.

Her joy lights up my day, and I want to savour every inch of that feeling, not throw it away.

But that's exactly what my mother did. She threw it away. Not just me, but Madison, too. I'll never understand why. Not now I know what she gave up.

"Thank you," Maisie says, bringing me back to the present as she licks around her cone.

I'm not sure if she is thanking me for taking her to ballet, or for the ice cream, but knowing I made her day feels better than I thought it would. An unexpected warmth spreads through me, melting the ice cream in my hands.

Maybe I could get used to being part of this little girl's life after all.

Chapter Twenty-Two

CALLUM

A loud banging from the hall jolts me out of the slumber I was in. The noise sends me into a panic, and I have to count out my breaths to slow my racing heart.

After a brief pause, the banging recommences and I'm forced to crawl my way out of bed. Grabbing a pair of shorts from the dresser, I pull them on before storming down the hall. The sky still has the peachy hue of sunrise and this morning was supposed to be my rest day after running all week. Whoever is waking me up with their constant knocking better have a good reason.

My hand reaches for the doorknob when I realise it might be Cass. The buzzer never rang, so it has to be someone from in the building, and I can't think who else it would be. I don't know why she would be banging on my door at the crack of dawn, but it can't be good.

I crack the door open an inch and am caught by surprise when I find the lady from apartment thirty one standing in front of me.

"Mrs Kelly?"

She gasps at my appearance.

"Go put some clothes on," she says, placing her wrinkled hands on my chest and trying to push me back into the apartment. "Or don't," she adds with a smirk when I stand firm.

I fold my hands across my front, forcing her to pull her own off me.

"What do you want?" I yawn.

"Hmm, not as pleasant as I thought you'd be."

"Meaning?" I don't have time for games, and since I was woken up early and haven't had coffee yet, my patience is wearing thin.

"I've seen you with your daughter, and Cassidy practically begged me to ask for your help. I thought you would be nicer to an old lady."

Sure, but the old lady woke me up, and still won't tell me what's going on. Even still, I clear my throat, pushing the frustration down before I respond.

"You knocked—no, banged—on my door while I was still asleep, and still haven't told me why."

"Oh." She takes a step back, wringing her hands in front of her. Her hunched frame is petite and frail. "I need your help. Well, we need your help. Cassidy thought she could do it herself, but the pot is too heavy."

Cassidy's name extinguishes the frustration that had been sizzling through my veins. For the past week we've been floating between friendship and something more. The sensual touches, lingering looks, have all indicated something more, but we still haven't had a chance to talk about what has changed between us.

I've never properly met this old lady, but if Cassidy needs my help for something, I'll be there. Even though I'm still a fraction confused at what exactly they are trying to do.

"Let me get a shirt." I close the door on Mrs Kelly and race back to my bedroom, pulling out the first tee I can find.

Returning to find the hall empty, I figure the old lady must have returned to her own apartment. Her door is open at the end of the building, so I let myself in, announcing my presence with a loud, "Hello?"

At the end of the building, apartment thirty one is a different layout to mine and Cassidy's. I know because I saw the floorplans when I first bought the building, but I can't help but peer into the rooms either side of her short hallway. One bedroom has a large queen bed with an oversized purple comforter, the other has been set up as a craft room, complete with sewing machine, baskets overflowing with wool, and an easel by the window.

"On the balcony!"

Cassidy's voice races through my body like lightning, and I find myself chasing down the high as I power walk to the tiny outdoor space.

Outside, a tree taller than Cassidy rests on its side in a giant terracotta pot, surrounded by bags of potting mix. The women stand back, staring at it. Both have their hands on their hips, but my gaze is drawn to Cassidy's face. The sun catches the green in her eyes, giving them a sparkle I didn't know was possible outside of fantasy movies. Rather than her signature messy bun, her hair is in a loose braid that sits over her shoulder. The ends dangle over her breast, drawing my attention to the perfect perky mounds. For the briefest moment, I imagine getting lost in them, until Mrs Kelly coughs and I am shocked out of my imagination.

"My lemon tree needs repotting," Mrs Kelly says, as she steps through my space to head back inside.

"She's up to something." Cassidy laughs when Mrs Kelly slams the sliding door shut behind her. "It's not repotting season but she insisted. She also told me she could move the pot herself."

Behind the giant pot, a second, even larger pot sits empty. Its thick black rim contrasts against the murky orange of the base.

"What exactly would she be up to?" I smirk at the way she grits her teeth.

"I told her we were friends."

Cassidy pulls the sleeves of her tight tee up and reaches for a pair of gardening gloves on the cast iron table.

"Is that what we are, Rogue? Friends?" Taking a step towards her, I reach for the second pair of gloves, intentionally brushing the tips of my fingers against hers.

She jerks her hand away to pull on the gloves.

Somehow, I manage to rein myself in while we repot the tree. Cassidy remains mostly silent, only speaking up to give me instructions.

Once the tree is standing tall in its new, contrasting pot, I step back. Cassidy looks up at me from her spot beside the trees.

The way she looks on her knees is excruciating. All the other things she could be doing from down there flash through my mind, causing an ache in my cock. I turn my back on her to hide my swelling length, pretending to admire the view of the buildings. It's not much, but the neighbouring buildings are all only two stories, so I can see the park, and beyond it, the taller buildings of the city.

Cassidy moves to stand next to me, leaning her elbows on the railing as she gazes into the sky.

"I love them."

I follow her line of sight to where the hot air balloons drift.

"Have you ever been on one?"

Shaking her head, she turns to look at me. A small "no" escapes her lips. She coughs. "I'm scared of heights, but it would be cool."

"Remember the last time you said that to me?"

"When we were at the fair and you made me go on the Ferris Wheel?" She pokes me with a firm finger. "Yeah, I remember worrying for my safety."

I can still picture her, frozen as we tried to step into the chair. With a little coaxing, and a lot of nudging, she finally stepped on. It wasn't until we reached the top that she finally opened her eyes. And she loved it.

"You enjoyed it," I reminisce, and she nods as she takes a tiny step towards me.

"I did." Her voice is a whisper that floats between us, urging me to close the gap.

I step forward, towering over her tiny frame. I stare down at her, my hands rubbing her shoulders. With every rise and fall of her chest, her breaths start to hitch. I don't care that we are on our neighbours balcony. All I can think about is kissing her, and never letting go. I drag one hand along her neck to cup her cheek.

"Are we friends, Rogue?" I repeat the question from earlier, the one she never answered.

A blush rises from her neck, coating her cheeks in a pink glow. Her mouth drops open a fraction, and she brushes her tongue over her lower lip. My thumb follows its path.

My heart stops. Cassidy does her best to control her breathing, filling her lungs as she draws in a long, unsteady breath.

I lean down to whisper the words in her ear. "Because this feels like something more. And I've never made a friend come with my tongue before."

Turning her head towards mine, she steps closer until I can feel her body pressed against mine. Goosebumps spread up my arms and across the back of my head, and she shivers as she trails her fingers along them.

"I feel like it's something more, too."

She speaks directly into my soul and fireworks explode around us, between us, through us. I run my hand around her neck, fisting her hair as I pull her mouth to mine. She tastes like coffee, but her kiss wakes me up more than a latte ever could. Her tongue explores my mouth and my hands explore her back. I run them down her spine, pausing briefly before I drop them to grab at her behind. Hoisting her up, I lift her body into mine. She wraps her legs around my waist, and I push her down against my growing erection.

"I need you, Cass." I moan the words directly into her mouth, never breaking the kiss.

She bites my lip, grinding her core against me.

A firm cough sounds from inside, and I drop Cassidy to her feet.

Her eyes widen briefly and she steps back, turning to face the tree. Regret floods through me.

I immediately know I came on too strong, and I hate myself for it. Cassidy's presence does something unnatural to my brain because it stops working whenever she is around. I should talk to her, before I jump headfirst into a relationship she isn't ready for. Tell her the only reason she thinks we wouldn't work is not enough to keep me from wanting her. Wanting us.

But the truth is, I am in too deep. I fell the moment I realised she lives across the hall, and I have no hope of finding my way out.

I'm terrified of Cassidy not feeling the same eventually, but I also know why she keeps teetering on the edge. It makes no sense to me that the best thing to ever come into my life, my daughter, is the one thing holding Cassidy back. But that's how she feels and I have to respect that. All I can do is hope I can convince her to give me a chance.

"We're done!" she calls as she walks back inside, and I'm left standing alone on the balcony when Mrs Kelly comes out to thank me.

"She'll get there," she croaks, patting me on the shoulder. *I hope so.*

Chapter Twenty-Three

CASSIDY

Maisie is still in her pyjamas when she slams her tiny fists on the door. Callum hangs back, inside his apartment.

"Will you come to the park with us?"

"There's a café there, we can get coffee."

Callum's addition was just what I needed to make my decision. Sadly, or maybe worryingly, I have nothing better to do on my Sunday. And with Amira working an early shift, all I've had this morning is my dirt flavoured coffee. I don't know what I do wrong with our little machine, but I couldn't even get through the whole cup.

Despite Amira's efforts to train me, I haven't been able to make a decent coffee. Our new machine will be delivered tomorrow, and I have a week to figure out how to make a coffee worth five bucks. I'm hoping the fancy machine is the magic wand I need. If not, I hope Madison can handle a few extra shifts so Amira doesn't have to work seven days a week.

I grab my bag and coat, leaning down to Maisie's level.

"Think your daddy will buy me a coffee if I come?"

She throws her arms around me giggling.

"Come on, Maisie." Callum guides his daughter toward her bedroom. On the table, an empty backpack sits surrounded by supplies.

Drink bottle, snack box, sunscreen, hat, spare pair of leggings and undies, allergy plan and medicine. It feels like a lot of stuff, but I'm not the parent here. I trust Callum's judgement and start loading it all into the bag.

From the sound of toys being thrown around Maisie's room, I figure they've had a rough morning. She squeals Taylor Swift at the top of her lungs, and while it was endearing at first, three mashed up songs in and I'm ready to put on my noise reducing headphones. And it's only 9.30 a.m. If I become part of their lives—for real—how would we cope? How would I cope with the broken sleep and stolen mornings?

"I need copious amounts of coffee today." Callum's voice shocks me out of my daydream and I zip up Maisie's bright pink backpack.

"I think I do, too."

He yawns, shoving his knuckles in front of his face. "I'd even drink your dirt at this rate, Rogue. But Isobel said the café was good."

"Safer to wait then, probably."

As I tuck her drink bottle into the side pocket, Maisie's tiny voice enters the kitchen a fraction before she does.

"What happens to my new clothes when I go back to Mummy's for a week?"

Maisie has shuffled her way out of the room, dragging Pavlova behind her. She's spent plenty of nights here, but Callum mentioned they were working towards full weeks.

Callum walks over to Maisie and squats down in front of her. "Well, if there are any you really like and want during the week you can bring them with you to Mummy's. The rest I'll wash so it's all clean for when you come back."

"Okay," she says, but her downward expression and stooped posture give the impression she still isn't certain about the whole situation.

"What if I don't want something now, but I want it before I see you again?"

"Then Mummy can call me and I will bring it to you."

Maisie fiddles with her doll's hair. Callum pulls her hands into his own to calm her nerves. I don't want to seem like I'm

216

eavesdropping, so I pick the bag off the counter and walk to leave it by the front door. These apartments are so small though, I still hear everything.

"I know it's hard having two homes, but I promise it will get easier."

I wonder if he knows when, or how it would get easier. It sounds like he is making promises he might not be able to keep, but I keep my mouth shut and stay out of their way.

Two happy homes are better than one shitty one, isn't that how the saying goes?

I hope Callum and Audrey can make their homes happy for Maisie, and once again, I'm finding myself wondering where I fit in that image.

"You can never break a promise," Maisie says. She steps back, holding out her pinky finger.

Callum hooks his finger around hers. "I know, but you have to give me enough time."

Their hands jerk in a firm pinky promise shake, before Maisie leaps into his arms. Callum falls back onto his heels as Maisie squeezes into the bear hug. Running off, she yells over her shoulder.

"I need the Elsa jumper at Mummy's!"

"It's in the basket," he calls back.

I'm impressed at how easily she can pull herself out of a bad mood.

The autumn day is balmy, the sun shining for the first time all week. What feels like hundreds of families have flocked to the park to take advantage of what might be our last sunny day for a few months.

"I haven't taken Maisie here yet," Callum says. After

ordering our coffees we do a quick walk around the perimeter with Maisie, setting boundaries of where she can and can't go before finding a spot in the shade to stand while she runs off to explore the playground. I try to remember if my mum or dad ever cared this much, but nothing comes to mind. Madison and I used to walk to the park by ourselves; entertaining each other for hours until the street lights came on.

Maisie stays close by, doing laps of a slide. Even from a distance, her giggles light up my soul in a way I didn't think was possible.

"She's pretty cute." I lean my shoulder against Callum.

He hums his agreement, a wide smile on his face as he watches his daughter.

A young couple cradling bright coloured reusable coffee cups settles down on the grass in my peripheral vision. They default into a cosy position with their legs twisted together and her head on his shoulder. When he reaches down to touch the grass with his hand, realising it's still damp with morning dew, they laugh at each other.

I can't help but watch them, envious of what they have.

I think of Callum and Maisie, and me, and where, or if, or how, we could evolve into something that looks like a happy family. I want what the couple on the grass has, so being told I couldn't have it has done irreparable damage to my heart. But with Callum, it feels like maybe some of the pieces are fitting back together.

I wonder how things would have been different if we had gotten the timing better. If we hadn't been young and dumb and run away from each other when we got scared.

He is such a natural dad, and now I know he is one, I can't see him as anything but. He always wanted a family, but that is something I could never give him. Maybe the universe knew before I did, separating us before we fell too deep. It would have broken him, broken us, if he had been in Blake's position.

I'd like to think he would have cared more about me than about my ability to give him a child. I'd like to think Callum would have stayed by me. But it would have stolen a piece of his future, and I'm glad we didn't have to walk that path together.

This was always where we were meant to end up. And I hope our paths continue to twine together.

I'm in so deep here, it feels like quicksand. I'm sinking further and further into something that feels a lot like love, and it's scaring the shit out of me. I don't know if I'm ready to be in this relationship one hundred percent. If I'm ready to tell not just Callum, but Maisie, too, that I want to be around forever.

They've been through so much, I need to be certain before I take that giant leap.

A lanky boy with a red face and blond hair comes running up to the couple on the grass. They sit up as he barrels towards them, and together they all collapse back onto the grass laughing. My eyes fall shut as I enjoy the sound of a happy family.

I lean further into Callum's shoulder, soaking in the sunshine and relaxing into the easy morning. It feels more right than anything else.

Something brushes against my fingertips. Callum's fingers thread between my own, but he jolts them away before I can grab them. Without a word, he runs toward the playground.

Maisie is lying awkwardly on the ground under the top of the slide. One arm twists underneath her body. She's silent, but it's more concerning than comforting to not hear her cry.

I hang back, not knowing what I can do that would be helpful. Callum comforts his daughter, sitting Maisie up. Tears stream down her pale face, but her eyes are dazed. Her shoulder hangs at an unnatural angle.

Scooping her up, Callum calls out as he walks past me. "We need to go to the hospital."

Chapter Twenty-Four

CALLUM

"**F**uck!"

Cassidy hits the brake as the light turns orange. After she fished my keys out of my pocket, I couldn't bear the thought of leaving Maisie in the back on her own. I'm squished next to her car seat while we race towards the nearest children's hospital.

Maisie's face is dry and salty. The tears have finally stopped flowing, but this is worse. Her tiny whimpers shudder through her whole body, and she clings Pavlova under her chin. Getting her seatbelt on was rough, getting it off will probably be even harder.

The break in her right collarbone sticks out, and I feel pain in my own shoulder just looking at the red, swollen lump. My coffee breakfast churns in my stomach and my chest feels tight. Cassidy curses from the front as another traffic light ahead turns red before we can get through.

I should call Audrey, but I don't want to take attention away from my daughter. My hands rest in her lap, and I lean across to kiss her cheeks.

"You're so brave," I whisper.

"I want Mummy."

My heart breaks. I want to be enough for her, but Audrey was always better at the comforting side of parenting. Keeping one hand in Maisie's lap, I push my hips up to pull my phone out of my pocket.

Audrey answers after half a ring, panic already in her voice.

"What happened?"

"Maisie is fine," I start, taking a deep breath as I glance at her tear-stained cheeks. "But we are taking her to hospital. I'm pretty sure she broke her collarbone."

Audrey drops the phone, and I can hear her scrambling to get everything she needs.

"What hospital?" she asks when she picks the phone back up.

She hangs up as soon as I've given her the details, and Cassidy pulls into the loading bay at the Emergency Room. Climbing out of the car, I unbuckle Maisie's harness and pull her into my arms, careful not to move her arm too much. Cassidy loops the backpack onto my hand. It bumps against my knee as I walk inside, but I'm too concerned about my daughter to care.

The smell of bleach burns my nostrils as I walk through the entrance way and into the ER. Nurses rush back and forth behind the desk. A short line of patients wait to be triaged, and almost all the chairs are taken. Someone is lying on the floor in the corner, coughing violently. Another person sways dangerously in the line ahead of me.

I sing quietly into Maisie's ear, trying my best to calm both our racing hearts. It does nothing to ease the deep pit in my gut or stop the twitch in my fingers.

After an eternity, we reach the front of the line. The triage nurse is kind, but blunt, as she assesses the urgency of our visit. When she sees the clear break in Maisie's shoulder, her attitude changes. Suddenly endearing, she hands me a form to fill out and fetches an icepack.

Squishing myself between a man holding a towel over his arm, and a lady with a very swollen ankle, I fill out the form. Maisie wriggles in my lap, a small gasp escaping her lips. Her eyes are puffy and closed, her breathing slow, and I wonder if she is sleeping. I turn my head back and forth, adjusting

Maisie in my lap. Holding tight with one hand and a forearm, I move to stand and return the form to the nurse.

"I'll take it."

Her voice cuts through the silent chatter like birdsong, and I look up to see Cassidy zig zagging her way around chairs towards us. I hadn't stopped to wonder if she would come in after parking the car. I didn't think to care. But now she is here, it feels odd. Maisie doesn't need Cassidy, she needs her mum. And we clearly established whatever happens, Cassidy doesn't need to be that person. After the divorce, I never thought I'd feel this way again, but I hope Audrey arrives soon.

Cassidy grabs the form in my hand, taking it over to the nurse before returning to stand in front of us. Squatting down, she lays a hand on Maisie's knee, rubbing small circles with her thumb.

"I'm so sorry," she whispers, although I'm not too sure what she is sorry about. None of this is her fault. It's all mine.

I got caught up in the imaginary scenario in my head, the one where we were a family. I was too distracted by the comfort of Cassidy leaning against me. Too focused on the couple ahead of us, and how much I want with Cassidy what they seemed to have. My thoughts were too removed from my daughter on the playground. I should have been watching her, and instead I was inside a happy family fantasy in my head.

I stroke Maisie's hair, making a silent promise to never let myself lose focus on her again.

I look up at Cassidy. Her long hair is windswept and knotted, and her eyes are red and glassy. "You don't have to stay."

"I want to," she responds. "At least until Audrey gets here."

As though Cassidy's words summoned her, Audrey bursts into the ER with a backpack flying behind her. She pauses to dart her eyes across the room, rushing over when she sees us.

Cassidy stands and takes a half step back, but Audrey pushes in front of her to crouch by Maisie.

"Is she asleep?" Concern laces her words as they hitch in her throat.

"I think so," I whisper. Maisie's breathing is still slow, but with every few exhales a slight whimper escapes.

Audrey shifts her legs as she sits on the floor. She leans back against my leg and drapes her arm over Maisie like a blanket. She sings softly, her breathy allure comforting me, even though it was intended for Maisie.

It's not until the nurse calls Maisie's name I notice Cassidy has left. My heart twists at the realisation, dropping low in my stomach. I hate myself for it.

My daughter is in pain in my arms, and I'm thinking about Cassidy. I'm feeling things for her I have no right to feel. Not now at least. Cassidy is a distraction I so badly wanted, but I don't need.

I was so worried about how me being with Cassidy would make Maisie feel, I never stopped to think she might actually get hurt. But she did. And I will never let that happen again.

Chapter Twenty-Five

CASSIDY

From this side of the cart, the roasted smell of coffee beans blend with the sweet aroma of syrups and the subtle creaminess of warm milk. Amira kicked me off barista duty after my second failed attempt at making a heart in the milk foam. Instead, I've resigned to writing names on paper cups and placing homemade biscuits into little paper bags—when I'm not assembling bouquets or relieving Madison behind the till.

Pride swells through me. Teachers who told me I didn't have enough motivation to work in the creativity field be damned. I spent years building my skills and business to the level it is today. And it's all thanks to an idea, and a best friend with a passion for coffee and sweets.

It's been busy. Hectic. None of us have stopped moving since we opened hours ago.

"I'm going live." Blondie bounces her way over, her expert waves flowing behind her.

Amira wipes her hands on her denim apron, tucking her hair behind her ear. "Okay, I'm ready." She tilts her head a little to the left, with her chin tucked down and her shoulders rolled back.

I attempt to straighten the collar of my shirt—denim, to match Amira's apron. My hands are still up around my neck when Blondie slides an arm around me. Phone in the air above us, she smiles at the screen. Hearts and thumbs float across the filtered image of us. I look odd. Good, maybe, but odd. My nose is smaller, lips bigger, and my skin is flawless.

"You guys have all seen the incredible floral wall in my videos and *guess what!*" Blondie pauses for emphasis, batting her lashes. "I am *back* at Betty Blooms Boutique and now they have *coffee!*"

Flipping the screen, she shows off our rustic coffee cart. Amira waves, leaning over the counter with a wink. Behind me, Madison coughs. Twice.

Turning to face her, I don't see him enter the room. Madison wobbles her head, trying to redirect my attention, but it's too late. I feel his presence before he speaks.

"Rogue." His voice is a warm breeze on a hot summer's day. Something that you want to feel refreshing, but instead leaves you burning. And sticky.

We've barely spoken since Maisie got hurt at the park. I haven't seen him. He's been staying with her at his ex-wife's house. The brief message he sent last weekend said Maisie had broken her collarbone and needed to wear a sling for six to eight weeks. Guilt jackhammered into me, and I still have no idea how to make it better.

If Maisie and Callum hate me now, I get it. If I hadn't been at the park, Callum would have been playing with Maisie. Paying attention to her, instead of me. The vision of Maisie lying on the ground in pain is seared into the back of my eyelids. I'd been too busy imagining a fantasy where Callum and I were together that I hadn't even noticed Maisie fall.

Kids get hurt all the time, that's what Amira said. And Noah. And Madison. And even Callum. But it doesn't matter how many messages he sent saying it wasn't my fault, I blame myself.

My shoulders tremor at his proximity. I can't turn to him, but I also can't turn away.

"Callum." His name is nothing but a whisper on shaky breath.

He runs his hands down my shoulders, bringing them to a stop. With a squeeze, he steps away.

My cheeks burn as he strolls toward the floral wall, remembering the last time he was in the boutique. And my chest aches as I remember why I can't allow myself to feel that way.

Even so, the distance I put between us over the past week has done nothing to eliminate the annoying way my insides flutter when he is near. Or the way I linger by his door, even though he isn't home. Now he is close, my feet itch to walk up to him. To throw myself in his arms and beg him for forgiveness. No matter how hard I try to fight it, the bead of hope still resides in my heart. The one that thinks maybe one day, somehow, we could make this work. Despite all the red flags that have shown us why we can't.

Because if Maisie getting hurt wasn't the universe's way of telling me I needed to back off, I don't know what it was. I've been fooling myself this whole time, thinking Callum and I could be something more.

My thumb scratches against my finger, the red skin now raw and painful. Silently cursing Amira for not letting me wear jewellery near the food.

"Food handling 101," she had said in the most know-it-all voice. *Fuck that.* I'm not even making the coffee now.

A gentleman distracts me, pointing out his partner and asking me to create a bouquet for her. Her yellow and white sundress is far too summery for this time of year, but I use it as my inspiration. Wrapping a combination of white peonies and daisies and wattle with white paper, I use a jute ribbon to hold it all together. The gentleman beams.

"It's perfect for her."

Once he pays, I tidy the florist benchtop, mostly trying to look busy. Madison is helping Amira clear her line, and there's no room for all three of us behind the tiny cart. In hindsight, the counter extension would have been helpful, but I had no idea we would see this much success. I cross my fingers and hope it continues past our launch day.

"Should I buy flowers for my sister again?"

I spin away from the bench. Callum stands before me, close enough that we can have a conversation in the busy space, but not so close that I can smell his woodsy scent amongst the sea of florals. Closing some of the gap between us, I rest a hand on his chest. He laces his fingers through mine, grabbing my other hand and tugging me closer.

"Callum I—"

He cuts off my apology like he knew it was coming. "You didn't screw anything up at the park. I'll tell you a million times if that's what it takes. Kids fall and get hurt all the time. It was never your responsibility to be watching her every move."

"It feels like my fault."

"It feels like my fault, too."

As if moving by its own choice, my head slowly tilts down to rest against the crook of his shoulder. The woodsy scent I craved moments ago soothes my muscles. My shoulders drop from their position near my ears and my neck loosens, falling into Callum's shoulder. With my fingertips, I trace the lines of his abs, teasing lower.

"Tall flat white and a skinny almond cap for Charlotte."

Amira's voice reminds me where we are. I snatch my hand away from Callum's waistband, but he wraps his arms around me, holding me close.

"I missed you." I utter the words under my breath, still unsure if I want Callum to hear them. But he does.

"I missed you, too."

Together, our chests rise with a long inhale. Callum rests his hands on my shoulders, taking half a step back.

"This is incredible. You are incredible."

It feels unjust, accepting his praise without directing

some of it to the woman still making coffees. "I couldn't have done it without Amira."

Callum shakes his head. "She said it was all your idea. She said you found the cart and researched all the commercial kitchen requirements and ran the marketing. She said it was all you, she just had some inheritance and knows how to make a coffee that doesn't taste like mud."

"I don't do anything different. She showed me exactly what she does and I followed every step. I don't understand what I do wrong."

Callum hums, tracing small circles on my shoulders. With gentle pressure in carefully selected spots, he eases the knots I hadn't noticed were forming.

"There are a lot of things you do right, Rogue. Who cares if you can't make a coffee. You don't have to be able to do everything. You don't have to be good at everything. You're allowed to learn as you go, and everyone is allowed to make mistakes. Even the people who have been making coffee for five years. You have to promise me that you won't give up. That you'll focus on all the things you can do, and you'll keep trying at the things you aren't sure of."

The blue of his eyes goes cloudy as he stares into mine and I don't think he is talking about making coffee anymore.

"I won't stop making coffee," I promise.

Chapter Twenty-Six

CALLUM

"Okay," I say as Maisie scoops another oversized mouthful of once frozen lasagne into her mouth. "If you could be any animal in the world, what kind of animal would you be?"

It's a silly question, but something I've started doing every meal with Maisie. Since I only get half of all her dinners, I want to make them count. No more eating with the TV on, we eat together, present. And as we talk to each other, I get to know her a little better every day.

Like last fortnight, I learnt her least favourite colour is "the poo green crayon colour," and that she would rather fly than breathe under water.

I hope, though, that through all the random and silly questions, she learns she can ask me anything, too. I want her to trust me to answer her questions, to be honest with her.

Maisie's forehead furrows as she chews.

"A kangaroo," she finally answers, stabbing her next adult sized mouthful onto her fork.

"Hmm?" I prompt whilst chewing my own food.

"I like how they hop."

"So why not a bunny?"

"Too little, I want to be big."

She fills her mouth with the last of the lasagne. The sound of mumbling and keys rattling breaks the silence. Through chews, Maisie looks at the entranceway. The sling pulls her arm tight against her chest when she tries to lift it to point down the hall.

"Can I see Cassidy before I go back to Mummy's? I want to show her my swing."

"Sling," I say, enunciating the 'el' sound. By the time she figures out how to say the word, she won't need to anymore.

Something weird happens to my thoughts. Maisie misses Cassidy. I miss Cassidy. But from the way she avoids my gaze every time we pass in the hall, I'm not sure if Cassidy feels the same. It's been almost two weeks since Maisie got hurt at the park. At first, I thought Cassidy was giving us some time. Some space I don't need, but I understand why she would think I did. I'd moved back into Audrey's place for the week to help her care for Maisie, but her responses to my attempts were short and closed off.

I don't blame her. I overreacted after Maisie got hurt. At the hospital, I pushed Cassidy away, believing we had both done something terrible. Thinking it was our fault Maisie fell. But after some time to think about it, I came to my senses. If Cassidy wasn't there with me, I probably would have been scrolling on my phone anyway. Her presence made no difference to the outcome. If anything, I'm glad she was there to help get us to the hospital.

I thought showing up to support her when she launched the coffee cart with Amira would break the weird ice that had formed between us. Would make her see I don't blame her at all. Instead, I left feeling more unsure than I had been before. We were close that day, she said she missed me. So why have our conversations since then felt so forced?

"You know what," I say as I lift Maisie off her chair. "Let's go see if she's home."

If she won't come to me, I'll go to her. I want to get back to all those nights we spent curled up together. Me and Cass. And the only way we can move past the weird tension between us is to actually move past it. I crave Cassidy, in more ways than one, and if the only time I get to spend with her is when we play happy families with my daughter, so be it. I know everything is still raw for her, and that the thought of being any kind of parental figure is unnatural and daunting. Especially after Maisie's fall. But I'm going to do everything in my power to show her, little moment by little moment, how right we are together. The two of us, but also the three of us.

Before I can stop her, Maisie runs through the hall, slamming into Cassidy's door. My knuckles tap against my sternum as I work to hold in the bubble of emotion that threatens to burst.

I'm still centring my thoughts when Cassidy appears in the hallway with a smile. Maisie's hand is still up, fist formed as though she wasn't finished knocking. In her work clothes, she looks exhausted, but also, enchanting. Dark jeans hug her hips, and her loose-fitting tee suits her perfectly. A laptop bag swings over her shoulder, with a denim apron slung over it. She just got home from work, hasn't even stopped to put her things down.

"Hi," she says as Maisie latches onto her leg in a hug.

"Will you come watch the rest of my movie?" Maisie asks.

Cassidy shuffles back out of her grasp. She looks between Maisie and me, her eyes catching on Maisie's sling.

"How's your shoulder?"

Stomping her foot, Maisie scowls. "It doesn't even hurt now but I still can't go to ballet."

Looking up at me, Cassidy fiddles with her fingers. "What about," she says as she drops to Maisie's level, "instead of a movie, I show you how to do some ballet?"

Maisie jumps up and down, but Cassidy places a soft hand on her good shoulder, pausing her.

"Some gentle ballet moves."

The bubble in my chest bursts in the most spectacular

way. But I can see the way Cassidy picks at her fingers in the absence of her ring.

Under instruction, I push the coffee table against the wall to create more space. Cassidy plays some classical music on her phone, and Maisie brings her ballerina doll out from her room to sit next to me on the couch.

"You're the audience," she tells me.

Together, Maisie and Cassidy practice their points. Twisting their toes out and stretching their legs. I lose focus on the specifics; the French words Cassidy uses to describe the movements. Instead, I'm lost in the beauty of my two girls dancing before me.

The swelling inside me intensifies. All those fairytale stories I told in my head are coming true, and I wonder if all the mess of the divorce was worth it to be here right now. To have found my way back to Cassidy.

My mind is stuck on how perfect this moment feels, and I can only hope Cassidy feels it, too. I want her to know how perfect the three of us are, and I need her to understand she doesn't have to be a mother to Maisie.

Maisie has that, with Audrey, and I would never try to replace my ex-wife in that way. Cassidy can be something entirely different to Maisie. I don't care what kind of role she takes, as long as she is a part of our lives.

I can hear the delight in Maisie's voice every time she talks to Cassidy. There is some connection between the two of them I can't explain. But I see the way Cassidy's eyes light up when they are together, and I know she feels it, too.

The weight of Maisie's head lands on my lap and the couch shifts as Cassidy sits next to me. They giggle through their yawns.

I'd known both Cassidy and Maisie would love the light and sound exhibit, it's why I pushed Cassidy to come with us. What I hadn't expected was how well the two most important people in my life would connect over the experience. Cassidy's 'real life ballerina' story became the foundation of their friendship.

That day, I wondered if we were standing on a precipice. If my second chance at love, my second chance with Cassidy, was here. All the baggage we both held was still there, but it didn't feel so heavy when the three of us were together.

After she told me about her infertility, and her subsequent decision not to become a mother, I understood why the whole situation would feel like skating on thin ice for Cassidy. But I will do anything to bring us on to solid ground. I've loved Cassidy since I was a teenager, I'm not willing to lose her again.

Maisie yawns as I scoop her onto my lap, careful to keep her shoulder in a safe position. Her head falls against Cassidy's arm, who shuffles down to lean against my shoulder. Images of every moment I've ever spent with Cassidy flash through my mind. Sharing lunch breaks and hiding in the cool room as teenagers, my first shift as supervisor when neither of us knew how to act. The intense shock and mild hope when I first saw her in the hallway the day I moved in. Our first kiss in some other kid's backyard, the life changing one on her couch. The way she danced with Maisie and how natural it had felt when the three of us held hands. The electricity in the air when we pass in the hall. And how perfectly our bodies fit together, just like our souls.

And now. This perfect moment.

The love that has been growing inside me expands until there's a pressure in my chest I can't contain. The woman I love is sitting right there, and I have no idea how to tell her what I feel.

I lean my head back on the couch, my neck stretched and my face towards the roof. I feel torn.

I love Cassidy. But the child in my lap, the child who

deserves all of me, and who I would do anything for, is stopping me from going to her.

Maisie's weight turns to lead, her breathing grows slow and steady in my lap.

"Is she asleep?"

Cassidy's whisper shocks me out of my stupor. I nod, awkwardly pushing myself to stand up.

I carry Maisie to bed, tucking her in and turning on the nightlight before creeping out of her room and back into the living area. When I get back, Cassidy stands from her spot on the couch. Her face is red, and wet marks trail down her cheeks.

My eyes sting, my chest heaves, and my hands rasp against the stubble on my cheeks.

"I should go," she says, her voice low.

"Don't."

I step towards her, reaching out my hands so our fingertips touch. With one hand on her lower back, I guide Cassidy back to the couch, laying her down against the pillows. I kiss her hand when she stretches it up to my face, then her forehead, then her cheek.

"I love you," I whisper.

Before she can respond, I kiss her. My weight settles against her as I throw every feeling I have for her into this kiss. With one arm still caught underneath her, I use the other to cup her cheek when I pull back.

Her eyes are glassy. She bites her lip, holding my face in her hands.

"I know," she whispers. "I think I could love you, too."

She runs her hands down my neck and over my shoulders. Her soft push guides me up until we sit, chest to chest.

"But I should go." Her attention is already over my shoulder, down the hall.

"You don't have to."

"But I should. This … us … it's hard."

A knife forms in my lungs.

"It doesn't have to be hard."

"But it *is* Callum. Every time I think I can do this, I think we can do this, the universe throws me some big giant reminder of why it won't work. Your alarm clock, Maisie's collarbone. Even now. It doesn't matter how much fun I had dancing with Maisie, we sit on the couch like a family and all I can think about is how you deserve so much more. How Maisie deserves more. I can't keep fighting for something I don't think is meant to be."

Resting my palm on her cheek, I wipe at the tear forming under her eye. My own tears flood down my cheeks.

"We are, Rogue," I choke on the words. "We are meant to be."

But she shakes her head. "It's really hard to feel that way anymore."

Stepping away from my touch, her shoulders roll forward.

Every inch of me burns with the need to stop her, but I let her go. I've been fighting for us this whole time, hoping, praying, she would feel the same way. I start to shake, my pulse racing as a darkness overwhelms me.

"So let me prove it."

She turns before she leaves. "I'm trying."

Chapter Twenty-Seven

CASSIDY

Amira finishes my hair as I rub some tinted moisturiser over my face. Once she has unrolled the final heatless curler from my bangs, I give her a quick squeeze.

"Thank you for doing my hair."

"If I didn't, you know you'd be at a fancy winery with a messy bun," she says, pulling out her own curlers.

She's not wrong. My idea of done up hair is a brief run through with my decades old straightener. But Amira has the skills of fancy hair and makeup that I can only dream about.

Amira looks at me through the mirror, rolling her eyes at my hair incompetence.

"I'm going to have to teach you one of these days."

Her arm reaches up to grab at me and I take the opportunity to tickle her.

"Fuck, stop." She squeals, batting at my hands and kicking my shins.

I step out of the bathroom, calling truce.

"Looking forward to choosing bridesmaid dresses?"

Amira groans, making a gagging motion with her tongue. Her cousin is in full wedding preparation mode, and as a bridesmaid, Amira has been dragged along every step of the way. That, plus her parents' extra pressure to 'settle down', I don't blame her for being exhausted, and over it.

"She said she wanted brown. Brown. Who in their right mind wants brown for their wedding colour?"

"You always call her a shithead, maybe she is sticking with her strengths?"

"Yeah, great, except she isn't the one who has to wear it."

My phone dings. My Uber has arrived.

"I'll see you later." I give Amira a quick kiss on the cheek.

As I race to the door and throw on my favourite boots, she yells down the hall, "Enjoy getting day drunk with your sister!"

I had Noah put our names on a table for my father's birthday lunch, but even though it's relatively close to the city, it's still a bit of a drive to get there. I settle into the back seat of the Uber and, like I often find myself doing, my thumbs open up the message thread with Callum.

Our text history reveals the intense ups and downs of our relationship, every high matched by an equal low. Reading through, it's clear I am the common denominator in every low. I freaked out at every step. The blank spaces where my texts should sit stare back at me.

The cursor flashes, and I know I should say something, to let him know I'm still here. But the words don't come. There's a line that needs to be drawn between us, but I don't know how to pick up the pen. I don't know *where* the line needs to go.

By the time the Uber drops me off in the tree lined car-park, I'm twenty minutes late.

"I'm so sorry," I announce as I walk up to the table where my dad, sister and brother in-law are all sitting.

Without the large bridal table and cake display taking pride of place, the winery has a cosy feel. Barn style wooden beams cross the cathedral ceiling, pendant lights hanging low above the tables. The walls are made entirely of tinted glass, with a wide doorway opening out to a stunning casual decking area. A walking track flows down the sloped grass, to the grapevine lined fields below.

"It's okay," my dad says, standing up to greet me, and I reach my arms around him for a hug.

"Happy birthday," I say as we pull apart, before turning to greet Madison and her husband. "Thank you for planning this, Mads."

Our relationship with our father is strained, to say the least. After our mother walked out, he turned in on himself, leaving us to fend for ourselves more often than not. It wasn't until we were young adults that he started making an effort. In trying to make up for lost time, he can be a little overbearing. I used to be the one protecting Madison from his incessant questions. But since she married her Oliver, and I moved back to Melbourne, the protecting tends to go the other way.

Grabbing my menu, I notice that despite the bottle on the table, Madison doesn't have a glass of wine.

"Are you not drinking, Madison?" I ask.

I cross my hands over my churning stomach, hugging myself. My hands link, a thumb pressing against my ring. Every movement hurts, and I can't bring myself to spin it.

Oliver smiles, looking at his wife. She is beaming, and I sense what's coming. I force my arm to the table to take a long sip of my water. I count my breaths, trying to swallow down the wave of panic rising in my chest.

Madison reaches out to touch my arm, and I look her in the face. And I know, instantly.

Like when she broke her arm after falling off her bike and I knew something was wrong before I even knew she had fallen. Or when I decided to move interstate and she called me asking what was happening before I'd told anyone. We've always shared an unexplainable bond. So somehow, right now, I just ... know.

My sister is pregnant.

I've known for a while now they were trying to get pregnant. She told me as soon as they started, knowing a surprise pregnancy announcement would be hard for me to take. Still, the news forces a knife deep into my lungs and a hiccup catches on the rapidly growing lump in my throat.

"Congratulations." I swat away the tears that risk spilling down my cheeks.

After Blake and I tried for a baby for over twelve months with no luck, we worked with fertility specialists to determine why it was taking so long. Months of blood tests and hormone injections and samples later, it was determined I have 'unexplained infertility'. The title felt like a kick straight to the uterus.

Technically, everything is right with my body and my cycle. I have good egg reserves, the right hormones, and my uterine wall is 'optimal'. But, for whatever unknown reason, I wasn't getting pregnant.

We were told we should "keep trying" and I was given a host of vitamins and hormone supplements that were supposed to help. When I still wasn't pregnant, they said to try artificial insemination. That didn't work either, so we were told to try IVF. Thousands and thousands of dollars later, I was done. Physically, emotionally, and financially.

Blake wanted to keep trying, but I couldn't handle the strain it was putting on our whole lives any longer. I failed. The joy and excitement about having a child had faded and the whole process had become such a chore.

Focusing on the ring spinning between my fingers, I wiggle my toes in my shoes, trying to force out the negative emotions. I need to be happy for my sister. She is getting everything she ever wanted. Everything I ever wanted.

She closes the gap between us, leaning away from her chair to wrap an arm around my shoulders, pulling me close.

"I don't need you to act happy," she says. "Take whatever time you need to feel sad and shitty and angry."

The corners of my lips raise up as I pick up my wine glass.

"Thank you," I say, before I down the whole drink.

"Woah," my dad laughs. "I think it's meant to be Oliver's job to drink for two, not yours."

The table erupts into cautious laughter. I stare up at my dad, who is trying not to let his humour show. When a waiter walks past, he catches their attention to ask for another bottle of wine.

Topping up the three wine glasses, he raises his own.

"To our little eggplant." He tilts his glass in a cheers, but the rest of us lose it.

We can't contain our laughter, erupting into fits that cause other patrons to glare at our loud display of humour. And my poor dad doesn't understand.

"What?" he questions, eyes darting between us trying to clue in on the joke he missed.

"We are not nicknaming my child after penis, dad," Madison wheezes out.

Dad goes bright red, scoffing because he clearly had *no* idea that an eggplant emoji is code for dick.

We eat lunch without any further mention of root vegetables or tiny humans. Despite our protests about it being his birthday, dad refuses to let us pay, and marches over to the counter to pick up the bill.

"So," I say, turning to Madison. I glance down at her tummy unintentionally. Her flowy top hides any hint of bump that might be there.

It's hard to believe a tiny bundle of cells is currently multiplying into a baby inside her belly. The fight I went through feels more unfair than it ever did, and I can feel a wetness in my eyes trying to escape.

I look up, attempting to blink away the tears but instead making it obvious they were there.

"Let's go for a stroll while we wait." Madison links her arm around mine and guides me outside. I spot her glancing over her shoulder and assume it's some kind of happily married couple signal that we need a minute.

The air outside is cool with a winter breeze, but the sky is clear and the sun bites my pasty winter skin. I pop up the collar of my linen shirt to protect my neck, and make sure my hair covers my ears.

"I would ask if you're okay, but it feels redundant," Madison says in a tentative voice as we follow the path towards the grapevines.

As we get closer to the field, I notice a stream that runs alongside it, hidden from view by the hill. Even with all the events I've done here, I've never walked down this far. The wet smell of moss and grass hits me, it's refreshing compared to the polluted air I'm used to at home.

"I'm okay," I say. "Well, I will be okay."

Madison pulls me closer and we fall in step, linked together, shoulder to shoulder.

"I'm happy for you, I am. Your life doesn't need to, should never need to stop all because I was dealt a shitty hand. I'll probably never be truly okay about not having kids of my own, but as soon as that little baby inside you is born, I'm going to love it something shocking. I'll be the coolest aunt the world has ever seen."

Madison's squeezes relax as she unlinks our arms. We're close to the stream now, the gentle flow of the water and occasional croak of a frog breaking the silence that floats between us.

"You'll be *the* coolest aunt," Madison repeats.

We stand, watching the water, contemplating life.

My heart aches for what I will never have, but I can't put that hurt onto Madison. It isn't fair for her when this should be the happiest time in her life. I will love this child, but it won't be mine.

My mind drifts to the conversations Blake and I had. After so many failed cycles, so many false positives followed by tests with single lines, so many babies that came and went before I could even hear their heart beating, I was exhausted. My body kept failing us, and eventually, it said enough. We spoke about what our next options were. We could look into becoming foster parents, or potentially adopt. We could try egg donation, although my obstetrician didn't think that would help. Or we could try a surrogate.

Blake was willing to try everything. He had one hand on his phone the second the doctor mentioned surrogacy, and on the way home he was listing off names of women he knew who might help. But there was only one woman I would have trusted. Madison. And I felt it was unfair to ask her before she had her own children. So we decided that was not an option.

Foster care and adoption were on the table for a while, but it all felt so *hard*. After all the strain and pressure I'd put myself under, trying to make sense of the adoption agencies and legalities was too much. I cracked.

"I can't do this," I say, staring at the paperwork in my lap.

For the fifth time this week, Blake has come home with information of yet another adoption agency. This one was apparently based closer to our suburb but was smaller.

"Okay, we'll look tomorrow instead," Blake replies.

Reaching across the coffee table, he grabs the papers off my lap and straightens them into a neat pile.

"No."

He looks up, eyebrows raised, mouth hanging open. I want to stick my finger in it like he does when I yawn, but I'm so exhausted with everything, I don't bother.

"You don't like this one?" he asks, continuing before I can answer. "You're right, maybe they are too close. We wouldn't want the baby's birth mother to end up living across the street. Good point. I'll bin this one, and we can check back through the others before deciding. It might be a good idea to sign up with multiple agencies, in case that increases our chances."

"No," I repeat when he finally stops to take a breath. "I can't do this."

I lean forward, elbows on my knees and my face buried in my hands. Years worth of tears erupt as the gravity of my life finally pulls me down.

The whole time, the whole fight for children we've been through, I was able to tell myself it was worth it. I never cried because I truly believed this was just our journey. That the light at the end of this tunnel would be our child.

But I don't believe that anymore. We're not in a tunnel, we're in a hole. And we keep digging ourselves deeper.

Blake sits next to me, one arm around my waist, the other hand caressing my knee.

"I'm sorry," I choke out between sobs. "It's been years and I'm done. Years of failure, and I can't keep doing that. I need to stop this hopeless dream."

I will away the memory. I didn't know it then, but that conversation was the beginning of the end for Blake and me. We tried to make our child free life work, but there was always something missing. The child we had both wanted, that we thought would be running around our feet.

Despite our love for one another, we started arguing more and more. Months after we stopped pursuing adoption, Blake brought it up again. He said he thought enough time would have passed and I would have been 'over my melt down'.

I wasn't though, and I could never look at him the same after that. In those months I had come to terms with never having a child, and I thought Blake had, too. But it turned out to be something he couldn't give up.

We parted ways not long after, and I moved back to Melbourne with my tail between my legs, and nothing to show for the years I spent in Sydney. I don't grieve my relationship with Blake, at least not anymore. A long time ago, I added Blake to the list of people who left me and moved on with my life. But after hearing Madison's news, I'm realising I still grieve the child we both wanted.

"Let's head back up," I say as I squeeze Madison's hand.

"I'll drive you home," she says. "I would have offered to drive you here, but I was worried you would have figured it out."

I nudge her off the path, and the heel of her shoe sinks into the soggy ground. I laugh as she stumbles, pulling on my arm to gain her balance.

"I would have figured it out."

Chapter Twenty-Eight

CASSIDY

It's not until I've walked into my apartment building that it hits me. The wine churns in my stomach, a physical representation of the storm in my mind. In my soul.

My sister, who I love dearly and will cherish always, is getting what she always wanted. What I also always wanted but can never have.

Since my diagnosis, I always held on to the idea that maybe it was my mother's fault. There was no medical reason for my infertility, so I blamed her in some roundabout way. As though maybe the universe knew the only maternal reference I had was a deadbeat, so I wouldn't know what I was doing. Maybe somewhere along the way, my mother running out on me made the powers that be think I'd run out on my child, too. Maybe the world wanted to stop the cycle before it began.

I truly believed it, and it made the whole situation feel, in some tiny way, okay. Like it wasn't my fault. Another thing I could blame my useless mother for.

Only now, my sister is pregnant. My sister, whose mother also ran out on her. So my infertility can't be my mother's fault. It's all on me.

I take the stairs slowly, pausing at each turn to stare out the tiny window between each floor. The sun is warm on my face, and I soak in the brightness, hoping it will spread through my veins.

I am happy for Madison, truly. And I'd be lying if I said I was shocked. Honestly, I've known this news was coming for a year. Every time I saw them, I would see today coming a little closer. I would come away and try to mentally prepare myself for the gut-wrenching mix of emotions I thought I would feel.

Nothing could have prepared me for this. I knew I'd be excited for Madison. I knew my heart would ache. I knew I'd feel jealous and envious and bitter.

Something different hits me now. Standing between the second and third floors, with my face in the sun. The twist in my stomach grows until my lungs are twisting, too. I fall forward, shoulders drooping and letting my forehead rest on the dusty window.

Guilt. I feel guilty, and for a while I stand, soaking in the emotion. Processing the feeling and wondering where it came from.

I did everything I could in my attempt to have a baby. Blake and I sacrificed the money we had saved for a house, for our wedding. I poked myself with needles until I was raging with enough hormones so that an even bigger needle could suck the eggs out of my ovaries. Then I was poked and prodded some more when we tried to put the embryo back in.

Blake stood with me the whole time, his defective girlfriend who couldn't give him the baby he so desperately wanted. No, the baby *we* so desperately wanted.

My eyes snap open and my hands flex at my sides and it clicks. I gave up. It was never about blood for Blake, it was about a child. It wasn't about bringing new life into this world, and spreading the love we shared. It was about raising a child and sharing in the joy of their exploration of the world.

And I took that from him. I held the physical pain with every failed month of trying and I decided I'd had enough. I let my hatred of my body fester until it spread. Until I couldn't bear the thought of bringing a child into our relationship. Until it forced a wedge between me and the man I loved.

I hadn't realised until now, or maybe I never took the time to process it. I couldn't have tried any harder, but we could have tried something different. And now I'm stuck, boyfriend-less, childless, alone.

While my sister gets it all.

The green, angry man is back on my shoulder, and it makes me want to throw up all the fancy wine and food I had at lunch. It makes me want to do something stupid like throw myself on Callum's lap again or reinstall all the dating apps on my phone. Anything to fill the void my sister becoming a mother has created.

I slam my palm against the window, cursing when I jar my wrist.

Shaking my hand, I move to head up the stairs. I trip up the first step, hurting my wrist further when I throw it against the wall to steady myself.

I'm trying to be happy for my sister, but it feels too soon. The uncomfortable blend of emotions rumbles through me until finally, I can't hold them in. Standing outside my door, fishing my key out of my bag, it erupts out of me in waves. I have no hope of holding in the tears that flood down my cheeks, instead, I let them fall.

And I still can't find my damned key.

I throw the contents of my bag onto the floor, searching for it. All the crap that was in there weeks ago is still there, with some extra bits of junk. Everything blurs into the grey carpet as tears continue to flood down my cheeks.

I hate myself. For adding more crap to my bag. For not getting a proper keyring like Noah said. For not leaving a key above the doorframe like Callum.

For not being able to have kids and for fooling myself into believing I didn't want them.

And for falling for my best friend. The man who left me once but promises to never do it again. The man who I can't escape because he lives across the hall. The man who has the most incredible daughter.

I hate myself for wanting to be a part of their lives when I'm so clearly not supposed to be.

My limbs vibrate as I collapse against my locked door, sobbing. Everything I've wanted feels miles away, trapped beyond an impenetrable wall.

I thought I might have been able to have it all with Callum, but now I'm not so sure.

I tricked myself into thinking I would be enough for him. And for Maisie. But my sister's news is another blinding reminder of why I'm not. Why I'll never be enough.

Sitting on the floor, tears stream down my face. I let them fall, waiting for the darkness in my heart to swallow me whole.

Chapter Twenty-Nine

CALLUM

I take the stairs two at a time, desperate to get home. My arms hang heavy by my side, the skin between my thumb and forefinger raw with forming blisters. I thought spending my Saturday afternoon playing golf with my brother-in-law would be a relaxing, calming experience. I was wrong. He plays, a lot. I ... don't. And I felt it. Every inch of my back aches.

Entering the third floor hallway, my eyes are closed in a yawn as I head to my apartment. My feet anchor to the ground when I look up and see her; sprawled on the floor in front of her apartment, sobbing.

Taking two long strides, I fall to my knees and pull her onto my lap. The sight of Cassidy crying is like a knife through my ribcage, piercing my lung. I can't breathe, knowing that something, or someone, has upset her this much.

She stares blankly across the hall. One hand twists at the ring she always wears.

"Rogue, what hap—" I start, before changing my words. "Who did this?"

There's an urge to go to war that conflicts with my desire to comfort her.

Finally, she looks up at me. Her gold-green eyes sparkle through the tears. She pulls her sleeves over her hands, bringing them up to wipe away some of the tears that pool on her cheeks. I pull back the hair that falls across her face, gathering the long strands into a low ponytail. I loop the hair tie I always have on my wrist for my daughter around Cassidy's chocolate waves.

"My sister," she chokes.

Her sister what? Her sister hurt her? How?

I keep quiet, willing her to continue when she is ready.

I check her over, from head to toe, searching for bruises despite the fact I wouldn't see them under her long sleeves and pants. The contents of her bag lay scattered over the floor, amongst them her solitary door key, still separate from the keychain holding her car fob. With one arm still surrounding her, I reach around us to gather her belongings.

"She's pregnant."

She mumbles the words under her heavy sobs, but they hit me. My throat closes and I blink away the tears I feel forming. I can only imagine how this must feel for her.

"I'm sorry," I whisper into her ear. Holding her close, I lean back against the wall, remembering the way she comforted me like this when I needed it.

My hands rub gentle circles on her back and along her arms. Neither of us try to talk, because we don't need to. Just like she didn't pressure me into talking when I wasn't ready, I do the same for her. Cass will talk when she is ready. If she ever is.

Eventually, Mrs Kelly toddles down the hall, crochet bag swinging over her arm. Cassidy and I sit silently as the old lady steps over our legs. She makes it three steps away before turning back to us.

"This your fault?" She glares down at me.

I shake my head as Cassidy lifts her head.

"No," she says.

Mrs Kelly's face is still full of bitterness as she stares at me.

"Even so," she croaks, "probably up to you to make it better."

"I will," I promise. Even though I have no idea how to do that.

Mrs Kelly walks down the hall to the stairwell, pausing before she opens the door. Seeing me looking up at her, she smiles with a gentle nod, clasping her hands together.

"Thank you," Cass whispers, "for staying out here with me."

I give her a soft squeeze, planting a kiss on her forehead. "You needed me."

"Can we go inside?" she asks as she stretches her legs out in front of her.

It's awkward when we stand, most of Cassidy's weight still in my arms as I grab her bag off the floor. I shift our position until I have her wrapped into my side, and reach above us for my spare key.

"I thought I told you that wasn't a safe spot for a spare key?"

Her tone is accusatory, but also light and teasing. A hint of her usual demeanour poking through the sorrow.

When she walks into my apartment, an odd mix of emotions stir within me. Her shoulders are drooped so low she could touch her knees. The sight of her in so much pain sends my heart twisting, plummeting into my gut.

Cassidy collapses onto the couch while I get her a glass of water.

"It's not fair," she blurts out when I sit on the opposite side of the couch. Her shoulders still tremble, but there's a determination in her voice now.

"You don't have to talk about it."

"I want to," she says. "My ex and I, we tried for a really long time, but it never worked. Nothing worked."

She reaches behind her, as though searching for her blanket.

"Wait," I tell her. Grabbing the lone key from her bag, I race out of my apartment and across the hall.

The dodgy handle takes longer than it should to unlock, but I get it open. In her apartment, I pull the scrappy pink blanket off the couch before rushing back.

As I approach her, I slow down. I wrap the blanket over her shoulders. She wears it like a cape, unmoving.

After a few breaths, she pulls the blanket tighter around her body.

"We never … we tried … I thought …" she starts a few times before she finds the words to go on. "After so long, I made peace. But he didn't, and we … I moved back to Melbourne."

My hands curl into fists. The thought that he walked away, over that, has me raging. I don't even know the man's name and I want to hunt him down. Make him realise the mistake he made when he hurt Cassidy.

"I was okay with it, really." Cassidy slumps back onto the couch.

"Until you found out about your sister?"

I knew she couldn't have kids, that for a while she hasn't wanted them. But the situation surrounding her eventual diagnosis … it hurts. It hurts me, so I can only imagine how it must hurt her.

"It took a lot of time and therapy, but I came to terms with my place in the world. I was even excited about being the fun aunt who holidays in Europe and drives a fancy car."

She sniffs, wiping her eyes with the back of her hand.

"I guess," she chokes on the words as they come out, "finding out I am about to become that aunt hit me a lot harder than I thought it would."

I reach forward to trace slow circles on her wrist with my thumb. Audrey and I got lucky. We had barely decided to start trying when everything fell into place for us. But I know how hard it can be for some couples, some women.

There's nothing I can say that will take away her pain, so instead I trace those circles, a silent gesture that I'm here, I'm listening.

"I was still processing that news, and I saw your door. And I thought of Maisie and how amazing she is and how lucky you are. And how much I—"

I can't help it. I move towards her, reaching out to cup her cheek. My thumb wipes at the tears as they fall.

Cassidy leans into my hand. Her breaths start to calm and my heart swells at the thought she finds comfort in me. Despite everything, my presence is helping her and I hold onto that thought.

"Maisie changed everything I had imagined in my head," she continues. "I thought I was okay with it, I tried really hard. But I can't be what you need."

Cassidy covers her face with her hands, pushing my own away as her palms press into her eyes.

"There is a reason I can't have a baby. And it's not my mother like I always imagined. It's me. You talk about the universe bringing us back together for a reason, but maybe the universe made me infertile for one, too. Maybe I'm not supposed to be a mum."

There's no air in my lungs as I realise what she is saying. I knew my daughter was holding Cassidy back. But I had believed I could convince her we were worth it.

"I don't know if I can do this," she whispers through her hands.

The confession sucks the air out of my lungs. All this time I held on to hope we could be something more than we are. That Cassidy could love me, and Maisie, enough to want to try.

"Maisie doesn't need a mum. And I just need you."

I knew she thought we would never work. I knew she didn't want kids, no matter how great she is with Maisie. But I also knew she felt things for me that friends don't feel about each other. I took that sliver of hope and I ran with it, and I hoped she would see how great we could be.

Until now. Cassidy shies away and the hope drains away until it hurts to breathe through the hole that's left behind.

"I still hoped," I admit.

Her hands pull away from her face and drop into her lap. She nods softly before changing her mind and shaking her head.

Her voice trembles as she rubs her thumbs together. "I still hoped, too. But I can't anymore."

"Because of her," I add. Not because I believe it, but because I understand.

Silence falls between us, broken only by my heavy sighs and Cassidy's quiet hiccup-like sobs.

"I should go," she announces, standing up.

"Rogue, no. Please."

I have nothing to say. No idea what, if anything, would make the situation better. This feels like an ending I'm not ready to accept. I won't accept it. But for now, dread cements me in place.

All I can do is beg, and slouch back into the couch as she ignores my pleas and walks out of my apartment, still wrapped in her blanket.

When my apartment is empty, I give the stabbing pain in my chest free rein. I feel every racing beat of my heart, every throbbing in my temple. The panic rushes over me, and I have no one to pull me out.

Chapter Thirty

CALLUM

"**W**hat the fuck did you do?"

His voice cuts through the dark, inky mess of my mind. Storming into my space, he finds me curled into a ball on the floor of my living room. I've shuffled my way between the couch and the wall, squeezing myself into the tiniest gap I could find. The plant my sister bought to brighten up the space leans against the wall, spilling soil onto the carpet rug.

I sniff as the room comes back into view, wiping away the wetness under my eyes. I should be more concerned that a random man has waltzed his way into my apartment. But nothing matters any more.

"She crawled into her room, Callum. *Crawled.* And not in some overdramatic exaggerated way. Amira said she crumbled onto the floor and literally couldn't get up. I will kill you."

The man hits an invisible wall when he enters the living room, finding me in my tiny little corner. I recognise his tan skin and golden hair, but the pained look on his face is nothing like the amusement that coated it the last time we met.

"Shit not you, too."

Dropping to his knees in front of me, Cassidy's cousin hovers his hands over my knees.

My head falls back into my arms.

One, two, three, four. I try to count out each breath to steady the erratic rhythm rushing through my body.

"Cass does this weird tapping thing on her chest, maybe you could do a weird tapping thing?"

I blow out all the air in my lungs, suppressing the chuckle that fights to escape. I taught Cassidy the tapping thing, all those years ago. I hate that she has to use it now.

But he is right, I should try the tapping thing.

Inch by inch, I unwrap myself from my spot on the floor. Cassidy's cousin moves back, giving me space to stretch out my legs and climb onto the couch. With my counts, I tap a steady rhythm on my sternum, focusing on the firm vibrations and willing my pulse to steady.

"You should go back to Cassidy."

"Amira is there."

I don't know this guy. I met him once and I can admit I was a jerk. But in my defence, I didn't know he was Cassidy's cousin.

He sits backwards on a chair, facing me from the dining space. From over the back of the chair, he waves a finger between us. "We're going to start again. I'm Noah."

I look up at him, giving a tiny shake of my head.

"Callum."

Noah taps on the back of the chair, his knee bounces as he takes in my apartment. The uncomfortable couch I sit on with its three bright cushions, the IKEA catalogue furniture, and the collection of colouring books on the coffee table. It only feels like home when Maisie is here. Or Cassidy. Preferably both. But that will never happen again.

Noah's tapping stops. "You ah ... want to talk about it?"

I don't. But the words fall out anyway.

"Her sister is pregnant. She said it was too hard."

"Okay mate. If there's one thing you need to know about me it's that we talk. None of this half communication bullshit, because it only gets you into trouble. You need to give me more than that."

This guy. I scoff at him, but he stares me down. There's

something about his bright eyes and the glimmer of a smile on his lips. He makes me *want* to talk to him.

"Fine. For months, I knew me being a dad was hard for her to come around to. She spent so long thinking that because she couldn't have kids it meant she wasn't meant to be around them. So it was hard, I get it. But I thought we were good, I thought she was falling in love with the thought of us. And my daughter fucking loves her."

Noah starts tapping again, humming his encouragement for me to continue.

"But Maisie got hurt, and she withdrew. And then she found out her sister's having a baby and now it's all too much. She said it was too hard and she should go. She gave up. And then she *crawled* to her bed."

I drop my head between my legs, sucking in the oxygen I need. It burns my lungs until I'm drowning with the pain.

"I don't know what's worse," I admit. "Me hurting this much, or knowing she feels just as bad, if not worse, and not being able to go to her."

Noah stands. Walking over to the couch, he sits beside me. Close enough I can feel the divot he creates, he nudges me with his shoulder.

"Give her time."

"I did. I tried."

"More. She has had a really rough run. Sounds like you have, too. But I know this isn't it for the two of you."

"How?"

"Because she was never like this when she broke up with Blake."

His name reignites something inside me. Her ex. The one who left when things got tough and she couldn't give him a child. The one who favoured her as a mother before anything else. I refuse to be anything like him.

"What do I do?"

Noah plays with his phone, typing out a text. "Give me a minute."

The whoosh of messages being sent and received hides the anxious shudder in my breath.

"Okay," Noah breaks the silence, putting his phone away. "Madison has a plan for Cassidy."

"Her sister?"

"Yeah. Cass needs some time to move past the shock of Madison being pregnant, that's all."

"And I just wait?"

"For now."

After he leaves, my thoughts scramble. I thought all was lost. It still feels like all is lost. *But maybe not?* Noah seemed to think so.

I hate the tiny raindrop of hope he gave me. It feels so fickle and unreliable, but it's all I have.

Chapter Thirty-One

CASSIDY

"I don't think I can do this," I say into the Bluetooth system of my car.

I was fine all morning. I thought this was a brilliant idea. I was excited Madison had asked me to come. But as I pull into the parking lot, a wave of anxiety rushes over me. My palms are clammy, no matter how many times I've rubbed them down my jeans, and a pit of nausea is growing deep inside me, worming its way towards my throat. Switching off the ignition, I close my eyes and try to slow my racing heart. One, two, three, four ... hold. I count as I suck in air, willing the panic away.

"Cassidy, my appointment is in five minutes, where are you?" My sister's voice is mechanical and echoes through the car's speakers.

"I'm in the parking lot but ..." I force another deep breath. "I'm frozen."

The beep as she hangs up shocks something in me, and I realise how much I've let her down. Most pregnant mothers don't have scans at this stage in their pregnancy, but when Mads was cramping and had some spotting yesterday, she went to the hospital just in case. The tests there went fine, and she says she's been feeling fine all morning, but they ordered an extra ultrasound to double check everything is okay.

With Oliver away on a book tour, support person duties fell to me. I hate that I have to do this for her. I'm still coming around to the fact she is pregnant, but right now, I have to show up for my sister. The thought of walking into a building full of pregnant women, full of women who are living a life I'll never get to live, though? It feels like I never learnt how to swim but am about to dive in the deep end of a shark infested pool anyway.

Rolling lavender oil on my wrists, I pick apart the scent, focusing on anything but the building in front of me. I count each spin of my ring, trying to ease the heavy feeling of dread that has settled low in my stomach. Right where Madison's baby grows in hers. A rattle on the window breaks my rhythm.

Red faced, with puffy swollen eyes and unkempt hair, Madison stands outside the car, fist still resting against the glass.

"Open the door." The closed window muffles the sound of her voice.

I do as she says, and she squats down until she is eye level with me.

"I know," she starts, before correcting herself. "Actually, no, I don't. I can't even imagine how hard it must be for you. But I need you. I need you to suck in a week's worth of oxygen, and put your blinkers on so we can walk through that building and into the examination room. I need you to hold my hand while they squirt cold goo all over me, and to listen to what they say because I know I'll forget something. I know it's not fair, but Oliver is away and I've just had the hardest twenty-four hours in my life, and right now I need my sister."

The anxiety doesn't dissolve into nothing because of her words, but I've survived through worse. I can push it to the side for her, if only for a moment.

"Okay," I reply gingerly. I hope my old therapist is proud of me.

As I move to step out of the car, Madison doesn't move out of the way. Instead she laughs, holding her hand out towards me.

"I also need you to help me get back up."

"You owe me ice cream." I laugh, and once we are both standing, she hugs me.

"I'll even get you a double cone."

Antiseptic cleaner fumes invade my nostrils as I walk through the automatic doors, obliterating the faint lavender scent that remained on my neck and wrists. Before I have time to take stock of the happy women around me, a man in scrubs walks towards us, glancing at his clipboard.

He greets Madison and gestures down the hall, "I'll be doing your scan today. This way please."

We follow behind as he rushes down the hall and into a small room lit only by a deep blue computer screen. Madison climbs onto the reclined bed, pulling her top up to reveal the small round of her stomach.

I marvel at the sight of her. For the first time since Madison announced she was pregnant, I take stock of the fact she is growing a human. A real life baby is in there growing and forming all the right organs and limbs.

Madison reaches out to take my hand. Her fingers squeeze mine as the slurp of the lubricant bottle breaks through the otherwise silent room.

I squeeze back, holding my breath to keep my unease at bay. Without warning, a familiar sound replaces the silence hanging in the room. It's backed by a dull, rushing white noise, but the heartbeat is unmistakable.

My vision blurs from the unexpected tears that form in the corners of my eyes, and I squeeze Madison's hand with a joyous force.

"Madison is that—?"

"Yeah." I can see all of her teeth through her smile. "That's our little girl."

A warmth spreads through me as my heart swells until it feels too big for my chest. Glancing at the monitor near Madison's feet, I can see the tiny outline of her baby. It doesn't look like a bundle of cells the way I imagine her first ultrasound picture did. It looks like a baby. I can see two legs and tiny hands bunched up around a pint sized face. Her mouth is opening and closing, and I faintly register the technician saying something about her swallowing being a good sign.

For the rest of the appointment I sit in wonder as the technician measures limbs, registers blood flow, and tracks movement. I'm the ideal support partner; taking notes as the technician explains that everything looks normal, and the midwife will go over the results in the appointment they scheduled for tomorrow. He tells her that sometimes women can have spotting through pregnancy, but that it was good Madison came in yesterday, just in case.

Madison wipes gel off her stomach and rolls herself off the bed. My incompetent uterus scratches at my insides. I rub against it and consider if I blew my chances at ever having a family. Again.

I was so caught up on doing what Madison is doing, on the conceiving and the being pregnant. Once again I lost sight of what really matters with the whole thing. It's the child. And sure, Madison's child is growing inside her, and that's a beautiful thing, but I know it's not the only way. I've known all along. I just kept forgetting.

The past month flashes in my mind. Dancing with Maisie, helping her point her toes and keep her balance. The way I held her hand to help her keep her balance, and always stood where I could catch her if she fell. How perfect it felt when we sat on the couch after to catch our breath. How comfortable it felt in Callum's arms, and how I didn't want to leave but felt like I *should*. And how I now wonder if I should have stayed instead.

If Callum, and Maisie, is exactly what I want. What I need.

The winter breeze is cool, but it doesn't stop us from sitting to eat our ice cream from the booth near the park.

"I think I made a mistake," I admit once I reach the cone.

"Hmm?"

"With Blake, maybe?" I admit.

I slouch back into the park bench and tilt my head up to where the sun fights to be seen through the clouds.

"I was so busy trying to get pregnant, I lost sight of the end goal." It feels cathartic, finally acknowledging and talking and processing my truth, so I keep going, letting all the words flow out.

"He wanted to foster, to look at adoption," I continue, "but I wasn't interested. That's why we broke up. For so long, I believed it was because I couldn't give him a baby, but with everything now, I can see that's not true. We broke up because I gave up on our dream of having a family."

"That's ..." Madison pauses to take a bite from her cone. For a beat the only sound between us is the crunch as she chews the waffle, barely audible over the magpies warbling and children laughing.

"Rough?" she finishes after she swallows. Looking at me with a raised eyebrow, she bumps my leg with her knee. "You didn't figure that out with all the therapy you went to?"

"I think for therapy to work, you have to be honest with yourself. And I wasn't."

"Okay, so what now?"

I shove the final pointy end of my ice cream into my mouth and drop my head into my hands. "I wish I knew."

I don't want my life with Blake back, I know that much. Because no matter how much I tried to fight it, no matter how much I pushed away, I love Callum. And now I'm scared it's too late for me to finally realise that.

Madison pushes herself to stand and I follow her up. As we start to stroll around the gardens, past all the families, my mind shifts back to the days I spent with Callum and his daughter. At the ballet exhibit it was the first, the only time I'd ever felt like maybe I could fit in as a mother. At the park when she hurt herself, I knew she needed her mum, but I was there to help in every way I could until Audrey got to the hospital. Maybe my place as a parent doesn't have to be the mother.

I must have stopped walking in my trance. My eyes are wet behind my sunglasses when I notice Madison has stopped, metres in front of me, to turn back.

"Cassidy," she calls out. Caution laces her voice and she takes slow steps back towards me.

I try to speak, but the words get stuck in my throat. My sister guides me to the closest bench. Two teenage looking girls side eye us as I collapse onto the seat next to them.

Madison coughs, making a show of her belly as she stares down at them. They look to each other, sharing a grouched expression before returning their gazes to their phones, giggling.

"Move." Madison's voice holds so much authority I scoot over. The girls jump up to walk away, their arms linked together, heads still down in their phones.

When she sits next to me, I feel Madison's warmth spreading from where our shoulders touch.

"Callum?" she asks, and all I can do is nod.

After a few shaky starts, I tell her everything. All the bits she knows, like the teenage crush and the friendship, and his daughter. And all the bits she doesn't, like how we'd spent the night together and how much I enjoy spending time with Maisie.

I sob into her shoulder. "I think I ruined my chance."

"Your chance at a family, or your chance with Callum?" Mads whispers into my hair.

"Does it matter?"

"Of course it matters."

With her hands on my shoulders she pushes me up to look into her eyes.

"Because you haven't blown your chance at a family. If this is just about how you want to be a mum, you need to suck it up because your time will come. And everything that happened with Callum was the giant leap the universe needed to give you so you could realise what you wanted most."

I feel the indent of her manicured gel nails on my shoulders as she squeezes them.

"But I have a feeling all of this is more specific than wanting *a* family. I think you want to be part of Callum's family."

My mouth opens to rebut, but instead of words, only a sob comes out, and I realise she is right. I never wanted to adopt with Blake because I felt as though that baby, child, would never really feel like mine. I felt like I would have to pretend. Having a family that way is beautiful, but it doesn't feel right for me. It never did and it still doesn't.

What feels right, is stepping in with Callum and Maisie. Being an *extra* parental figure for her, not the main one. Being in a relationship built on so much friendship and history that we accept one another's flaws and baggage unconditionally.

I want it so bad, and now I've acknowledged it, it hurts. Somehow even worse than before.

"What do I do?" I sob.

"Talk to him?"

A snort escapes, threatening to become a laugh I'm not ready for.

I pull away from my sister and stand, reaching out a hand to help her off the bench. We finish our walk in silence, my head still racing with all the what-ifs.

Walking up the first flight of stairs to my apartment, the loud clack of a door opening sounds from above me. The air in the stairwell is dank and silent, but the opening brings in a lightness I can't explain. Until I hear the unmistakable giggle of a five-year-old.

My heart beats too many times, or skips a beat. I can't be sure what it's doing wrong, but it certainly isn't behaving like it should. The effect steals my breath, and despite taking the stairs at a leisurely pace, it feels like I've been out for a run. I slow down, knowing when I turn the bend I'll come face to face with Callum.

I'm not ready. I just realised I want to spend the rest of my life with the man coming down the stairs, and his daughter. But I'm not ready to tell either of them that. I freeze, contemplating turning back down the stairs and hiding in the first floor corridor.

But before I can make up my mind, Maisie swings herself around the corner, giggling as she hangs on the rail with one arm and flips her legs out behind her. Her right arm is still in a sling, but she pulls off the move with a surprising amount of grace. It's part cartwheel, part leap, part pirouette, and all adorable. She giggles as her feet find the floor again.

Her face lights up when she sees me. The joy in her face catches me off guard and I fight to wipe my discomfort off my face.

"Cassidy!" She drags out my name with her grin. "Did you see my spin?"

"I did." I manage to add a joyous tone to my voice. The pitch raised to match the smile painted on my face. "It was very cool."

Callum stands behind Maisie. Arms crossed, the soft ballerina doll hanging by his side.

"Callum," I choke out through the knot forming in my throat.

He growls in response, and my insides swim. I remember that growl. How good it felt against my core. But I also remember how strained it was when his daughter was hurt at the park, and how painful it felt when I told him I had to go. How forced our interactions since then have felt.

A blush rises up my neck and I attempt to cough it back down. I think of my sister's ultrasound, of her growing child and the family she will have. I think of what Callum and I could have been, about how I could have fit into his family. I think of Maisie, and of how easily we got along and how nice it was to be a part of her life.

Love mixes with grief, swirling around in the pit of my stomach. I can't hold it in, but I don't want them to see.

"Sorry." The word barely comes out as I rush past them to retreat inside my apartment.

Chapter Thirty-Two

CASSIDY

The orange glow from the rising sun peeks through the curtains. Yesterday is still playing on repeat in my head and I'm struggling to make heads or tails of my emotions.

Everything hurts, no matter how tightly I wrap myself in my grandma's blanket.

Seeing Maisie in the stairwell right after my conversation with Madison, I panicked. Her sling was a crushing physical reminder of all the reasons Callum and I shouldn't be together. When Callum rounded the bend, every hair on my body stood on end. Like always, I've found myself wanting something I can't have. And it feels like a stone slab sits on my chest.

My sister is at the shop with the barista we hired, and Amira left far too early this morning. I should have woken up late to wallow, to contemplate, to figure out what it is I'm going to do with my life. Instead, I'm curled in bed, on the verge of tears.

My phone rings, the sound echoing through the apartment while I stretch across the pillow to find it.

"Wha—" I choke on the phlegm caught in the back of my throat when I answer.

"Are you still in bed?" Noah groans down the phone. "I don't have time for this, I need flowers."

Grunting as I sit up, I hear him add, "I'll pay double."

Adrenaline surges, the creative outlet exactly what I need. I always think better when I'm making art.

"What for?"

"There's an … event. I forgot to add it to the calendar. Bring whatever you can at short notice."

I race to the store to pick up as much stock as I think we can spare, not stopping to explain the situation to Madison, before driving out to the winery to set up. Noah wants a floral arbour at the start of the pathway that leads through the vines, with as many scattered flowers hidden through the rows. He never told me what they were for, but I'd imagined a couple on a romantic stroll through the vines.

After I finish, I find a spot on the grass and lie back.

"Here," Noah says when he comes to say thanks. He hands me a bottle of Rosé and a glass, "Madison said you might need this. Enjoy the sun."

Grass tickles my toes as I push myself up to pour a glass of wine.

I would enjoy the moment, soaking in the unusual winter sun, if only my brain would shut up. I wonder, now, if there was a last minute event, or if it was all a ploy to make sure I didn't spend the day in bed. Madison has a way of knowing just what I need, and I wouldn't put it past her to call Noah into her tricks.

The thought reminds me of all the things I've ever wanted, how I never got what I wished for.

For my mum to come back. For Callum, all those years ago. For a baby. For Callum, again. Only this time, for Maisie, too.

Callum is a package deal, and at first that was hard to accept. Now though? It feels right. Callum and me as a couple feels right, but so does Callum and Maisie and me as a family. I want to be part of his daughter's life almost as much as I want to be part of his.

Two weeks ago, at Madison's ultrasound, a desire I'd long ago snuffed out was reignited. Only, it's different now, like the flame of a scented candle instead of a cheap birthday cake one. It has more depth, more meaning. I don't want a baby, I don't even want a child.

I want Maisie. I really like her. I liked sharing my love of ballet with her. I liked helping Callum look after her.

It's as though my heart knows she belongs with Callum, and accepted Maisie with every piece it had. And now it's aching, knowing she's always going to be so close, yet so far.

I drink the last sip of my wine, before leaning back down to tap my head on the grass. Groaning, I roll over and push myself to sit. When the sun hits my face, a lightbulb clicks in my mind and I know what to do.

All this crap swirl of emotion is because I love Callum. But I made it clear, many times, we would never work. And I finally pushed hard enough that he listened. We've shared nothing but tight nods and thin lipped smiles as we passed each other in the hall for the past two weeks.

So, if I can get over my love for Callum, everything will feel better. Right?

Returning to the cellar door, I head towards the bar to deposit my now empty wine bottle and glass. Aside from the group of women on a boozy bridal brunch, everyone seems to be paired up.

There's an older couple sitting by the window, holding hands across the table as they sip at their red wine and gaze out the window. The younger couple, possibly on a first date, sitting in a booth and looking deep in conversation. The family with young kids, both parents looking equal parts exhausted, happy, and in love.

It feels like love and coupledom is surrounding me. It makes me gag.

"Need another?" a baritone voice reaches across the bar as I approach.

Looking up, I'm shocked at the man I see before me. He feels too young to own such a deep voice.

"Rosé, right?" he adds, gesturing to the empty bottle. "Although my RSA tells me you probably don't need it."

I laugh, although it's more like a choking giggle. He's right. I've downed the whole bottle on a mostly empty stomach, I probably *don't* need another glass. Let alone another bottle. But I want to drown my sorrows.

Shaking my head, I take in the man in front of me. His short sandy hair reflects a hint of ginger in the sunlight. I wonder if he is one of those men that carry a ginger beard, but his face is so clean shaven and smooth, I also wonder if he'd even be able to grow one. There is nothing remarkable about him.

He isn't buff, isn't skinny, isn't large, or small. He's just average. His azure eyes match the cloudless sky, without being overpowering. His nose is a fraction too big for his face, but his too small ears somehow compensate to balance everything out.

My Rosé coloured glasses are making him much more appealing than he should be.

"I'm Cassidy." I lean across the bar and smile, ever so slightly, and look up at him through my lashes. Batting them a few times for good measure.

Lord, I'm cringing at myself. It's been so long since I've flirted with a guy, I have no idea what I'm doing.

"No, you're drunk," he replies with a smirk. His gaze lingers on my breasts for just long enough. I feel a weird bead of satisfaction in my core.

Cheers erupt behind me and I twist to see the young couple standing, wrapped in each other's arms.

"Yes," the girl is squealing. "Yes, of course, yes!"

I turn away from the brutal reminder of my aching heart, the stark display of the love I want but will, apparently, never have.

"Good for them," the bartender's deep voice catches my attention.

"Lucky for some." I wave my hand around, losing my balance and toppling off the stool.

A laughing cough sounds behind me, as someone catches me before I fall. Steadying myself in his firm grasp, I peek through squinted eyes at Noah. He stands with his hands on his hips and a deep crease between his brows.

"How much did you let her drink?"

Although I want to say it was none of Noah's business, instead I find myself clinging to my cousin's shoulder.

"He wouldn't let me have any, this is all you, cousin." The words slur a little.

"Come on." Noah guides me away from the bar. "I'll drive you home."

With the window down, and having polished off a bottle of water and a toasted cheese sandwich, the Rosé buzz starts to wear down about halfway home.

Staring out the window, I groan inwardly.

I still feel like I need something to take my attention off Callum and Maisie, but finding that distraction by getting day drunk at the winery my cousin manages, and that I provide floristry for, wasn't the best idea.

"You want to talk about it?"

I groan again, outwardly this time, leaning back on the chair.

"Not really," I whine. "I'm a mess, my life is a mess."

"No, you're not."

"I am. I'm depressed over something I learnt about *years* ago. I'm in love with a man who has a child, but I forced him away because I was convinced I didn't want to be a parent. And I made an absolute fool of myself with someone who is technically a colleague. Kind of." I sink as low into the chair as my seatbelt allows.

Risking a brief glance at me, Noah shakes his head.

"Cass," he says, "I've lost track of how much crap you've been through. You're allowed to get a little day drunk—my fault by the way because I should have known you wouldn't have had breakfast, and I gave you a whole damn bottle of wine at 10.30 a.m.—and you're allowed to have a little self-pity flirt with the fill-in bartender." He laughs.

My cheeks burn with embarrassment and I hide my face in my hands.

"He won't be back," Noah states, shaking his head. "We had three people call in sick so he came to help from another bar."

I turn my head towards the wind rushing through the open window. The air is fresh, but damp. Clouds have rolled overhead, hiding the sun. Rain is coming, and I'm glad I enjoyed the sun while it lasted.

"But seriously, Cassidy. Talk to Callum. I've never seen you like this. Even when you and Blake broke up, it didn't crush your soul enough for you to flirt with a guy ten years younger than you are."

Noah's right. Everything he says makes more and more sense as I continue to sober.

I should talk to Callum about what I want. But I'm also hesitant to open up. My heart is too fragile to be broken. I don't want to risk opening myself up to hope. I can't risk it.

A lone tear escapes and trickles down my cheek, until the wind catches it. The salty drop is flicked into my nostril and I snort when I accidentally inhale it.

My mood sours because although it was just the wind, it feels like I can't even cry right.

I sigh as Noah pulls into the parking garage under my apartment building.

"Why is love so hard?"

Reaching across the centre console, Noah pulls me into an awkward, back patting hug.

"It's not love that's hard. It's accepting what you can't control. Love is what happens when you open your heart to the unexpected."

That's exactly what I have to do. There are a lot of things I can't control. I can't control my infertility. I can't control the choices I made in the past or the fact Callum has a daughter. I can't control Madison being pregnant. But I can accept all of those things.

I just hope it's not too late.

Chapter Thirty-Three

CALLUM

"**D**addy?" Maisie questions, as the movie credits start to roll.

I shift to face her when I answer, "yeah, chicka?"

"When will you start having sleepovers?"

Her question rattles me. We spoke about her having sleepovers here when I first moved in, but she stays here every second week now. She doesn't have sleepovers anymore, she lives here. I can feel the crease forming between my brows.

"What do you mean?"

"Well, last week, Mummy's friend, Michael, had a sleepover after dinner. And you never have friends stay over."

I pinch the bridge of my nose and let out a long, slow breath before I formulate a response. Fire broils in my chest and my heart races. I pull Maisie onto my lap, tensing the muscles in my feet in a pathetic attempt to release some of the anger racing through me. I can't let Maisie see it.

"I thought maybe we could ask Cassidy for a sleepover, and she could teach me more dancing like she promised." Maisie's voice is a faint whisper, slow and rasping as she drifts into sleep. "But she lives so close she could go back to her bed at bedtime." She yawns the final words while they slice open my already bleeding heart. I don't tell her I'm not sure if we will see Cassidy again. I don't tell her Cassidy broke my heart.

Instead, I carry Maisie to bed, tucking her in and turning on the nightlight before creeping back to the living room.

After pacing three laps around the tiny shoebox, I creep

back to Maisie's room and pull the door shut. I've felt so many emotions in the space of about an hour, and the storm they are brewing is making me dizzy. As I continue to pace, I try to process what Maisie told me, to read between the lines of what she did and didn't say.

Audrey has been having "sleepovers" with her friend "Michael".

So Audrey is in a relationship.

And Maisie seems … okay with it.

Acid burns through me. I can't believe Audrey would introduce someone to Maisie without keeping me in the loop. Would invite that man to spend the night while our daughter was sleeping down the hall. I had a right to know before all this happened.

As Maisie's father, my whole job is to keep her safe. Protected from things, and people, who have the potential to cause her harm. And although I trust Audrey's judgement in a person, it still angers me I didn't have a say in the matter.

I charge across the room, heading for my phone.

"You've been having *sleepovers*?!"

I expel the words as soon as Audrey answers the phone. My blood boils, my ears so hot I'm sure steam is rising. I pace laps around the living area, forcing the built up adrenaline to release. Because as angry as I feel, this needs a civil conversation, and I need to keep my voice down.

I can see my ex-wife's sigh as much as I can hear it. The way her eyes would close and she would rub the middle of her forehead with her finger.

"Like you can talk with that bitch from across the hall?" Audrey slaps back at me.

I explode. I'm not normally a violent person, but I punch the back of the couch as I storm past. Cassidy is anything but a bitch, and it's infuriating anyone would label her as such. Never mind the fact she's never stayed the night while Maisie was here. Or the fact it's apparently over now. That my life was too hard for her to accept and I have to be okay with that. Even when I feel anything but okay.

I explain it all to Audrey, doubting she would listen anyway.

"And besides," I add, "Cassidy is a long-time friend, it's different. I trust her. And I told you about her."

"Oh, fuck off," Audrey is insistent. "You can have your new partner and I'll have mine."

"It's hardly the same," I scoff. "How would you have felt if I introduced Cassidy into Maisie's life without letting you know? If she stayed here while Maisie slept in the other room and you didn't even know about her?"

Audrey is silent.

"See." The word spits out through gritted teeth as I collapse onto the couch. "You wouldn't like it."

She sighs again. It's less forced this time, and I imagine the way she, too, might have sat down or leaned her weight against the counter.

"No," she admits. "I wouldn't. It would feel like I was being replaced."

I hold in an exasperated breath of my own because that's not what I meant. I'm not comfortable with a stranger sleeping in the same house as my daughter.

"What if Maisie woke in the night and went to you? But instead, she found some guy she's only known for a few weeks?"

Audrey falls silent again.

"I didn't think of that," she finally says. Her tone has softened, and I get a glimpse of the woman I married. Her caring nature, how she would always put others before herself.

Becoming parents changed both of us, for the better in some ways, but certainly for the worse in others.

Falling out of love with someone is much harder than

falling in love with them. Because although we changed, although we realised how incompatible we were, I'll always love the woman she was when we met. And I'll always cherish the good memories.

Without Audrey, I wouldn't have Maisie, so a part of me will always hold her dear. But I've realised it's time for both of us to move on with our lives.

"We both deserve to move on, to love again and to be loved," I tell her.

Despite the anger I felt earlier, I find as much comfort in the words as I hope to give her. When she hums her agreement, I continue.

"There is no rule book for divorce. Just like there was no book for marriage, or parenting. We are all making this up as we go. Both of us are going to make mistakes, Audrey. All we can do is learn from them. I don't care that you're seeing someone, I don't care who it is or how you met or how quickly you fall into a relationship. Your dating life is your dating life."

When she sucks in a breath, I get the sense Audrey wants to refute what I'm saying, but I keep talking. I'm telling myself these words as much as I'm telling Audrey, and it feels like I need to get them out in the open.

"But when your dating life collides with our daughter, that's when I need to know. And that's when you will know about my dating life."

Audrey whimpers a tiny "okay" before repeating herself. "Okay," she says, and I can hear the smile forming on her face.

It reminds me of all the good Audrey and I once had. Of the holidays spent with my family, the love we shared when Maisie was born. Although things got as rough as they did by the end, we shared something special for a while. Maisie will always be the perfect reminder of that.

Audrey and I are resting on the turning point in our divorce and I wonder if things will be easier from now on.

She is an incredible mother, and everything she does—everything she has done—has been with Maisie's wellbeing front of mind.

"Will Cassidy—"

"No," I cut her off. "I don't think so."

"Maisie likes her."

Her voice is muffled through the phone but the words light up behind my eyes.

"Whatever happened, I think you should try to make it work." Her words shock me, but they light a tiny spark in my soul. I thought I was done trying to make things work with Cassidy, but maybe there's a little fight left in me after all.

"I don't even really like Michael. Like, he is a good guy. But he isn't right for me. I just didn't want to be alone, getting replaced, while you found the love of your life."

"Oh, Audrey."

I want to hug her through the phone. I grab at one of the cushions on the couch and squeeze it instead.

There's a lot to process and I'm not sure where to start. Maisie liking Cassidy is a good start. Or the fact that even Audrey can recognise how special what I have with Cassidy is.

"Promise me something," Audrey forces out after a large sniff.

"What?"

"Promise me Maisie will always come first."

"Our daughter will always come first."

After ending the call, I sit for a while. Contemplating everything, regretting so much.

Laughter in the hallway distracts me from my musing. My legs move of their own accord as they creep toward the door, and I'm thankful for my 'no shoes in the apartment rule' when my socks muffle my footsteps.

Cassidy's laugh fills my ears, along with another woman who I assume is Amira. Their voices are faint and broken from inside my apartment, but I can make out the sounds of one of them searching through a handbag. For keys, I guess.

"Ugh, we should leave a key above the doorframe like Callum," Cassidy says as I inch closer to the door to hear better.

Amira laughs in response before shouting, "Found it!"

Their door opens, then slams shut and I'm left standing sideways, my ear centimetres from being pressed against the wooden panelling between me and them. Between me and her.

I can't breathe. What started as a swirling of emotions inside every piece of me, has grown to a cyclone sized storm. My chest constricts, my neck aches, my brain races.

Cassidy is right there across the hall, and I know she is the woman I am meant to be with.

I know almost nothing of my ex-wife's relationship with this Michael, and I'm still angry I had to find out through Maisie. But so help me if it hasn't fuelled me with something else.

A heat that won't stop rising from my core. I can have that, too, in fact, I can have something even better. And the woman I want it with is mere metres away from me. Noah told me to wait, but I'm done sitting around and waiting for her to fight for us, because Cassidy is worth fighting for.

I'll fight every day until she knows she belongs with me. Until she knows she fits.

Without thinking, I undo the latch on the door, crossing the corridor in two long strides. I don't stop to knock, stepping straight into their apartment.

"Rogue," it comes out on an exhale, breathy and hot from deep in my throat.

The two women appear at the end of the hallway and for a brief second, I register that Amira still has her shoes on. But like always when she is in a room, it's Cassidy who catches my attention. She has, presumably, already changed. The fluffy socks on her feet give way to bare legs. I allow myself the time to peruse them slowly, dragging my gaze up to where the long dark tee brushes her thighs. It's clinging in all the right places, and I can see the outline of her hips, her breasts, underneath it.

Her face is pink with blush, her mouth open in a tiny 'o' shape. The storm rushes through my limbs, lightning sparking around me.

Amira coughs, stealing both our attention.

"I am so glad I'm going back out." She laughs as she speed walks down the hall. She passes me with a wide berth, sidestepping as though to avoid the heat I'm sure is radiating off me.

As soon as she has passed, I move for Cassidy. My arms wrap around her waist and pull her in until I can feel every inch of her pressed against me. I trail my hand up her back and into her hair, fisting it around the chocolate waves to tilt her head up so she is looking up at me.

We breathe in unison and her tongue darts out to wet her lips.

"Uh, Callum, your door is open?" Amira calls from the hall.

"Fuck," I call back, "leave it."

I let out a sigh and dip my head until my forehead collides with Cassidy's. The raw energy and need between us competes with my instincts as a father.

"Maisie?" Cassidy whispers, and all I can do is nod.

Pulling away from Cassidy, I bring my hands down to hold hers.

"This was … I'm …" I can't find the words, but I feel like I'm losing Cassidy, losing this moment. "Sorry," I whisper as I pull away.

Cassidy's hand firms on mine, preventing me from

walking. She pulls me back, spinning me around to face her again. With half a breath, she is up on her toes and our lips crash together.

The kiss is hard and fast and short before she pulls away again.

"Don't be."

She walks through me, and I'm frozen as she moves towards the door, grabbing her key from the hall table. As she gets to the door, she turns to face me. Her eyes are molten, and her hair is a mess from where I sunk my hand into the lower side of the bun.

"You coming?" she says with a knowing grin.

And it's all I have in me not to run.

Chapter Thirty-Four

CASSIDY

"Wait," I choke out as Callum backs me against the wall in his hallway. To his credit, he freezes in place instantly, his lips so close to my pulse point I can feel how hot and heavy he is breathing.

"What is this?" I ask, and I hate myself for it.

Callum pulls back until we are eye to eye. I wonder about how comfortable the hunched position is for his back, but the intensity in his eyes gives the impression it doesn't matter to him.

"I don't know," he admits. The raspiness in his voice penetrates my being and shoots a wave of heat to my core. "But I'm not done trying to fight for us, Rogue."

His hands find the sides of my thighs, below the hem of my baggy oversized shirt. Looking down between us, I cringe that I had already changed into my comfort clothes when he stormed into my apartment. The flowy dress and boots I had worn to dinner would have been far more appropriate for whatever this moment is.

"I've wanted to do these things to you for as long as I can remember," Callum whispers into my mouth. He pulls me into the kiss. It's somehow delicate and heavy all at once, and he groans as I open my mouth to let him in. Our tongues clash as we become frantic, tasting each other. It's not the first time, but something tells me this time is different from all the others.

Those ones had meaning, had feelings. But this one, it's loaded with emotion, and promise.

"I had to stop myself when you were a teenager. You'll never know how many times I imagined you bouncing on my lap, or pictured your mouth wrapped around my cock while I made myself come."

I turn to putty, and if it wasn't for Callum holding me against the wall, I would fall to my knees. All those times I wanted more, he did, too. But we weren't ready.

"We weren't ready," he agrees and I realise I said at least that part out loud.

"And now?"

I'm so scared of the answer, but I have to know. His daughter is in her bedroom down the hall, and I hope me being here shows him I'm willing to try. I should say those words, I know it should be on me to get the words out, but I can't. They get caught in my throat and instead, I force our lips together again.

"I am," Callum says into my ear as he pulls away and runs his tongue along my neck. The fingers of one hand still tease at the hem of my shirt, as his other hand finds the back of my neck. "I know it's a lot for me to ask you." He nibbles my earlobe and I run my hands up his body, settling them on his shoulders to ground myself.

I pull away to look in his eyes when I answer. "I'm here."

There's more I want to say, more I should say, but our mouths collide again in a fury. As Callum's hand ducks under my oversized shirt and up my thigh, I whimper.

"I need you to be mine." Callum groans as his hand reaches my panties. His strong palm cups my core, squeezing firmly.

Our chests rise and fall in sync, our tongues and teeth still moulded to each other.

"Tell me you're mine, Rogue."

His voice is guttural and demanding, and I moan into the sound. Wetness pools where his palm still cups me and I want more, I want to feel everything. Nodding, I lift my leg and wrap it around Callum, hooking him closer until I can feel how hard he is under his sweats.

Pulling away from our frantic kiss, Callum reaches behind me and lifts me up. On instinct, or out of an undamped desire, I wrap my legs around his waist. Grinding myself against him sends waves crashing through my core and into my soul.

Somehow, Callum has carried me to his bedroom, and I finally register the intensity of the moment as he lowers me onto the bed. I drag him into a kiss, pulling his shirt up and over his head and tracing my fingers over his abs. When he pulls away, I whimper.

"I need to hear you say it, Cassidy. I don't just want to fuck you. I want all of you. Your body, your heart, your future."

The pulsing in my core intensifies and my heart thuds.

"*Our* future, Callum. I want this, I want you. I want us."

Because God, I do. I'm done fighting against the words etched deep into my soul. I've spent months tossing and turning, struggling to find the balance between my feelings for Callum and my built-up trauma. But I know what I want now, I know this is where I'm supposed to be.

I didn't have the words or the strength to tell Callum I made a mistake when I said it was too hard and walked away. I still don't have the words. But I can show him.

For a second, Callum closes his eyes, humming as he opens them again. His pupils are wide; love and desire written all over his face.

He trails slow goosebumps all over me as he lifts at the hem of my shirt. I push off the bed, falling back as he flings the flimsy material away.

Starting at my mouth, he leaves a trail of wet kisses down my front, pausing as he sucks a nipple into his mouth. A hand palms my other breast before pinching at my nipple.

A mewling sound escapes as the hint of pain shoots electricity straight through me.

As he kneels beside the bed, he pushes my legs apart and settles himself between them.

"I need to taste you again."

He turns to kiss the inside of my knee. I shiver as he licks up my leg until his head is dipped between my legs and I feel his hot breath against my clit.

He licks and sucks like I'm his last meal and I feel my release building.

I groan, but before the sound is fully formed, Callum slams his palm against my mouth.

"Shh," he growls.

My eyes widen, and I suck in a breath as I remember why we need to be quiet, and I wonder if we are doing the wrong thing. *But God, if it's wrong why does it feel so right?*

As if sensing my hesitation, Callum dips a finger into me, caressing my inner walls. I moan into his hand, as he moves up to hover over me.

"Are you okay?" he asks as our foreheads touch, pausing to wait for my answer. "Is this okay?"

My mind stretches, trying to find all the reasons it shouldn't be. Trying to remember why I pushed him away in the first place. But all those reasons have dissolved into nothing at the realisation of how perfect we are together.

And I know one wild night won't make all the hardships go away, that I still have a lot of growth and acceptance to get through. But I also know this is worth it. Callum is worth it. We are worth it.

"It's more than okay, Callum."

My inner teenager squeals in excitement as I pull Callum closer so I can kiss him. Tasting myself on his tongue sends a wave of pleasure I was not expecting deep into my belly, and I lift my hips to meet him. He pulls his finger out before thrusting back in with a second. Hooking them inside me, he strokes against my inner walls. Electricity burns through my veins as he pulls me closer and closer, and I ride his hand through the explosion.

Callum kisses me as I shudder through my orgasm.

Pulling back, he licks his hand clean and reaches across the bed to the drawers.

"I have a—"

"You don't need it." I cut him off.

"Are you sure?"

I nod, and he moans as he brings himself back over me. Pulling his face into mine, I kiss him, biting his lip as I lift my hips into him again.

His cock glides through the wetness of my pussy. He rocks back and forth, coating himself with my arousal. Reaching a hand between us he adjusts himself and pushes into me.

I feel full and stretched and whole. His size taking my body to its limits. I suck in air as I will myself to relax, to let him in. Pleasure builds slowly while he waits for me to be ready. I rock my hips back and forth against him until he bottoms out inside me. We kiss, deep, and long, and loving as we move in sync.

The intensity in my core builds again until I can barely breathe, and I can tell from his quickening movements that Callum is close, too. Pulling away from our kiss, I suck in a deep breath as Callum reaches between us to rub my clit with his thumb.

And I'm lost, somewhere outside of my body as the final wave of pleasure crashes into us both. I can feel the hot spurts of Callum's orgasm as my muscles quiver around him until we are both spent.

Callum collapses onto the bed and I pull him close to

me. We are sweaty and sticky and God, if I'm not in love I don't know what this feeling is.

"I love you," he says, kissing my forehead.

I blush, worried I said the words out loud. They feel big, and scary. Another step that feels impossible to take right now. I want to say them, but I need to wait.

We lay, part appreciating the way our bodies fit together so seamlessly, part dozing in bliss. Eventually, we peel our bodies apart where our sweat dried sticky. But it's not awkward or uncomfortable. It feels right, to be so vulnerable with each other like this.

Once we've showered we return to the bed. I'm wearing one of his shirts and nothing else, and Callum pulls on a pair of bed shorts. He curls me into a loving embrace.

"I don't want this to end," I whisper into his chest, before sucking in a breath of courage. "But I don't think I should be here when Maisie wakes up."

I pull back to look him in the eye. "I'm not running away. I just don't think that's the best way for her to find out about us."

Leaning back down, I plant a kiss on Callum's cheek and whisper into his ear, "If there is an us."

With a firm grip, he grabs and turns my head so I'm looking at him again.

"There will never not be an us now."

Our lips crash together again, his fingers still gripping my chin. Not like he thinks I'll run, but in a tender way because he knows I won't.

But also in a firm, loving way, like he is claiming me. And I like it.

Chapter Thirty-Five

CALLUM

"Where are we going?"

Cassidy laughs from the passenger seat as I drive along the windy roads towards her cousin's winery. Dawn is yet to break, and with the morning mist in the air, visibility is low. I yawn, reaching for my coffee between turns. The bitter liquid from the takeaway cup has lost all its warmth, but the caffeine is welcome. Blindfolded— so she can't guess where we are going—Cassidy hugs her own cup, patting it against her lips to find the spout.

After all the unspoken confessions we shared the other night, it's been a few days of lingering glances. I was busy with Maisie, and neither of us know the right way, the right time to bring the topic of 'us' up with her. Audrey didn't know the right way either, but we will figure it out. For now, I wanted to plan something special, just for me and Cass.

Because one night of sex, no matter how incredible, was never going to be enough to show her how I feel.

Cassidy hiccups a little into her fist, reaching forward to put the window down. "These roads are making me sick."

She tugs at the blindfold. Reaching over, I pull the fabric off her face. My hand lingers on her cheek a little longer than necessary, but she leans into my palm.

"I didn't think of that, sorry. But you'll figure out where we are going now."

The sun is nothing more than a glow on the horizon as we wind down the country road. As I manoeuvre the car into the winery car park, Cassidy scrunches up her nose in confusion.

"I thought we were going somewhere special."

"We are, trust me."

I step out, wiping my sweaty palms on my jeans and grabbing our coats from the back seat. I walk around to open her door, reaching my hand into hers.

As she climbs out of the car, I suck in a breath, hoping this will be enough to surprise her. With her work for the winery, there's every chance Noah has kept her in the loop with his plans.

"Why are we at Noah's winery at 6.30 in the morning?" she questions as I guide her down the path toward the back garden.

She doesn't know the truth about whose winery this is, so I find it odd she calls it Noah's winery, but I let it slide. I was sworn to secrecy when I found out. All Cassidy knows, all she needs to know, is that Noah organises the events. Like the one I'm surprising Cassidy with this morning. When I told him I wanted to surprise Cassidy with a date, he said he knew just the thing.

For months he has been working on securing a hot air balloon vendor for the coming spring/summer season. Today is their maiden voyage. Technically only for staff and 'selected guests' so the company can take some promotional photos before they launch in a months' time.

Noah clearly has a soft spot for his cousin and gave up his tickets. He had choked when I asked who he had been planning to take, brushing off the question as though it meant nothing.

"Oh my God," Cassidy squeals as we make our way around the cellar door building to see the giant balloons spread out across the lawn.

She jumps up and down on the spot before cowering into herself.

"Remember the fair, you had fun."

At the reminder of the last time she put aside her mild fear of heights, Cassidy turns to leap into my arms. Her body collides with mine and I scoop her up. She wraps her legs around my waist. I hold her tight, planting a lasting kiss on her lips and soaking in the feeling of her body against mine. Even through so many layers, the feeling of her legs on my waist, her core against mine, sends electricity coursing through my veins.

We spot Noah, standing by the closest balloon, with a clipboard under his arm.

"Hey lovebirds." He laughs from across the field.

Writing something on his clipboard, he tucks it under his arm to walk over. Turning to me his voice is stern, "you better make this worth it."

Squished in like sardines with the other guests, it's claustrophobic in the basket, despite the wide open air spreading for miles around us. Cassidy's fear of heights forgotten, she gazes out into the distance as the sun rises behind us. The wind drifts the scent of Cassidy's tropical shampoo my way, and I pull her close to nuzzle into her neck.

"I love you," I whisper, for her ears only.

She turns to face me, nodding with a smile that lights up my world more than the sun at my back.

We turn toward the horizon together, taking in the sweeping hills and the picturesque shadows they make as the sun ascends into the sky. Beside us, a gentleman pushes back, trying to make space where there is none.

When he realises we have nowhere to go, he takes a step back toward his partner, reaching a hand into his pocket and pulling out a tiny box. His words are lost in the wind, but from the girl's squeals and the kiss they share, it's clear they got engaged.

Cheers of congratulations ring out from the basket of witnesses. I clap the man on the shoulder as I say, "congrats mate."

Cassidy turns to me, there's a hint of hope in her eyes that feels like a knife in my throat. I love her, but it's too early for something quite so grand.

"Hope you weren't planning to do that. Because if so, he definitely stole your thunder."

Hugging her from behind, I run my hands down her arms before holding her hands. My fingers find her ring finger and I press down where an engagement ring would go. Where my engagement ring will go. Eventually.

"One day," I say, "but it'll be better than that."

"I'll hold you to it." She laughs, leaning back into my shoulder. "But not yet," she adds.

The knife in my throat dissolves and I hug her closer as we begin our descent.

A complimentary brunch picnic awaits us between the vines once we are safely back on the ground, along with the huge bunch of flowers I had Noah order in secret.

"You bought me flowers?" Cassidy drops to her knees on the picnic rug, smelling the colourful blooms.

I follow her to the ground, hugging her from behind and kissing her neck. "Even florists need someone to buy them flowers."

She hums as she leans back into me, nestling herself between my legs. Leaning back on one hand, the other wraps around her waist.

The champagne swirls with anxiety in my stomach, my

breaths shaky as I prepare to recite the speech I practised last night.

My hands on her waist, I twist her around to face me. "Cassidy, I've been kidding myself about a lot of things for a long time. I thought I had no space for someone new to enter my life, and that held me back for a while." I pause to inhale, drawing in oxygen and savouring her lavender scent. My heart feels somehow heavy and light at the same time.

"But you aren't new," I continue. A stray piece of hair falls from Cassidy's messy bun and I reach out to tuck it behind her ear. My hand lingers on the side of her face, and I rub my thumb along her cheekbone. "My soul has known yours for so long, Rogue. I didn't need to make space for you, because all the space you need in my heart was carved out years ago."

Her eyes start to glisten, and when she holds them closed, a single tear escapes. I wipe it away with my thumb. My own tears form as I hold back the lump in my throat to force the words out.

Cassidy looks up at me, shaking her head against my hand. "I'm sorry I took so long to figure it out. But you fill up all the space in my heart, too." Her hand covers mine, holding it against her cheek. "I spent so long thinking I could never have kids of my own, I convinced myself I was never meant to have a child in my life. I pushed you away because I thought I couldn't be what you and Maisie need."

She pulls my hand away from my face, holding it low in her lap as she shuffles away from me. The morning air between us is frigid and feels like ice in my chest.

"I can't give Maisie a sibling." Her voice is soft, almost carried away on the wind but full of uncertainty. "I want to be there for Maisie, but it's not just about me not having a baby. I made peace with the fact I would never become a mother. It took a lot of growth and therapy for me to accept

311

that I never will be, I can't go back through the pain of trying everything again."

The tears are spilling down her cheeks and I fight the urge to kiss them away. Instead, I rub her hands with my thumbs, encouraging her to continue.

"Maisie is enough for me," she says, "but I still worry I'm not enough for you and Maisie."

Her hands pull away from mine and reach to hide her face. She turns away from me to wipe her tears, and a wave of panic rushes through me. It feels like I'm losing her, and fuck if I'm going to let that happen. I launch myself at her, scooping her into my lap. One hand wraps around her waist, and the other reaches up to cup the back of her neck. With care, I force her to look up at me.

I hate myself for not bringing this up between us sooner, but I had no idea this was how she felt. No idea this was the reason holding her back. I don't want another child. And sure, Maisie might ask about having a baby, but all kids do that. She doesn't really get a say.

"You should know something." I don't mean to sound so stern, but my voice is rough as I force out the words. I'm angry at myself for not making sure Cassidy knew. She pulls back at the change in tone, but she keeps her eyes locked on mine.

"Maisie has always been it for me," I tell her. "As soon as she was born and I held her in my arms, I knew that was it. I was always meant to be her dad, and no one else's. It was the first thing her mother and I fought over."

Cassidy's mouth opens as she tries to respond, but I cut her off before she can start.

"I don't believe in fate. But I believe the world brought us back together for a reason. And I have to believe the timing is right now, because I can't imagine not knowing you again."

Leaning down, I plant a kiss on her still open lips before

adding, "And you are more than enough for me, and for Maisie. But we need to stop talking about my daughter now."

She kisses me again, furiously.

Her core rocks against me, and the way she straddles my hips creates a deep friction that causes my cock to press against the inside of my pants. My hand still on the back of her neck, I tilt her head to deepen the kiss, running my tongue against her bottom lip.

"Let's go home." Cassidy moans the words into my neck as I thrust my hardening length into her.

"Good plan," I choke out.

Chapter Thirty-Six

CALLUM

My balls ache. My cock is firm against the zipper of my jeans, and my fingertips are red as I squeeze the steering wheel. The drive back to our apartment building drags. We're not even halfway, but the windows are fogged from the anticipation in the air.

Cassidy hums in her seat. Her knees bounce in time to my rapid pulse. Peeling a hand away from its grip on the steering wheel, I reach over to caress her thigh. I stroke upwards from her knee, stopping mid-thigh and trailing my fingers back down. Back and forth, I trace her upper leg, inching higher with every pass. Her hands stretch above her head, pulling hair off her face. My fingertips graze against the rough seam of her pants. She moans, lifting her hips to increase the pressure. I rub the seam against her clit.

On a straight stretch of road, I glance over at Cassidy. Her hair now sits in a messy bun atop her head, and she bites her lip with a twinkle in her eye. Pushing my hands out of her way, she twists in her seat. She tugs at her seatbelt, stretching the strap down so she can lean over the centre console. She plants a quick kiss on the corner of my mouth as she reaches down to stroke the bulge in my pants.

"This looks uncomfortable," she coos.

I huff my agreement.

"Rogue, I'm driving," I add when she rubs her palm along my length.

She kisses my cheek, leaning close to whisper in my ear. "But I'm not."

I should protest, but in one swift movement she unbuttons my jeans and pulls down the zipper. Reaching into my jocks she frees my cock. It springs up for her as she leans over it.

With a moan, she runs her tongue along the underside of my shaft. At the tip, she licks the bead of pre-cum that wasted no time spilling out.

I grip the steering wheel, checking my mirrors and easing off the accelerator. There are no cars around us, but the country road winds through the fields, and I need to concentrate. *But God.* Cassidy sucks me into her mouth. Her moans send vibrations down my length and up my spine.

This is … fuck … this is no longer safe. A smaller, back country road appears ahead. I throw on the indicator, even though there hasn't been a car behind us for miles, slowing to take the turn in a way that doesn't throw Cassidy into the dash. Pulling the car off the road and onto a grass bank, I throw the seat back to give her space.

She shifts her weight onto the floor in front of me.

"Look at me, Rogue."

She does. And from her spot on the floor she keeps her eyes on mine as she licks her lips and stretches them back over my throbbing erection. Bobbing her head, she swallows me deep into her throat and I fight the urge to throw my head back.

Reaching down, I palm her neck, feeling myself inside her. My fingers trail around to the back of her head, fisting at her hair as I resist the urge to take control. She draws back, her mouth making a popping sound as she releases my cock.

Her voice is husky and strained. "Do it."

I do nothing but suck in air, willing my brain to compute what she said.

"Please," she says, blinking up at me. "Master."

And so I do. Because fuck that old nickname, now, of all times.

With my hand on the back of her head, I guide her back down until her nose brushes against my pubic bone. Her thumb rubs gentle circles on my thigh.

"Tap if it's too much," I warn her.

She hums, and I pull her up, only a fraction so I can thrust my hips to meet her. Cassidy hollows her cheeks and I revel in the wet warmth of her mouth. My balls draw tight and Cassidy, as if sensing it, reaches under her chin to massage them. My ears rush and my lungs are tight. My release is coming but I pull Cassidy back.

Lifting her up I find she has already pulled off her leggings. Ripping her thin panties to the side, I run my cock along her pussy. She's so wet already and I groan at the thought of being inside her again. I pull her tee up to her neck, leaning my face between her breasts. Yanking her bra out of my way, I pull an already tight nipple into my mouth.

Cassidy gasps as I bite down on her nipple and slide her down onto me.

"Fuck, wait." Her walls constrict against the size of my dick buried all the way inside her. I wait as her muscles relax. It's excruciating, but I wait, toying my tongue over her nipples. She moans again as she rocks her hips back and forth, pleasuring herself on my lap.

I lift her up, slamming her back down onto my cock. She grabs my face between her hands, pulling my head up and sucking my lower lip into her mouth. She kisses me like she is dying. Devouring every inch of my mouth while I thrust in and out.

My balls draw tighter, higher than they have ever felt. The vibrations spread up my spine as Cassidy's walls clamp around me. With her release, she draws mine out until I'm spurting inside her. I hold us together as we ride out our orgasms.

Cassidy leans back, catching her breath as she fixes her bra and top. Her elbow hits the steering wheel and the horn blasts.

"Shit." She falls back into me, trembling at the sound.

My shoulders shake as Cassidy wheezes through her own laughter. I grasp her chin, tilting her head to kiss her again.

"I love you."

And for the first time she whispers back, "I love you, too."

Chapter Thirty-Seven

CASSIDY

The warm glow of the sun on my bare back coaxes me back into the waking world. I'm thankful for the quiet moment, knowing it's sure to end soon. I don't want to think about getting up. I want to savour the sun and remain in this cosy cocoon of love.

As though it knew I was hoping it wouldn't, Callum's alarm finally beeps behind me. I nuzzle into his shoulder, willing the sound to cease.

Despite everything we spoke about yesterday, we never discussed what would happen next, and I hold my breath in anticipation.

Callum rolls and reaches over me to turn the alarm off. His forearms squeeze my chest and I feel that familiar wave of heat rush through me. Moaning, I glance up at him through my lashes.

His black hair is scruffy from sleep or perhaps from all the pulling and tugging I did yesterday, and his eyes darken as he gazes down at me. Lust coats his face, but he shakes his head as though he can will it away. He runs a hand through his hair as he groans, before letting out a long breath that turns into a yawn.

"I have to, ahh—" he stumbles over his words, so I finish for him.

"Maisie?"

"Audrey has a date."

He snorts. I snuggle closer into his shoulder, desperate to show him I won't run away again.

I've done a lot of growing over the past few months. When I first found out about Maisie, a relationship with a man who had a child felt completely out of my boundaries. Even with Callum, as perfect as he is, I couldn't cope with the thought I would eventually disappoint them both.

Now, though, my whole thought process has changed. I no longer hold on to a belief that my infertility is a sign I should never be a parental figure. Weirdly, it was accepting my becoming an aunt that made me realise I can open up my heart to a child. And more importantly, her dad. And I trust and believe Callum when he says he never wanted more children.

After yesterday, I feel confident in my place in Callum's life. I feel confident in how I can fit in with his family. And I need him to know that.

"What time do you have to pick her up?" I push myself up, leaning my weight on my elbow. Callum's eyes dip and I feel their intense longing as he takes in my naked body. My nipples pebble under his gaze.

Instinct makes me want to reach and pull the cover up, but years of knowing this man have left me wanting to be open and vulnerable around him now. I pull my bottom lip into my mouth, willing my pulse to remain steady, at least until I know if we have time to spare.

Callum sucks in a breath, the hand still under the sheet stretching down as he adjusts himself.

"We have time." He leans over and takes one nipple in his mouth. The gentle suction combines with the roughness of his beard, sending a rush of sparks over my body.

I reach down to pull him up to me. Kissing him, I keep the contact short and innocent. Despite the throb in my core, I feel sticky with last night's sweat. Our exploration of the way our bodies combine lasted well into the early hours of the morning, and I'm spent. And I really need to pee.

"We have all the time in the world now," I whisper as I guide him back off me.

It takes us longer than it should to get ready. No matter how tired I thought I was. We get distracted in the shower. And again when I'm walking around the apartment, wrapped in a towel as we search for my underwear.

I duck across the hall to change into clean clothes, while Callum finishes cleaning up the house. As I pull out a khaki sundress, I'm thankful Amira has already left for the day. Although, I'm desperate to tell her, well *almost* everything, I know Callum's ex can be a stickler for time. I don't want to ruin their newly forming peace.

Callum's face lights up when I burst back out into the hall. Dressed in chino shorts and a simple white tee, his arms are on full display. When he reaches out to take my hand, it hits me why I recognise his dragon tattoo.

"The black dragon," I say as I grab his hand and use the other to trace the lines of its wing around his forearm. "From that game we used to play."

He pulls me in for a kiss and I can feel his smile against my mouth. When we pull apart, I'm smiling, too. Still beaming, I turn my back to lock my door. The beaded keyring Noah bought me jingles as I return it to my bag.

"Some of the best nights of my life, even now."

Nostalgia washes over me because I still look back on those game nights sometimes, too. Remembering how fun it was to put on a persona and play out a literal fantasy. To call him Master while he called me Rogue, the nicknames far more innocent then than they are now. Nodding, I lean into him as we enter the stairwell.

It's not until Callum pulls open the heavy lobby door that I consider the huge step I've assumed we are taking. We hadn't spoken about me coming with him to pick up Maisie. And while we discussed how I would fit into their father-daughter relationship, I don't want to expect something he isn't ready for.

I hesitate before walking through, asking, "Should I be coming or?"

"I want you to come, but if it's too much you can wait."

My mouth widens to a grin as I take two little skips towards him.

"It's not too much."

The car rumbles on the long gravel driveway, and when Callum pulls up to park under a tree, I keep my seatbelt on and settle into the seat. What Callum and I have found feels fresh and new. I'm ready to introduce it to Maisie, but not sure I'm ready to introduce myself to her mother.

Callum pauses after climbing out, turning back to see I haven't moved. As though he can read my mind, he gives a small nod before heading to the house.

I sit and scroll through my phone while I wait, enjoying the stuffy heat that forms in the morning sun. I'm about to step out for some fresh air when footsteps crunch along the driveway. One set quickens to a run, but I still jump when Maisie yanks the passenger door open.

"Cassidy," she squeals as she climbs on top of me to throw her arms around my shoulders.

The giant pink bow is back in her hair, holding a high ponytail in place. Maisie looks like the perfect little fashionista in her denim pinafore and white shirt. I'm amazed at how white her little sneakers are, and hope they are new. If not, a five-year-old is better at keeping her shoes clean than I am.

"I missed you," she whispers into my ear before climbing across the centre console and into her car seat.

A cough sounds from outside the car, pulling my attention from Maisie.

I step out, straightening my dress as I stand.

Audrey.

Her eyes squint in the winter sun and something that feels like dread swirls in my stomach. I shouldn't have been so bold as to come today. But more than that, now I'm here, I should have introduced myself.

"Callum said you were nervous, and I get that. But I wanted to say thank you."

"Thank ... me?"

I push my hair off my face, scratching at my temple.

"For taking Maisie to her first dance class, and for dancing with her when she couldn't go. I have two left feet, it would have been a nightmare if I tried."

"Oh, it was nothing."

But it wasn't, it was everything. And to be thanked for it feels unnecessary. The tiny hole that existed in my heart starts to fill, knowing I was able to offer Maisie something that's just ours.

Audrey pulls at her sleeves, crossing her arms in front of her. "And for driving Maisie to the hospital and leaving before I did something dumb like make a scene. But let's not talk about that."

Callum steps closer, wrapping an arm around my shoulders. Audrey glances up at him with a smile.

"You two look good together." She shifts her gaze back to me. "We never fit, his hair was too dark next to my pale skin and blonde hair. I'm glad you found your way back together."

We say our goodbyes, Maisie climbing back out of the car to give her mum a hug.

"Enjoy your date with Michael," Callum says through the window as we drive away.

"Michael?"

"Yeah, some big beefy dude. Audrey said he is smitten."

It can't be. I shake off the random thought.

"Why are you here today?" Maisie asks from the back seat.

Her question is nothing more than excited curiosity, but I have no idea how to answer.

I consider what to say, how much to give away.

"Cassidy and I were spending the morning together, so she came to say hi." Callum saves me from saying the wrong thing.

Maisie beams. "Did you have a sleepover like I said you should?"

My mouth drops open. Her question has come out of nowhere, but Callum rests a hand on my knee, tapping his fingers twice. I'll leave this one to him, too.

"Yeah, chicka," he says, "we did."

Maisie jumps in her seat as much as her tightened harness will allow, and I can't help but smile at the level of excitement she is showing. I had no idea she would even care, so to have her excited at the idea of Callum and I being together, in whatever capacity she is imagining, makes my breath catch in my throat. The morning sunlight streaming in through the window is too bright and my eyes water.

I realise I am happy. So beyond happy, I'm at a level I never imagined would be possible.

I might not be a mother, but a young girl cares deeply for me, and I can't wait to have her as an important part of my life. And her father? It feels like I spent my whole life loving him, wanting him, and now I have him. Closing my eyes, I appreciate how full my heart feels, knowing I've finally found where I'm meant to be.

Epilogue

CASSIDY (5 YEARS LATER)

"So." I lean into Cal's chest, "When should we tell her we are taking her to Disneyland?"

"At least twenty minutes after we tell her the two of us are going." He laughs.

I spin to face him, my mouth wide open in playful shock. He pops a jelly snake in my mouth, the sweet taste lingering on my tongue.

"I think we should make her sweat for it a bit first. It'll make the whole thing even better."

The hardest part of keeping the secret was getting passport photos. Maisie's pre-teen urge to poke out her tongue or throw up a love heart with her fingers runs strong, so getting a photo that was serious and straight faced was almost impossible. In the end, Audrey had helped us feign the need for a school ID photo for her private high school applications. I had no idea we had to start those this early, but apparently to get into the best schools, you do. And we all want the best for Maisie.

The girls' laughter carries through the open kitchen window. Audrey rounds them out of the pool, handing out towels to Maisie and her friends. I hold back tears as I push the last candle into the cake. Amira made it, and I'm continually impressed with her skills. The two-tiered white cake has a rainbow waterfall cascading over the side, falling into a pool of rainbow frosting. It's extravagant for a ten-year-old, but then again, so is taking her to Disneyland. And so is building a pool so she could have a pool party, but that's what her step-dad did. She's not normally this spoiled, but we all went a little overboard for this birthday. Double digits is a big deal.

It's still hard to believe our little girl is ten. Harder still to believe we call her 'our' little girl. It took a long time for all of us to fall into our respective parenting roles, but I'm glad we put in all the work.

Even more so, I'm glad for the whole tribe of kids we now have in our little circle. Maisie has her cousins, and most importantly she has her siblings. The ones I knew she deserved but could never give her. When Audrey announced she was pregnant, Maisie was beside herself with joy. She loves her brothers with all her heart. Surprisingly, I do, too.

Just not quite as much as I love Maisie.

My favourite part of the week is when we go to ballet class together. Every Monday, whether she is with us for the week or not, I pick her up from school and take her dancing. Our tradition started five years ago, and I've never missed a class since. I hope she never wants to stop.

Cal kisses the nape of my neck as I light the candles. A gentle shiver washes over me, my fingertips tingling as I take in the moment. I never thought I'd end up here, and I'm grateful every day.

"You okay?"

Placing the lighter down, I shift to face him. "More than," I whisper as I plant a kiss on his lips.

I reach up behind his neck, tugging his hair as I tilt my head. My lips part and together we deepen the kiss. It's the kind of all knowing, all-consuming kiss we've had countless times over the years, but every time Callum kisses me, my knees go weak.

We lose time, lost in our kiss, until I hear the sparkler extinguish. Pulling away from Callum's embrace, I take another one from the box.

Once it's lit, Callum picks up the tray.

"Happy Birthday to you …"

The girls sing as soon as they see the cake, crowding around the birthday girl.

I hang back, finding somewhere to sit. I squeeze between Noah and Amira and throw my arms around Amira's growing belly.

"How's the little munchkin?" I ask.

"She's perfect."

Amira rubs her hands over her stomach, stretching her back into me.

"Heavy though," she whines.

Noah rolls his eyes with a huff. Standing, he roughs his hand through Amira's hair before strolling off towards Callum and the guys. Madison waddles over, one hand rests on her own swelling middle, the other holding a plate of cake large enough to share. She sits in Noah's place, handing us forks.

"You should add this flavour to the shop's cake list," she says with a mouth full of icing.

Since opening the coffee cart, Betty Blooms Boutique has continued to evolve. After a few months, we rebranded to become "Betty's." Amira's love for baking spread further into the business. As well as flowers and coffee, we now offer a full range of sweet treats, from donuts to macarons, to full sized cakes. When the gift shop next door closed down, we took over the space—and some of the stock—and spread even further.

We now have five employees, and I can't think about our success without tears forming in my eyes. All of it, from one coffee craving influencer who planted the tiny seed of an idea.

The sound of laughter and splashing from the pool brings me back to the present.

"Look at what we have," Amira muses.

My gaze shifts between Maisie and Callum, and I can't help the smile that spreads across my face.

Read on for a sneak peek of

Because of Them
MICHAEL

The morning sun is hot on my back, waking me up with its burning glaze through the window. I carry my pillow with me as I roll over, covering my face. I must have slept in, with the way the sun streaks lines across my sheets from the windows I never bother to close. I live on the top floor of the tallest building in the suburb; no one can see me anyway. Not that I care if they do.

Stretching my arms above my head, the pillow falls onto my lap as I push myself to sit and swing my legs off the side of the bed. Baxter's head pops up from his spot on the floor, plodding over for his morning pat. He lets out a bark when he sees the pillow in his favourite resting place, giving me his best puppy dog sad face until I move it away. Crouching on the floor beside him, I soak in his unconditional love. The only kind I'll ever get.

RDO Fridays. My favourite day of the month, the best part of working for my dad's construction company. A whole day to do whatever the fuck I want.

Baxter lets himself out onto the balcony and I flick on the coffee machine in the kitchen. After adding a splash of cool water, I down the shot of espresso in one go. Tastes like fucking shit, but I need the boost first thing in the morning. Without it, I'll never get through my session.

Weights line the walls of the spare room, an all in one lifting machine sits in the middle. My one Friday off every month might be my favourite day, but Friday workouts are the ones I hate the most. Leg day.

I tried to be one of those gym guys who neglected his legs. I hate the exercises and frankly, I didn't see the point.

But the competitions demanded I build form in my thighs and calves, so I did. It became a habit. And although I haven't done a comp in over a year and I loathe the exercises and the way I struggle to walk down the stairs after them, it's kind of nice having some form where a lot of guys don't. Gives me an edge, and something to stir shit over.

After my rounds of calf raises and lunges and squats, I emerge from my makeshift gym on shaky legs to the buzzing of my phone.

Weird. No one calls me, especially not in the morning.

My dad's face lights up the screen when I pick it up from the charging pad on the bench. Not today. It's my RDO and the very last thing I want to do is spend it talking to my father about his business. About how he wants me to run the thing one day. I can't think of anything worse.

Rejecting the call, a stabbing in my heart reminds me of the one person I wish *would* call me. I fucked things up with Audrey. Bad. But no matter how many times I try to call her, how many texts I send. She never answers, never replies.

My mates all say to forget about her. The guys at work tell me to get over the wild few weeks we had. I can't. I tried.

It doesn't matter how big—or little, technically—the red flag was. I can't forget about Audrey. I can't forget about how her body moulded under mine, the way her breasts pushed against my chest when I sunk myself between her legs. We were perfect together, physically at least. And I doubt I will ever find another woman who fits so perfectly against me.

We had something most couples spend their relationships wishing for. An unmatchable sexual chemistry. But when it started to evolve into something more, I began to freak out. Audrey's older than me, not by a lot, but by enough. I shoved down my worries, hoping they would ease with time. Thinking that maybe I was destined to be with someone after all. Until I was rudely shocked out of the daydream.

I knew she had a daughter. She never tried to hide it. I figured I would get used to it. A kid is different to a baby, and for some reason it felt easier to grow into the idea of a kid being in my life than the thought of one day having a baby. I never knew how to act around her, but I was getting used to her being around. And that was something.

Until all my wishful thinking was destroyed in one tiny moment, by one tiny voice. I woke up, erection pressed against the small of Audrey's back. Moaning in to her, I imagined all the things we might get up to before ever leaving the bed. My hand snaked down her front, toying with the band of her panties.

"Mummy!" Her daughter's shrill voice had called down the hall. "Can I put *Bluey* on?"

Audrey had groaned at the rude awakening, calling out yes and pressing her behind into me. But the moment was gone, along with all hope I had that Audrey and I could work long term.

Maisie's tiny little voice had awoken a panic in me and I rushed to get dressed, leaving before breakfast had even been served. I wasn't ready to be such a big part of the little girl's life. I still don't know if I am, but I'm willing to try. Properly.

If only Audrey would let me. I ghosted her for weeks after that day, so I don't blame her for not wanting to give me a second chance. And now she is the one ghosting me.

I fucked up. But I'll never stop trying to make things right.

A message pings from my father.

Dad: I know it's your RDO but call me. As a son, not an employee.

Well fuck, his message hits a chord, but it's the chain under it that catches my attention.

A little blue dot next to Audrey's name. She messaged

me. In my haste to open the thread, I fumble with my phone, dropping it to the counter. Picking it up, I have to read the message four times before the words sink in.

Audrey: Hey Michael, can we chat?

My body screams to type *Yes* and hit send, but my brain holds me back. Chat? In what way?

There's chatting like how I used to chat with multiple women at a time, trying to find the one that felt right. I haven't done that since I met Audrey though. Or chatting like catching up on each other's lives. Or—and God I hope it's not this—chatting like a final talk. I have no idea where she wants this chat to go.

The message log says she sent the text this morning, while I was doing my stupid leg workout. My stomach cramps, part hunger, part a ball of anxiety at the thought of calling her back. I have to call my dad back too, even though it probably will be work related despite his message. I reach for a banana, needing fuel before I attempt anything else.

When I've shoved the final bite in my mouth, my stomach feels a little better. Audrey first, then I'll tackle the call with my dad.

The phone rings twice, but when Audrey answers, the sound of cartoons blasts into my ear.

"Maisie turn it down!" Audrey yells. I hear her shuffling away down the hall, muffling the obnoxious music.

"Sorry Michael, how are you?"

She sounds out of breath. Dread mixes with the anxiety in my stomach, swirling against my pre-breakfast snack.

"Audrey, I'm ... good. How are you?"

"Oh you know, work, motherhood, life."

The conversation feels like forced small talk, doing nothing for the storm inside me.

"Audrey what's—"

"Can we see—"

We cut each other off. "Sorry, you first," I prompt.

Audrey blows out a long puff of air. "Can we see each other? Like, go for coffee or something?"

My cheeks burn. She wants to see me, finally. I can't help but wonder what prompted her swift change of heart. But then, I suppose it must have felt the same for her when I started calling her again too.

"I'd like that. Today?"

"Not today, I have to get Maisie to school and get to work."

Right, I forgot the whole world doesn't get these blissful days off like the trade industry.

"On the weekend. I'll see if Maisie can go to her dad's. Can I text you?" Audrey gulps down her words.

"Okay," I strip the concern and confusion from my voice. "I'm looking forward to it."

I try to convince myself it's true as I end the call. I try not to think about the way each word caught in her throat, or the way she sounded on the verge of tears. I try to imagine all the ways it could go right, instead of focusing on the way my hairs stand on end like they know something I don't.

Because of Them

Michael

My life is changing, and I'm not sure I like it. I'm definitely not ready for it.
My dad wants me to take over the family business, my mum wants me to settle down. And Audrey wants me to be the man she deserves. The man they deserve.

I want to be him too, but I keep messing up.

Audrey

Just when I thought I was settling into my new life, two little lines threw all my plans out the window.
I was building my career, adjusting to life as a single mum, and had no desire to ever change a dirty nappy again.

But plans change, just like I need Michael to.

Because of Them is a steamy romance about falling in love, fighting for it, and accepting the changes it brings. A standalone story, it is the second novel in Bookstagrammer Devon May's Because of Love series.

Because of Them will be released on November 7, 2024

Acknowledgements

I want to start (end?) by saying something that, as a society, we don't often allow people to say... *Fuck, I'm proud of myself.* I was no more than ten years old when the tiniest spark of a dream was ignited in my soul. As a preteen girl writing fan-fiction and fairy tale retellings, I promised myself I'd become a published author one day. It might have taken me more than 20 years to get here, but gosh it feels good. I hope that in achieving this goal of mine, I can show all the other 30-something year olds out there that they can do the same.

That said, there is no way I would have made it here without the incredible troupe of cheerleaders behind me.

Sarah H, thank you for reminding me of my love for books. Who knew a book left on a doorstep during lockdown would be the match to start the fire?

Shannon, I will always thank you for being my biggest supporter, my rock, and my muse.

My BETA team: Ashleigh, Brittany, Jess and Bonnie. This book never would have made it off the ground without your advice.

There is an ever growing list of incredible authors who have stood by my side, shoving me along this journey. Kylie Orr, your constant encouragement forced this story out of me. You were there before I even knew what I wanted to write about, and when I finally figured it out your support was priceless. Anne Freeman, you passed me a shovel and reminded me to keep filling the sandbox. Without that advice, I'd still be stuck 10 chapters in. Also, Alexis Menard, Dyan Layne, Lauren Ashley, and all the others who answered my needy DMs. I wouldn't have finished this book without you.

And to every bookish friend I've made on social media over the past few years. I truly feel like I've found my people, and I love you all for it.

About the Author

When she was 10, Santa brought Devon a "how to write a book" journal. Publishing her debut novel more than 20 years later, she's glad it finally got put to good use.

Devon May resides in Melbourne, Australia with her husband and the two tiny humans who call her mum. When she isn't breaking up fights, she enjoys books that either break her heart, or turn her on. She carries her emotional support Kindle everywhere, drinks far too much coffee and will never be caught without a hair tie on her wrist.

Find her on Instagram @booksbydevonmay
or join her in her Facebook group:
DM me - Devon May's Readers

Printed in Great Britain
by Amazon

56784650R00199